Acclaim for Radclyffe's Fiction

Lambda Literary Award winner *Stolen Moments* "is a collection of steamy stories about women who just couldn't wait. It's sex when desire overrides reason, and it's incredibly hot!"—*On Our Backs*

Lambda Literary Award winner *Distant Shores, Silent Thunder* "weaves an intricate tapestry about passion and commitment between lovers. The story explores the fragile nature of trust and the sanctuary provided by loving relationships."—*Sapphic Reader*

Lambda Literary and Benjamin Franklin Award finalist *The Lonely Hearts Club* "is an ensemble piece that follows the lives [and loves] of three women, with a plot as carefully woven as a fine piece of cloth."—*Midwest Book Review*

ForeWord's Book of the Year finalist *Night Call* features "gripping medical drama, characters drawn with depth and compassion, and incredibly hot [love] scenes."—*Just About Write*

Lambda Literary Award finalist *Justice Served* delivers a "crisply written, fast-paced story with twists and turns and keeps us guessing until the final explosive ending."—*Independent Gay Writer*

Shield of Justice is a "well-plotted...lovely romance...I couldn't turn the pages fast enough!"—Ann Bannon, author of *The Beebo Brinker Chronicles*

Lambda Literary Award finalist *Turn Back Time* is filled with "wonderful love scenes, which are both tender and hot."—*MegaScene*

Lambda Literary Award finalist *When Dreams Tremble*'s "focus on character development is meticulous and comprehensive, filled with angst, regret, and longing, building to the ultimate climax."
—*Just About Write*

A Matter of Trust is a "sexy, powerful love story filled with angst, discovery and passion that captures the uncertainty of first love and its discovery."—*Just About Write*

"The author's brisk mix of political intrigue, fast-paced action, and frequent interludes of lesbian sex and love...in *Honor Reclaimed*...sure does make for great escapist reading."
—*Q Syndicate*

Change of Pace is "contemporary, yet timeless, not only about sex, but also about love, longing, lust, surprises, chance meetings, planned meetings, fulfilling wild fantasies, and trust."—*Midwest Book Review*

"Radclyffe has once again pulled together all the ingredients of a genuine page-turner, this time adding some new spices into the mix. *shadowland* is sure to please—in part because Radclyffe never loses sight of the fact that she is telling a love story, and a compelling one at that."—Cameron Abbott, author of *To The Edge* and *An Inexpressible State of Grace*

"*Innocent Hearts*...illustrates that our struggles for acceptance of women loving women is as old as time—only the setting changes. The romance is sweet, sensual, and touching."—*Just About Write*

"*Sweet No More*...snarls, teases and toes the line between pleasure and pain."—*Best Lesbian Erotica 2008*

"*Word of Honor* takes the reader on a great ride. The sex scenes are incredible...and the story builds to an exciting climax that is as chilling as it is rewarding."—*Midwest Book Review*

In Pursuit
of Justice

by

RADCLY*f*FE

2010

ISBN 10: 1-60282-148-8
ISBN 13: 978-1-60282-148-4

This Trade Paperback Original Is Published By
Bold Strokes Books, Inc.
P.O. Box 249
Valley Falls, NY 12185

First Bold Strokes Printing: April 2010

Credits
Production Design: Stacia Seaman
Cover Design by Sheri (graphicartist2020@hotmail.com)
Printed in Canada

Dedication

To Lee, my heart's pursuit

Chapter One

*E*verything hurt. Her jawed throbbed where he had struck her; her wrists chafed beneath the rough nylon cord that bound them tightly behind her back; and her breasts, exposed in the chill damp air, ached. The cavernous room was alive with shifting shadows, turning her fear to horror. His hands were rough—holding her down, violating her body, invading her soul. Helpless, she screamed silently, casting into the dark for salvation.

Please, please help me.

And then a voice—strong and certain and sure—called her name. A woman, blazing with strength and purpose, stepped from a darkness deeper than night to light the corners of her terror.

She's here. I prayed for her help, and she heard. She came.

With the cold circle of impending death pressed to her temple, she realized her mistake. Dread followed quickly on the heels of relief. Desperately, she shouted a warning that made no sound. She begged not for her own life, but for that of the woman she had summoned.

No, no! I didn't mean it. Don't come here. He'll kill you. I'm sorry. Oh God, don't do this.

A thundering explosion, deafening her. A searing trail of fire, dazzling her vision, blinding her. A thick red torrent—warm against her cheek; all that remained of her tormentor—his blood on her face and the hole in her heart.

Not my heart, *her* heart—oh, My Heart, don't leave me like this.

Stumbling, falling, her breath tearing from her chest in slivers of pain, she forced herself to look upon her own soul dying. There on the floor in the flickering candlelight, all of her hopes dissolved in a river of crimson, pumping past her hands with inexorable force. Relentless, pitiless, victorious death. The stakes had been set; the trade had been made—one life for another. She had been spared and, in the sparing, had lost everything. She would live, empty and forsaken. Guilt did not do justice to the agony of remorse she suffered for having called this one woman to her destruction.

On her knees in her lover's blood, her neck arched as if pleading to be sacrificed, begging to be taken instead, beseeching to be freed from the torment, she screamed again.

"Catherine."

Cold, she was so cold. Drowning in an agony of loss and self-recrimination. So dark, no air. "No…"

"Catherine, it's all right."

"Oh, my God." Dr. Catherine Rawlings shot upright in bed—gasping, sweat-soaked, and disoriented. Frantically, she turned in the dark room to the woman beside her, her hands roaming over the naked figure, reassured by the solid heat of her. *Alive, she's alive.* Finding her voice, she whispered hoarsely, "I'm sorry."

"No." Detective Rebecca Frye pulled the trembling woman into her arms, stroking the damp wisps of auburn hair back from her cheek. "Don't apologize."

"I woke you," Catherine said, her voice still shaking. "You should go back to sleep."

Rebecca gathered her closer, fitting their bodies together, breast against breast, thigh between thigh. "Let me comfort you, just this once."

"You do."

"Not often enough."

"Having you next to me is all the comfort I need."

"Well, then, let me believe I'm slaying your dragons. It makes me feel important."

"Oh, you are that." Catherine shivered, the image of Rebecca lying in a pool of blood chiseled indelibly on the tablets of her memory. She didn't need to be asleep to revisit that moment. Every time she looked at her tall, blond lover, she saw her precious life ebbing away with each heartbeat—seconds from death—having willingly sacrificed herself for Catherine.

During the first few weeks after the shooting, she had been able to shrug off the swift rise of terror and dread that so often took her unawares and left her shaking—sometimes when she was awake, more often when she slept. With Rebecca in the hospital, so critically injured, she'd had enough to occupy her thoughts that she had managed to ignore her own sleepless nights and anxious days. But Rebecca had been out of the hospital for more than two weeks, and the episodes were getting more frequent, and more terrifying.

Smoothing her hand down Rebecca's chest, lingering for a heartbeat on the thick scar tissue above her left breast, she murmured, "You're very important. Without you, I'd never get that great table at DeCarlo's, and I'd so miss having dinner there."

"We'll go tomorrow then."

"Rebecca...let's wait another week."

"It'll be fine. It's just dinner," Rebecca murmured, running her hand upward along the curve of Catherine's side until she cradled her breast in her palm. "Besides, I'm ready for a night out. I'm going stir crazy—for a lot of reasons."

"I know, but it's too soo—oh—" She caught her breath at the sharp point of pleasure that sparked from her nipple through her stomach as fingers closed hard on her breast. "Don't."

"Why not?" Rebecca teased, her mouth on Catherine's neck, tasting the salt, reveling in the pulse of blood beneath her lips. "I've missed you this way."

"You're still recovering," Catherine gasped. *You're not healed. You're still too thin; you're still so pale.*

Rebecca smoothed her palm down Catherine's abdomen, fingertips brushing lightly through silky hair. Catherine moaned—a faint strangled gasp of longing. *Oh, my God, don't do that. I want you so much. I was so afraid I'd lost you.*

When Catherine's hips lifted involuntarily beneath her fingers, Rebecca smiled and promised, "I'll be very still—just let me touch you. It won't hurt me." Shifting lower, she found a nipple with her teeth. Biting lightly, she slid her hand between Catherine's thighs, hovering a whisper above her, her palm warmed by the heat. "But I want you so much. Please."

"Yes. Oh, yes." Catherine relented because she needed so desperately to know in her bones that Rebecca was safe, to burn with the desire only this woman could stir in her, to extinguish fear with passion. "Touch me, Rebecca. I need to feel you. Make me…"

She choked, unable to speak, as Rebecca's fingers danced lightly over her straining flesh, stroking her fleetingly, dipping into the shimmering depths of her desire to spread liquid fire over her painfully engorged tissues. Turning her cheek to her lover's chest, Catherine closed her eyes, struggling to contain the avalanche of release that thundered demandingly through her blood. Trembling, she filled her hands with Rebecca's body, fingers digging into her arms, needing to be connected to her—everywhere. Only the tiny fragment of her mind still functioning kept her from pushing her hand between her lover's thighs to claim her, too. But she resisted with the last fiber of her strength, rocking against the fingers that tormented her.

Too soon…toosoon…ohI'mcomingtoosoon…

"Yess…" Rebecca held back as long as she could, listening to the cadence of Catherine's breathing, feeling her heart hammering against her own chest, sensing the tightening of muscles deep inside. When the woman in her arms went rigid, a strangled cry escaping her throat, Rebecca slid into her, filling her completely in one swift, sure motion. Muscles clenched, then spasmed, and Catherine arched, shouting in surprise, before finally convulsing in sweet, sweet surrender. Rebecca Frye closed her eyes and, secure in her lover's embrace, rode the crest of passion like a conquering hero. Never, never had she felt more alive.

❖

"What time is it?"

Rebecca rolled over and peered at the digital clock. "Almost six-thirty."

"Ugh," Catherine groaned, pushing back the covers to get up. "Thank God it's Friday. Ohh…I can't believe I just said that."

"Wait a minute," Rebecca said quietly, pulling her back down. When Catherine moved against her with a sigh, Rebecca settled onto her back with her arms around the still-drowsy woman. "So. Tell me about the nightmare."

"It was nothing. Just a dream."

"The third one this week?"

Catherine traced her fingers along Rebecca's ribs, down her

abdomen, remembering what it was like to make those muscles flicker with urgency when they made love. *What if they never...* She came back to herself with a start. "It's a bit of stress. Nothing to worry about."

"Because of me?" Rebecca insisted, tightening her hold. "Something I did?"

"No," Catherine assured her quickly. *It was hardly your fault...*

"Is it Blake?"

Catherine's stomach turned over. She should have realized that Rebecca was much too astute not to make the connection, although she doubted the detective realized exactly what about that night plagued her. For Rebecca, the idea of sacrificing herself in the line of duty was a simple reality of her life. "It scared me, almost losing you." At least that part was true. So terribly, terribly true. "When you were shot, I saw it. Your body jerked backward as if a giant hand had struck you. And then you fell. You were so still, so quiet, and there was so much blood."

"Catherine..."

"I was terrified...I remember, I was so cold. I felt something inside of me begin to die."

"I'm all right now."

"Not quite," Catherine said fervently, running her fingers over the scar tissue even as she pushed the lingering memories away. It was over. "But you will be."

"It's true," Rebecca insisted vehemently. She hated knowing that Catherine still suffered because of what had happened to her. The sooner she was back on her feet, the sooner this would be behind them. "Listen, I know you've had to take care of me the last couple of weeks, but I'm *fine* now. Everything is back to normal—at least it will be as soon as I pass the physical, re-qualify with my weapon, and jump through hoops for the shrink...uh...sorry. But you know what I mean."

"Yes." Catherine laughed finally, loving the certainty in her detective's voice. "I know what you mean. And you should remember that I *am* a psychiatrist. So believe me when I tell you I'm fine and there's nothing to worry about."

Rebecca pushed up against the pillows until she was sitting and looked seriously into her lover's eyes. "I'm still going to worry until those circles under your eyes go away."

"Well, then, just concentrate on getting well."

"That's exactly what I intend to do. Starting today."

❖

"Thank you for seeing me on such short notice. I'm sure you have other more pleasant things to do at home on a Friday evening."

"When you call me for a session, I know it's important," Hazel Holcomb replied, indicating the two overstuffed chairs flanking a low coffee table. The furniture was arranged upon a thick oriental carpet in front of a stone fireplace; the walls on either side were lined with floor-to-ceiling bookcases, and a large antique mahogany desk sat before bay windows that looked out on a well-tended flower garden. It was a functional but decidedly comfortable space. "Sit down. Do you want coffee or…let me see, I think I have some soda."

"No, I'm fine. I've been drinking coffee all day."

"You look tired, Catherine," the chief of psychiatry said kindly, thinking to herself that the woman across from her looked more than tired. She'd lost weight; there were new stress lines around her green eyes and a few more wisps of early gray in her hair. "Even considering the fact that it *is* Friday evening, with your clinical load and the recent events, you have every right to be weary."

"I am. That's why I'm here…in part."

"From the beginning, then," Hazel urged, settling back and looking for all the world as if she had nothing better to do than to listen indefinitely to her younger colleague.

"I'm not sleeping." They were in Hazel's private home office, and the warm comfortable atmosphere was a welcome relief from the too bright, too impersonal spaces of the university clinic. Still, Catherine found it difficult to relax as she leaned forward, her clasped hands on her knees, her fingers intertwined to hide the faint tremor. "I think I have post—"

"Let's wait before we worry about the diagnosis, shall we? Just tell me what's happening."

"Of course." Catherine smiled ruefully and ran a hand through her collar-length auburn hair, then regarded her friend and mentor apologetically. At sixty, Hazel was fit and vigorous, her quick blue eyes catching every nuance of expression, and she allowed nothing of consequence to pass without comment. "Is there anything worse than a physician as a patient?"

"Not many I can think of right offhand."

"This is hard…"

"Being a psychiatrist doesn't make it any easier. That's for television programs. Maybe I can help. This isn't about work, I take it? You would have come to the cafeteria for that."

Catherine smiled. When she needed a curbside consult, or just assurance that she was following the right clinical course in a difficult case, she sought out Hazel's advice during the chief's morning ritual of coffee and danish in the hospital cafeteria. "No. It's not work. It's the shooting."

"What about the shooting?"

"My…part in it."

Hazel regarded her steadily. "What part was that?"

"I insisted on going to meet him," Catherine said slowly, looking beyond Hazel's face into the past. "Rebecca didn't want me to go, practically begged me not to get involved. But I wanted to. I *wanted* to. I thought I could stop him." She brought tormented eyes to meet Hazel's. "My arrogance almost got her killed."

"Why aren't you sleeping?" Hazel asked, choosing not to comment but to let her talk. She had known Catherine since the younger psychiatrist was a resident, and she considered them friends as well as colleagues. What Catherine needed was for her to listen, not to point out the obvious fallacy in her reasoning. Reason carried very little weight where the emotions were concerned.

"I dream," Catherine replied, her voice choking. "I…feel him. He's hurting me, and I want Rebecca to come. I want her to make him stop. I want her to *kill* him."

"Go on."

"I'm so cold. He's torn my blouse." She shivered, rubbing her arms unconsciously. "I call out for her, and she comes for me. I'm so glad, so relieved. And then he shoots, and she's bleeding. She's bleeding and there's so much blood…oh God, there's so much blood…"

Catherine pushed back in her chair, as if pushing away the images, breathing rapidly, struggling to erase the vivid memories. "It was my fault."

"No, Catherine," Hazel said firmly. "It was the fault of the man who pulled the trigger, and I suspect you know that. I'll wager that's not much help, though, is it?"

"Not at the moment, no."

"I know. We're going to need more time than we have tonight to talk about why you feel that you're to blame. What I'm more interested in right now is a quick fix so you can get some rest."

Catherine smiled. "Such heresy."

"Fortunately, no one will ever know," Hazel replied with a grin. "How do you feel about medication?"

"I'd rather hold off for now." Catherine blew out a breath. "I was hoping it would be better when *she* was better. But it isn't. It's worse."

"How is she?"

"Recovering well. Chomping at the bit to get back to work."

"How is *she* sleeping?"

"So far, she seems fine. She's so focused on getting back to work that I don't think she's allowed anything else to really register consciously. Not Jeff Cruz's death, not even the fact that *she* almost died."

"She intends to resume active duty?" Hazel asked noncommittally, watching Catherine carefully, knowing that ultimately her friend would have to deal with how her lover dealt, or *didn't* deal, with these issues.

"Yes. The minute she's able."

"And there's no possibility she would change her mind…if you asked?"

"No, and I couldn't ask her. She loves being a cop. It's more than a job; it's who she is."

"So, she'll be on the streets again soon."

"Yes."

"And how do you feel about that?"

Catherine stared at her friend. Finally she admitted, "It terrifies me."

"I should think it would. I don't need to tell you about the fear that every partner of someone in a life-threatening occupation lives with on a daily basis. And you have not only *that* general anxiety with which to contend, you also have the actual experience of seeing her almost die in the course of doing her job." She shrugged. "You need to give yourself a break."

"That's it? That's your medical opinion?" Despite herself, Catherine was smiling.

"In a nutshell, yes. That and the fact that you need to see me on a regular basis for the time being. If your detective intends to go back to work, I suspect there'll be some things you need to sort out."

"Yes. I know," Catherine said quietly. If she and Rebecca were to have any future together, she would have to accept the fact that every time Rebecca walked out the door, it might be for the last time. She would have to learn to say goodbye, and she wasn't at all sure that she could.

CHAPTER TWO

The next morning, Catherine watched Rebecca pack with a sense of loss. It had taken her by surprise when after breakfast Rebecca had announced that it was time for her to move back to her own apartment "before the super rents it out from under me." That excuse was so thin Catherine could practically see it hanging in the air between them like a curtain of smoke.

The news shouldn't have been unanticipated, because in the last week Rebecca had improved dramatically; nevertheless, Catherine's first response had been one of disappointment. It was an occupational hazard to ask herself why she should feel abandoned, especially when she was genuinely elated at her lover's rapid recovery, but it was her nature to be reflective. So, as she leaned against the dresser watching Rebecca carefully fold jeans and T-shirts into a duffle, she struggled for perspective.

Too many conflicting emotions, that's all it is. Things will settle down in a week or two. As soon as I get used to the fact that she's all right, I won't feel as if my world is teetering on the brink of disaster. She jumped as the sound of the bag's zipper rasping closed cut sharply through the silence, a knife severing ties with heartless finality.

"I'll miss you."

Surprised, Rebecca looked up, a crease between her brows. "I'm not planning on going anywhere. But I can't stay here any longer."

Why not? But she knew why not. Her heart might not, but her head did. *Too soon. We've spent most of our time together in crisis mode, first in the midst of a high-pressure, horrifying case, and then in the aftermath of the shooting. That kind of intensity can push things too quickly. We need time to know one another better. There are far too many secrets still to tell.*

"I don't want us to end up practically living together by accident," Rebecca continued, placing her bag by the bedroom door. *You might discover you've made a mistake. You might decide I'm not relationship material, just like the others did when they spent enough time with me. Maybe if we're not so close, you won't be disappointed.*

The detective slipped on a dark gray blended silk blazer and automatically reached under the left side to adjust her shoulder holster. Of course, it wasn't there and wouldn't be until she was no longer on medical leave and had re-qualified on the range. Some rule from the city council about preventing impaired police officers from having access to service weapons. *Impaired.* Its absence was a constant reminder that she was not herself. At least they hadn't taken her shield. The weight of the slim leather case in the inner pocket of the jacket was some comfort—small comfort perhaps, but a reassurance that she *would* be whole again. *And soon. Today I start getting my life back.*

"And I especially don't want it to be because you were taking care of me."

"I was hardly taking care of you. You barely tolerated me cooking dinner every night without trying to do the dishes before you could even stand upright. I don't consider grocery shopping and a few loads of laundry a hardship. Skilled nursing it was not." Smiling wistfully to herself, Catherine thought about the three weeks she had taken off to spend with Rebecca after her discharge from the hospital and realized that they were some of the most relaxing weeks she'd had in months. Vacations had become a rarity as she tried to juggle private practice with her university teaching responsibilities. While she was at home with Rebecca, they'd watched a dozen movies on DVD, discovered that they shared a passion for screwball comedies, and managed to actually complete the Sunday *Times* crossword puzzle together—a first time for them both. Solitary and private by nature, she had never shared that much of her life with anyone before, other than her parents, and that had been far in the past. It had been surprisingly easy. "Besides, I liked it, you being here."

"So did I," Rebecca said softly, quickly crossing the bedroom to her side. She lifted Catherine's chin in her palm, searching her eyes. "I like a whole lot of things about being with you—having dinner with you, unwinding with you, and especially being there when you wake up." She blew out a breath, searching for the words to explain that she didn't want to build a relationship on the foundation of her own weakness. Finally she said, "When things are back to normal, I'll feel as if I deserve you."

"What makes you think you don't already?" Catherine realized even as she asked that Rebecca would only feel worthwhile if she was also a cop. "There isn't some test you have to pass with me, Rebecca. You don't have to *qualify* at anything to be cared about."

"I'm no good to anyone like this," Rebecca said in frustration. "I can barely carry my own suitcase!" Unconsciously, she'd taken a step back, putting distance between them. *You've only seen me when I was hurting or hurt. First Jeff's death and then this. I need to be able to give you something. I want to feel as if I deserve you, whether you think it matters or not.*

"It hasn't even been two months. You just need a little more time."

"Yeah, well," Rebecca said as she reached for her duffle, "it's time for me to get back to doing what I should be doing."

"Meaning what, Rebecca?" Catherine asked, her voice rising sharply. "Putting yourself in the line of fire before you've even healed from the last gunshot wound?"

"What?" Rebecca stopped dead, staring at her, completely perplexed. "You don't think what happened is normal, do you? It's a one in a million thing. Most police officers never even have to draw their weapons in the line of duty their entire careers."

"I don't care if it's 'one in a million' when it's you," Catherine replied softly, unable to keep the tears from her voice. "You're the only *one* I care about."

Rebecca's frustration at her own sense of helplessness disappeared in the face of Catherine's clear distress. "Hey," she said gently, moving quickly back to her and slipping firm arms around her waist. "Are we fighting?"

"No," Catherine sighed, leaning her cheek against Rebecca's chest. "*We're* obsessing."

"Uh-uh...cops don't obsess. We just act." There was a playful tone in her voice, but on some very basic level, she meant it. What she did, she did by instinct and reflex. Part of it was training and part of it was just her. When you stopped to think, you got yourself—or someone else—killed. Unfortunately, it probably wasn't the best approach to relationships, but it had never mattered so much before. "Cops don't go in too much for self-analysis. Nothing worse than second-guessing yourself out on the street."

Catherine snorted. "Don't think I haven't heard that before—from every cop I've ever talked to."

"Well then, see? It must be true."

"Detective?"

"Hmm?"

"Shut up." And then Catherine kissed her, forgetting for the moment that her detective was still healing, forgetting that she was worried about her safety, and even forgetting that she was angry—so angry—for her risking her life with no thought to how Catherine would survive the loss. She kissed her hard, enjoying the feel of those familiar arms tightening around her, thighs pressing close, hands claiming flesh. She kissed her until her own breath fled and her trembling legs threatened to desert her. "Much better," she finally murmured.

"Yeah. I'll pick you up at 7:00 for dinner," Rebecca said, her voice low and throaty. Another minute of that and she could forget the gym, because she wouldn't be able to walk.

"Yes."

As the door closed, Catherine listened to Rebecca's footsteps fading to silence. A silence so deep she thought she might drown in it.

❖

"Well, well, well…will you just look at what's arrived to brighten the mornin'," a voice bearing a hint of Ireland crooned in her ear. "And looking mighty fine as ever."

Rebecca finished the upward motion of her arms, deposited the barbell on the cleats, and turned her head on the slant board to eye the redhead kneeling by her side. Sparkling sea-foam eyes, faintly frizzy shoulder-length red hair pulled back in a haphazard ponytail, a dusting of freckles across pale skin. And a smile to light the darkest night. "Flanagan know you're loose?"

"Oh, no," Maggie Collins, the senior crime scene technician, whispered conspiratorially. "The general is mighty busy combing through a raccoon coat with a magnifying glass lookin' for dandruff and whatnot. She didn't see me sneaking away on my lunch break."

"She gives you a lunch break now?" Rebecca asked, sitting up on the end of the weight bench and toweling off. Her navy blue T-shirt with the police logo on the left chest was soaked through, as were her sweatpants, and she'd only been working out for fifteen minutes.

"Aye. Something about human rights requirements in the workplace."

"Huh. Amazing. What's she trying to find—DNA from the shed scalp skin?"

"That or from a hair follicle that isn't too desiccated to type." Maggie offered the detective her unopened plastic bottle of water. Frye was shaking, and she looked like she'd dropped twenty pounds off a frame that had always been lean. Her blue eyes were still the same, though—sparkling chips of ice, hard and penetrating. If anything, she looked more austerely handsome than before her injury, but Maggie sensed she was hurting. "Here—it won't be doin' you any good to get dehydrated before you've had a decent workout."

"Thanks." Rebecca took a long pull before asking, "What's new in the body shop?" She was referring to the crime scene investigations unit, or CSI, which was headed by Dee Flanagan, Maggie's lover. It was not just the morgue—which, strictly speaking, was the purview of Andy Corcoran, the medical examiner—but rather an extensive evidence analysis lab that examined all physical material collected at a crime scene and from the bodies involved. What Flanagan and her techs turned up was often instrumental in pointing the detectives in the right direction to solve a crime and virtually essential for proving a case in court. Means, motive, and opportunity were no longer enough for a conviction. You needed cold, scientific evidence—prints, ballistics, chemistry, DNA, serology, toxicology—and anything else that would link a suspect to a crime.

"Oh, every day it's a surprise. People keep inventing new and different ways to kill themselves and others. We've been missin' your company, though."

"Oh, I'll bet." Rebecca laughed. Dee Flanagan made it no secret that she didn't like cops in her lab, "bothering her techs and messing with evidence," as she so scathingly remarked, and she suffered their presence with very little patience. Like any good cop, Rebecca made it a point to review the forensic evidence herself, despite Flanagan's protests. "I'm sure she's been happy to have one less person bothering her."

"No," Maggie said softly, smiling a fond smile that Rebecca had seen before when Dee was the topic of conversation. "You she's been missin'."

"I'll stop down in a day or two. As soon as I get back to work."

"You're coming back soon, then?" Maggie tried to hide her surprise. Many officers injured a lot less severely than Rebecca took advantage of the disability premiums for as long as possible. But then she should have known that Frye wouldn't be one to sit at home. *Goin' crazy, probably.*

"I'm seeing Captain Henry first thing Monday morning."

"Well then, you'd best get back to pumping that iron. You need a spot?"

"No. I'm not pushing. Just easing back in." In truth, she'd been about to quit when Maggie'd come along. Her chest was on fire, and even though she'd reduced her usual weights by half, she'd been struggling. What worried her the most, though, was how short of breath she got after ten minutes on the treadmill. Although the doctors had assured her that her lung—collapsed by the bullet that had entered between her third and fourth ribs, an inch above her heart—had not sustained any permanent damage, it felt like something wasn't working right. And if she couldn't run, she couldn't work. "I'm doing okay."

"Right," Maggie agreed. "Good to see you back, Rebecca."

Yes. It will be good to get back. All the way back. When she went into the locker room to shower, despite the pain and the fatigue, she felt more like herself than she had since the moment two months before when she'd come to in a sea of agony to find Catherine bending over her, terror in her eyes. All she needed now was to convince everyone else that she was fit for duty. She had a lot of unfinished business to attend to, and she couldn't begin to take care of it until she had reclaimed her place in the world.

❖

"Is something wrong?" Rebecca asked quietly. They were seated at a small candlelit table in the nook formed by floor-to-ceiling bay windows in DeCarlo's, a very exclusive restaurant that occupied the ground floor of a century-old mansion. A bottle of imported champagne sat chilling in a silver ice bucket beside them and the appetizers—grilled figs and sweet sausages—had just been placed in the center of the linen-draped table. Despite the elegant décor and the intimate atmosphere, she had a feeling that her dinner companion was absorbed in something other than the fine meal and her own stellar company.

"Hmm? Oh, no." Catherine reached for her hand, smiling apologetically. "I'm sorry. I drifted away there for a minute. Work."

"Don't apologize; I know the feeling. Even been guilty of it a few times myself. Anything you can talk about?"

"No, not really."

Rebecca nodded understandingly. "No problem."

"Thanks." Fortunately, Rebecca had appreciated from the first that Catherine's work was something that she could only allude to in the most general of terms, for obvious reasons of patient confidentiality. It had been just that conflict that had brought them so explosively together just a few short months before. It was one thing, however, to have the barrier exist professionally and quite another to have it crop up in their personal dealings. Because she'd never before had a relationship that had been so central to her life, Catherine had never had to contend with the fact that she couldn't discuss some of the ramifications of her work with the person closest to her. She was still learning how to navigate those murky waters, and, thankfully, Rebecca, who was used to compartmentalizing her life, didn't push. It helped defuse the awkwardness, but there were times—like tonight—when Catherine wished she *could* talk. The session earlier in the day kept returning to her thoughts.

"Let's get the paperwork out of the way first, okay?"

"Sure."

"No significant medical, surgical, or psychiatric conditions in the past?"

"That's right."

"Ever been hospitalized for any reason?"

"*No.*"

She'd wait to ask about the obvious bruise under the left eye and what looked like finger marks on the neck. "Any drug allergies or current medications?"

"*No.*"

"*Recreational drug use?*"

"*I drink now and then. Nothing else.*"

"*Do you smoke?*"

"*When I drink.*" *Faint laughter.*

Catherine smiled. She had found that with new patients it was best to start with something basic and unthreatening such as reviewing the data the patient provided on a standard medical questionnaire. It established a bit of rapport, although the young woman in her office didn't seem particularly nervous. Upright posture, no apparent tics or nervous habits. Her button-down-collar pale blue cotton shirt and dark tan chinos were meticulously pressed, her oxfords polished and shined, her thick wavy hair cut short, no make-up. If anything, the clear-eyed brunette with the sharp blue gaze was watching her with just a hint of suspicion—or was it something else? Intense curiosity? Not unusual from patients, but it usually developed later in the course of treatment—that need to know the therapist as a person and not as someone who merely existed for fifty minutes once or twice a week and to whom you exposed your most intimate secrets. But about whom you knew almost nothing.

"*My secretary, Joyce, made a notation that we'll be billing insurance,*" *Catherine remarked, checking the intake form. It was Saturday, and she didn't usually see patients, but after Rebecca had left with all her belongings in tow, the apartment had seemed so empty— almost lifeless—that when she'd picked up her messages and found one about a request for a semi-urgent appointment, she'd decided she might as well work.* "*I see you have a good plan that doesn't cap the number of visits, so that will be simple.*"

"*I don't think I'll be coming long enough for that to be an issue.*"

Her tone was level and matter-of-fact, no hint of aggression or combativeness. Just a statement.

"*And that brings me to the next question,*" *Catherine responded just as evenly.* "*It says your reasons for coming are work related. Can you tell me about that?*"

"I've been ordered to see a therapist and to obtain a written statement that I am fit for duty."

"Ordered? I'm sorry, I don't understand," Catherine said, glancing down at the form, confused. Joyce had left a message that a new patient had called asking for an appointment as soon as possible, but there had been no indication that it had been any kind of official consultation. She often performed evaluations of city employees—mostly work-related disability claims, and occasionally confirmatory profiles on detainees—but someone from the appropriate city department usually called ahead to set up the meeting. *"What do you—"*

"I'm a police officer."

"I see." Catherine pushed the folder aside, leaned back in her chair, and met the young woman's eyes. Now it was time for them to talk. *"Is this a disability situation, or something else?"*

"It's a disciplinary investigation."

"I didn't get any referral papers. Usually someone sends me a summary of the incident."

"It's probably in transit. I'll call them on Monday."

"No need—we'll take care of it. How did you get to me? Isn't there an in-house psychologist who signs off on an officer's duty status?"

"There is, but the department has to provide alternate choices for reasons of impartiality. You're on the short list."

The lesser of two evils? *Actually, she hadn't even realized she was on any kind of list, and the only reason she minded was that, had she known, she would have asked Joyce to screen new patient calls differently and to prioritize calls from police officers. Her already busy private patient schedule could only accommodate so many therapy sessions per week, but she always made time for emergencies.*

"Is there some reason that you didn't *want to see...is it still Rand Whitaker doing the psych evals for the department?"*

"Yes."

The young officer shrugged, a move that reminded Catherine of Rebecca's dismissive gesture when she considered something unworthy of her attention. Lord, do they stamp them out of some mold somewhere, these silent women with suspicious eyes?

"I'm asking why you went outside channels because I need to know if there was a conflict or problem within the department that will affect how you and I communicate, or that we need to discuss."

"No problem. I just want my private business to stay private. And..."

For the first time she looked the slightest bit uncertain.

"And...?" Catherine asked gently.

"And I wanted to talk to a woman."

"Fair enough. Let me tell you a little bit about how I do this, so that we're on the same page. It helps to avoid confusion if you have an idea of how long this might take."

A curt nod, an attentive expression, despite a faint frown line between dark brows. Catherine sensed her ambivalence—she had come because she had been ordered to, but she was also cooperating. Perhaps, on some level, she wants to be here.

"As I said, the department will send a summary of why you're being referred, but I want you to tell me in your own words. Then I'd like to spend some time getting to know you. General background kinds of things. When I feel that I can make some determination about this event within the context of your professional life, I'll file my report."

"How much of what we talk about will be in it?"

Two references in less than five minutes to issues of privacy and confidentiality. She's worried about keeping something in her personal life a secret.

"You may see my report. I will not discuss your case with anyone without informing you and obtaining your consent. You understand that I will need to include some details of our meetings to substantiate my findings, and that this will become part of your personnel record?"

"Yes."

A bit of anger there. She feels violated. Betrayed by her superiors, by the system that sent her here?

"Do you want to proceed? You could still see Rand Whitaker."

"No. How long will this take?"

"I don't know. Have you been suspended?"

"No. But they've got me riding a desk."

Stiff shoulders, condescending tone of voice, one quick, frustrated fist clench. She's chafing at the restrictions.

"More than a few sessions, most likely. I'll see you on an accelerated schedule, but that's as definite as I can be. What do you say?"

Several beats of silence.

"Okay."

"So. Tell me what happened."

"If there's something you *can* say, I'm here if you want to talk," Rebecca remarked.

"I'm fine. I was just daydreaming about something that happened in a session today—something that brought up more than I realized, apparently. Rather like a waking version of what Freud said about dreams. He called them day residue, things we are still trying to process that we didn't finish before sleep."

"He said a lot more than that about dreams, didn't he?" Rebecca commented dryly.

Laughing, Catherine nodded agreement. "Yes, quite a bit—most of which I take issue with." Linking her fingers through Rebecca's, she continued, "Nevertheless, even if I could talk about it, I certainly wouldn't want to take up our time together tonight with business. After all, this is a date, right?"

They'd made love, spoken of love, but they'd never had the time to fall in love. As much as she missed Rebecca's subtle presence in her apartment—the extra clothes in the closet, two coffee cups in the sink, her keys and wallet on the dresser—she liked this new distance, too. It was a distance heavy with promise and hope, a kind of charged separation she'd never experienced before. It was the very opposite of lonely, because even though they still had a lot to learn about one another, Rebecca was a part of her life now.

"Well," Rebecca mused, feigning thought, her thumb playing over Catherine's palm, "I got all spruced up in my best suit and I washed the Vette. And I'm trying like hell to impress you with the dinner and the wine."

Watching a pleased smile flicker across Catherine's elegant face, Rebecca thought of how much she'd missed her that afternoon when she'd opened the door of her own apartment to be greeted by the musty scent of abandonment. Out of years of habit, she'd dropped the duffle inside the door and walked directly across the rugless living room to the single window, pushed it up, and leaned out to breathe the aroma of car exhaust and Saturday dinners. Home. As familiar as a favorite bar, and as lonely as the tail end of the night with only a bottle for company.

She leaned closer across the table, her gaze claiming Catherine with the intensity of a caress. When she was with her, the places inside that always ached stopped hurting. "And I was hoping that you chose that dark green blouse with me in mind, because it reflects in your eyes—like shadows in a forest—calling my…"

"Rebecca," Catherine murmured, her heart hammering, "we're in a restaurant."

Undeterred, she continued in a low, husky tone, "And I've been thinking all afternoon about the way my skin burns when—"

"Stop. Right. Now. We are going to sit here and consume this very fine food, or Anthony will be so offended, he'll never recover." Her voice cracked, and she had to swallow. The way Rebecca was looking at her made her blush, from pleasure and something far more primal. She had never been the focus of such undiminished attention in her life. It was a heady feeling, and she suddenly understood how people made fools of themselves for love. "Is this how you seduce women?"

"Only you."

"It's working."

"Good."

Reluctantly, they sat back in their seats, breathing a little erratically, fingertips just barely touching on the fine linen. The first time at DeCarlo's, they had just met. They'd been strangers, uncertain, wary, but drawn to one another nevertheless. In the weeks since, they'd shared fear and passion and near-death, but, in so many ways, they were strangers still.

"There is something wrong with the appetizers?" Anthony DeCarlo asked anxiously from beside them.

"No," Catherine answered, smiling quickly at him before glancing back at Rebecca, whose eyes had never left her face. "They're perfect."

Chapter Three

Rebecca rolled over and opened her eyes. She smiled when she found Catherine, arms wrapped around her pillow, lying close beside her and watching her with a tender expression in her soft green eyes.

"I fell asleep last night, didn't I?" Rebecca asked sheepishly.

"Uh-huh. Actually, you fell asleep several times last night." Catherine ran her fingers through Rebecca's thick, tousled blond hair, finally resting her fingers in the curve of her neck. "Let's see. First, you fell asleep in the car. I was very glad that I didn't drink more of Anthony's wonderful champagne, because I wouldn't have been able to drive us home. You were literally out on your feet by the time we got to the Vette."

"I'm sorry," Rebecca said, completely chagrined. She'd had very different plans for Saturday evening, none of which had included falling asleep at nine o'clock.

"Don't be. You obviously needed to rest, and I am very fond of sleeping next to you."

"Well, I'd like you to be fond of a few other things *before* the sleeping part," Rebecca murmured, shifting closer until their bodies touched along their entire length. Instinctively, effortlessly, their limbs entwined, and they pressed even nearer until their lips were only a breath apart. "It was supposed to be a hot date, remember?"

"Oh, I remember that very well." She didn't seem to have any control over what happened to her body when Rebecca was against her like this. The feel of Rebecca's skin hot against her own, a heat so much more consuming than any fever, set her blood on fire. It was hard to think; it was hard to remember that she meant to go slowly and carefully this first time. She hadn't made love to Rebecca in almost two months, and her hands were already shaking with the need to touch her. Valiantly, she tried to distract herself with conversation, because she was a heartbeat away from forgetting her good intentions.

"When we got home," Catherine continued, her voice a little breathless, "you managed to make it up the stairs with just a little help from me, but by the time I had my shoes off, you were asleep again." She ran her fingers down the center of Rebecca's chest, pausing to brush her fingertips over a taut pink nipple. The swift intake of breath and the automatic surge of Rebecca's hips were exactly the reward she had been seeking. Moving her lips along the edge of Rebecca's jaw, she finally reached her ear and whispered, "I had a really good time taking your clothes off, though."

Rebecca couldn't help but laugh. "I am thoroughly humiliated. What a putz."

"Oh, you are so far from that," Catherine replied, laughing, too.

"Well, I've had smoother moments. I guess the workout tired me out a little more than I realized."

"How are you feeling?" Catherine asked, suddenly serious, her hand stilling on Rebecca's skin. She'd seen Rebecca work for days at a time with no sleep, but never had she seen her as physically depleted as the previous night. Even knowing that it was a perfectly natural occurrence at this stage in her recovery didn't eliminate the quick rush of fear.

"I'm feeling way better than fine," Rebecca replied soundly, claiming Catherine's mouth for a kiss.

"Ah…" she sighed when she could find her voice. "I can tell."

Rebecca kissed her again, and it was the warmth of her tongue that was Catherine's undoing, or perhaps it was the way Rebecca pressed her fingers into the shallow depression at the base of her spine, or the way she—

"Rebecca," she gasped, "I can't possibly wait another minute."

"Then don't."

Rebecca shifted Catherine beneath her. Bracing her arms on either side of Catherine's shoulders, she fit her hips between Catherine's thighs and rocked into her, the rhythmic pressure making them both hard in a matter of seconds.

Sighing, Catherine ran her hands up and down Rebecca's back, cupping her buttocks, squeezing the tight muscles as she thrust, forcing them together even harder. Watching Rebecca through eyes dim with need, she found her desire mirrored in Rebecca's intense expression. Even as she felt Rebecca's strong shoulders and arms beneath her fingers and the insistent pressure of her hips working between her thighs, she couldn't help but see the irregular, bright red scars on her chest.

"How do you...feel?" Her words were punctuated by short gasps as she found it increasingly hard to catch her breath.

"I'm...perfect," Rebecca assured her, but all she could really feel was the growing heaviness in her stomach and the slowly rising tension between her legs. Her arms were trembling with the effort of supporting her upper body, but she didn't care. It had been so long, too long, and she needed this more than she needed air to breathe.

"This is torture," Catherine gasped, linking her fingers behind Rebecca's neck and pulling her head down, bruising her mouth with a kiss. Their tongues trysted with the same seeking need as their hips thrust, until the tempo of blood pounding and muscles clenching and lips searching echoed the pulsing beat deep inside. "I need to taste you. It's been so long. I feel like I'm starving."

"I won't last if you do," Rebecca groaned. It had been a very long time for her, too, and she was already crazy to come.

"I don't care." Gently but insistently, Catherine placed her palms on Rebecca's chest and pressed until she relented and rolled over onto her back. Following in one smooth motion, Catherine settled between her lover's thighs, her breasts resting for a moment in the moist heat between Rebecca's legs. Then she caught the rim of skin edging her navel and tugged it between her teeth, drawing a deep groan from Rebecca that made her head swim.

Following the insistent pressure of Rebecca's palms against her face, she inched lower until her lips brushed the fine hair between Rebecca's legs. The scent and heat of her was like being welcomed home. With a grateful sigh, she rested her cheek against the soft smooth skin of her lover's inner thigh and slowly, reveling in the first sweet taste, took her between her lips. She had intended to go slowly, had meant to savor every sensation, but Rebecca's sharp cry at the first touch of her mouth and the tightening of the muscles in Rebecca's thighs told her how very close she was. Suddenly, all Catherine wanted to do was lose herself in Rebecca's pleasure.

"Oh, no," Rebecca moaned, her voice tight and choked. "You're going to make me come right away."

It was enough to make Catherine's heart shatter. She loved having her like this, feeling the two disparate elements of Rebecca's being fuse at the moment of final release—strength and surrender, power and need, wariness and trust—all of her trembling, quivering on the edge of dissolving. So...so unbelievably beautiful.

"It's not enough," Rebecca whispered hoarsely when her body finally stopped shuddering. "I want you somewhere...somewhere inside..."

"I know."

The first time had been fast, furious—a wild, frantic reclaiming of body and soul after the threat of separation far greater than time or distance. The next time, and the next, followed on a swell of arousal that was no more possible to quell then it would have been to stop the revolutions of the earth. It was a force beyond volition and just as natural. They'd met in the midst of crisis, and during those few hectic weeks, they'd made love in moments of need, and in moments of gratitude, and in moments of nearly desperate passion. But they'd had very little time for happiness, let alone elation. On this particular Sunday morning in early September, with sunlight painting their skin in shades of gold, they made love for the sheer joy of being alive...and being together.

❖

"Pizza or Chinese?"

"Chinese," Catherine answered drowsily, trailing her fingers along the crest of Rebecca's hip. "More green vegetables."

"Oh, yeah. I guess I need to preserve my strength if we're going to keep this up." Rebecca shifted, moving the arm that she had just realized was numb. In fact, now that she thought about it, a lot of her seemed to be pleasantly enervated. "We *are* going to keep it up, right?"

"Don't tell me you still need more."

"Well, not right this very minute," Rebecca conceded, wondering if she'd ever walk again, "but soon."

Catherine leaned up on an elbow, pushing strands of damp hair back from her face, and stared at her. "Are you serious?"

Rebecca grinned. "Okay, maybe not until the morning."

"Thank God, because I am exhausted." She settled back in the crook of Rebecca's arm and drew one leg up over her lover's thigh. The room was dim, afternoon somehow having slipped into dusk, and the day held that timeless quality that only late Sundays in waning summer could. It reminded her of the naïve innocence of childhood when life seemed to be nothing more than an endless stretch of warm, lazy afternoons. Bicycles and tennis and a favorite book under the shade of a tree—no concept of disappointment or loss. Not even then, and certainly never as an adult, could she ever remember having been so satisfied or so completely content. She couldn't think of a single thing to worry about. Somewhere in the back of her pheromone-saturated mind, that fact rang danger bells, but she couldn't bear to break the spell by probing for the source. "I'd rather be here with you like this than do anything else in the world."

For a second, Rebecca's heart stopped, and she could hear the blood stilling in her veins. The idea of being that important to this one incredible, remarkable woman was terrifying and exhilarating and like nothing she'd ever experienced. Nothing in her life had ever struck her with the power of that single sentence, not even getting her shield. Not even the bullet. "Why?" *Why me, of all the women you could choose?*

"You remind me of what's important."

Rebecca turned on her side so she could see Catherine's eyes. "What things are those?"

"That's the funny thing about love," Catherine mused, tracing the side of Rebecca's neck with the fingers of one hand. "They're different things for all of us, but being in love makes us feel them just the same."

"You know what's really scary?" Rebecca asked quietly, wondering if she'd ever be able to take a full breath again. Her chest was so tight, and it had nothing to do with getting shot.

"What?"

"I know what you're talking about."

"Yes," Catherine whispered, her voice thick with so many feelings, and her skin still raw with the aftermath of passion, "I know that you do."

"How hungry are you?" Rebecca gathered Catherine's breast into her palm, rolling the nipple under her thumb.

"Starving," Catherine replied, tilting her head to catch a full lower lip between her teeth. *And I never even knew it.*

❖

"Are you going to eat that?"

Catherine studied the last shrimp in Szechwan sauce. It looked inviting. "I want it, but I think I'm full."

"I've heard that before," Rebecca commented as she quickly captured it with her chopsticks. "There's no time to waste then."

They were sitting naked on the bed, the *Times* stacked at the foot and open containers of food, paper plates, and napkins between them. It was dark outside Catherine's bedroom windows, and they'd turned on the shaded bedside reading lamp.

Catherine watched Rebecca deftly manipulating the slim slivers of wood, remembering the way those fingers had felt on her skin. "You're going in tomorrow, aren't you?"

"Yes."

"Does your captain know you're coming?"

"Not yet." Rebecca's smile was thin. "He'd probably refuse to see me until after I did the thing with Whitaker."

"The department psychologist."

"Uh-huh."

"But you *are* going to see him, right?"

"No choice. There's been a lot of bad press the last few years—reports of excessive use of force, vigilantism, escalating suicide rates among the ranks, and a million other things. So now, *anything* involving an officer—whether it's a complaint or an officer-involved shooting or even sometimes just *drawing* your weapon—can land you in counseling."

"But with you there's reason," Catherine offered gently, knowing that no officer wanted to be reminded of their vulnerability or of the fact that emotions were one thing outside of their control. Rebecca had said very little about the shooting or about the fact that she had almost died.

It was hard keeping silent, but Catherine knew that she could not be the detective's lover *and* her therapist; she would have to rely on Whitaker to help resolve whatever the experience had brought up for her.

"Maybe." The silence grew heavy between them, and finally Rebecca asked, "What is it?"

"I'm worried about you," Catherine confessed.

"Don't be. I feel fine. I'll be fine."

"All right." Her fears would make little sense to Rebecca, for whom life was so much more black and white. Cops like her did not fear possibilities, because only the facts mattered. Reality for her detective was defined by events, not eventualities. "Just…be careful."

What an inadequate request. *Don't get hurt. Don't get killed. Don't leave me now, not after touching me like this.*

"I'll do everything by the book. I promise." She'd seen the uncertainty in Catherine's eyes, and it killed her to know she'd put it there. She'd keep her word, too. As much as she could, and still do what she had to do.

❖

It had been more than two months since Catherine had last watched Rebecca's transformation from the woman she had held through the night into the cop. Oh, the cop was always there—whether on duty or not—surfacing for an instant in the sharp appraisal of a stranger who approached on the street or evident in the fleeting shadows that marred her clear gaze when some memory momentarily escaped her ironclad control, but never so much as when Detective Sergeant Rebecca Frye began her morning routine.

First she pulled on a crisp, starched shirt, creased tailored trousers, and a matching blazer. Then, she slid the case that held her gold shield into the breast pocket of her blazer. Her holster, empty now, she gathered in one hand, but later it would be snugged against her chest. As she assembled the symbols of her identity, Rebecca's expression became more remote, her carriage more guarded, and her eyes more distant. It was a frightening thing to witness when what Catherine needed most from Rebecca were the parts she so naturally hid away.

"You're awfully quiet," Rebecca remarked as Catherine gathered her briefcase, beeper, and cell phone from the small table just inside the front foyer. They'd showered separately, and when she'd joined Catherine in the kitchen, they'd barely had time for a cup of coffee and toast. Nevertheless, there was a shadow of discomfiture in Catherine's face that wasn't usually there.

"Am I?" Catherine smiled, realizing that she had indeed been preoccupied. "I suppose I am. You would make a good psychiatrist, Detective."

"And you're doing that shrink thing again—avoid and divert. Ask a question, change the subject." Rebecca's tone was teasing, but she leveled her eyes at the woman in the understated elegant jade suit. "That's a cop's trick."

They were only two feet apart, but the air between them was thick enough to walk on. It was a distance that if left unbridged would grow, and Rebecca had reached out. Catherine dropped her briefcase and stepped across the gulf, sliding her arms around the tall blond's waist.

"I'm trying to get used to the fact that things will be different now."

Rebecca put her hands on Catherine's hips, under the edge of her jacket, and kissed her softly. A moment later, she said firmly, "No. They won't."

"Call me later?"

"Count on it."

❖

At 7:10 a.m., she walked into the squad room and sensed the knot of uncertainty and unease in her stomach loosening. Everything looked, and smelled, the same. Same shabby mismatched desks fronting each other in randomly placed pairs, same sickly institutional green paint on the walls, same worn gray tiles on the floor. The odor of stale smoke, old coffee grounds, and honest sweat permeated the air. She couldn't help but feel a wave of relief when she saw that her desk was exactly as she had left it. Her mug was there in the middle of a stained blotter, a pile of dog-eared file folders balanced precariously in one corner, and the phone was angled precisely the way she always placed it when she was working. Even the rumpled hulk of a man seated at the desk opposite hers looked exactly the same. Fiftyish, gray-haired and balding, forty pounds over his fighting weight—stereotypical flat foot right out of Ed McBain.

"Is that your only suit, Watts?" she asked as she shed her jacket to the back of her chair.

William Watts looked up at the sound of the deep, cutting voice, his expression impassive but his eyes quick and sharp as they took her in. *Thin, still pale, and edgy. Not too bad, considering.* He smiled, but it didn't show on his face. Not much did. "What, did I miss the memo about the dress code?"

"Yeah, the one that recommends the laundry for that suit every few months."

He grunted, watching her slide open the bottom left hand drawer of her desk and place the empty holster carefully inside. She didn't look right without it, but she still looked damn good to him. He was relieved to find that he could look at her and not see the river of blood spreading over her chest. For a few weeks, especially while she was in the ICU, he'd been afraid he'd never stop seeing it.

"How come the cap didn't say anything about you coming back?"

"Because he doesn't know it yet."

Her smile was thin, and there was a new hardness in her eyes. He'd thought her tough before; now she was stone. Maybe that's what it took to come back after what she'd been through. He didn't really want to know. "Well, if it will get me off these goddamned cold cases, I'll go in with you."

She studied him, a big part of her wanting to dislike him still. Mostly because he was sitting in Jeff's chair, and Jeff Cruz, her partner of six years, was dead. But Watts, in his typical roundabout way, had just offered to back her up with the captain. He'd had her back once before, when it really counted. When it had been the only thing that mattered more to her than the job. When it had been Catherine's life. But right now, she needed to stand alone. To prove that she still could.

"I can handle it."

"Right," he replied uninterestedly, reaching for another file on another old case that hadn't been solved and never would be.

"Thanks, Watts."

When he glanced up in surprise, all he got was her retreating back, but he smiled anyhow.

❖

"Come in."

"Morning, Captain."

Captain John Henry looked up from the stack of departmental reports he'd been perusing as the door to his small office closed, and he registered the identity of the unmistakable voice he hadn't heard for weeks. "Frye."

They eyed one another for a few seconds, taking stock. They'd worked together for eight years. They respected one another. And they took nothing for granted. She stood in front of his desk as relaxed as she ever got, which was to say, hands loose at her sides but muscles coiled and set to spring. He leaned back in the leather chair, his one concession to comfort, with his summer-weight blended gabardine jacket on, tie tightly knotted beneath a snowy white collar, his handsome mahogany features inscrutable. He placed his pen on the desktop.

"I take it you have something to say?"

"Yes, sir. I'm ready to work."

He sighed. "Sit down, Sergeant."

She did, crossing one calf over the opposite knee, her hands motionless on the armrests. The last time she'd sat in this room, she'd come perilously close to insubordination and had nearly torpedoed her career. Catherine had been sitting beside her, and Henry had asked the psychiatrist to put her own life in danger to catch a psychopathic killer. Rebecca had disagreed with her superior—vocally and repeatedly. She still didn't know why he hadn't slapped her down that day but had put her in charge of the operation instead. The one time she'd seen him since then had been in the hospital, when she'd awakened to find him sitting nearby. She vaguely remembered him saying that she'd done the department proud.

"I don't suppose you remember that there are protocols for this situation." Frye was his best detective, but she didn't always play by the rules, at least not the bureaucratic ones. Most effective cops didn't. But there were some rules he couldn't bend.

"I know that," she replied. "I was just hoping to speed up the process." She waited a beat. "And I wanted to check out the lay of the land."

"Spit it out, Sergeant. I've got a busy day."

"My desk is still out there. I want to make sure my job is, too."

Henry got up and walked to a small side table where an antiquated coffee machine stood warming a half-filled pot. He poured a mug full and answered with his back turned. "If things hadn't turned out the way they did, you could have been suspended for ignoring any number of basic rules of procedure. You didn't call for backup; you endangered yourself and a fellow officer, not to even mention putting a civilian at risk. Jesus. What a field day the press could have had with that if she'd been hurt. You were lucky."

The scar on her chest picked that moment to start itching. When it did that, she wanted to tear through the hard red flesh until it bled. She didn't move a muscle. Calmly, she said, "Yes, sir."

"No one cares about that, now. You're a hero." He settled a hip against the counter and sipped the coffee. His wife bought the blend for him. He was grateful she'd consented to marry him for more reasons than he could count, and every time he poured a cup, he remembered it. Smart woman. "I can't say you haven't been missed." He almost smiled at his own understatement. Jesus, when had he become a bureaucrat? "With you out and Cruz...gone, I've been hurting for senior detectives."

"Watts is experienced."

He studied her, remembering quite clearly her vociferous objections to working with—what had she called Watts—a lazy fuck-up? He'd give a lot to know what really went down out there between the two of them that night. Whatever it was, Frye was standing up for Watts now. "He's not sergeant material. Here's the drill—you'll have to ride a desk until I have every piece of paper authorizing your return signed and in my hands."

The tightness in her chest began to ease. "I'm going to the range this morning. There's nothing wrong with my shooting arm. I'll re-qualify and get my weapon back, so I should be okay for street duty after that."

"Nice try, Frye. Not until the shrink signs off, and you know how slow they are." He held up a hand when he saw the fire jump in her eyes. "But, maybe we can work around it." He walked back behind his desk, took a thick blue folder off a pile by his right hand, and opened it in front of him. "This just came in. The brass wants us to be part of a task force the feds are setting up—"

"Uh-uh. No way. Not a combined jurisdictional deal. That's a dead-end job. Making nice with assho—"

"Sergeant."

She clamped her jaws closed so hard she was certain Henry could hear them snap. She'd expected some kind of repercussions after what had happened with Blake. The press might have made her out to be a hero, but that didn't make it true. Henry had every right to be pissed off about the way she'd skirted the chain of command, but she didn't figure he'd bury her in some back room, pushing paper with the feds. Okay, fine, she'd crawl if it meant street duty.

"Captain, please…"

"Hear me out, Frye." His tone was surprisingly conciliatory. Continuing to scan the memo, he read, "Justice, Customs, and the Philadelphia PD are to set up a multilevel task force aimed at identifying and apprehending those individuals and/or organizations responsible for the production and distribution of child pornography, including the procurement of subjects."

Rebecca blinked. "What does that mean? Some kind of sting operation?"

"I'm not entirely sure," Henry admitted. In fact, the way the entire thing had been dumped on him was odd. He'd gotten a call from *his* boss and been told to put a team player on it, and that's all he'd been told. Well, it was his squad and he'd assign whom he liked. "The thing is in the formative stages from what I can see. But it's been blue-lined—top priority. Since Special Crimes has the best working knowledge of the street side of things—child prostitution, kiddie porn, the whole ugly mess—we've been fingered to provide the local manpower."

"For how long?" Rebecca asked suspiciously. It might be an entrée back to the streets, at least she could parlay it into one, but she didn't want to be stuck in bureaucratic limbo indefinitely. There might be another important perk involved, too. While she worked the child prostitution angle, she could do a little digging into what Jimmy Hogan had gotten himself into while undercover, what he had wanted to tell her partner, and what he knew that had gotten both of them killed. "Weeks, months?"

"Couldn't say." He shrugged. "I can't imagine it will move all that quickly, but who knows. For the time being, it's the closest thing to street duty you're going to see."

He closed the folder and fixed her with a steady stare. "You've got a few choices, Sergeant. The commissioner would love to promote you—they like good press, and a hero cop is good press. Accept the lieutenant's bars, make the department look good, and you could probably transfer to some nice administrative position downtown."

"Behind a desk."

"Yes."

"Or?" Rebecca queried, although she already knew the answer.

"Go through channels and get your psych clearance, take this assignment, and when I think you're ready, I'll move you back to catching active cases."

There wasn't much to think about. She stood, her expression nearly blank. "Who do I contact?"

He opened the folder, jotted down a name and number, and handed it to her. "Avery Clark, Department of Justice. That's the local number. You can have one of our people for legwork, and we'll pull a uniform to handle the paperwork from our end. Organized Crime probably has people undercover working the prostitution angle, and you'll have to be careful to preserve their cover. I don't have to tell you that whenever we've got people in that position, any move that might expose them can be risky."

She thought about Jimmy Hogan and Jeff Cruz. Two dead cops. "No, sir. You don't."

"And this is an *administrative* position, Frye. Advise, coordinate, provide background. You need street intel, you get someone else to pound the pavement for it. Am I clear?"

"Perfectly, Captain."

CHAPTER FOUR

At 7:35 a.m., Catherine opened the door that separated her office from the patient waiting area. Joyce had not arrived yet, but her first patient had. This morning, she was in uniform. Creased navy blue trousers, pale blue shirt with placket pockets over each breast, a narrow black tie, small bits of silver shined to a high polish on collar and cuffs. She was standing, her hat tucked beneath her arm, her blue eyes nearly gray. Thunderclouds, hiding a storm of feelings.

"Come in, please, Officer."

"Thanks for seeing me so early."

"That's all right. It works out better this way for my schedule, too." Catherine gestured to the leather chairs in front of her desk as she walked behind it. "I take it you're on your way to work?"

"If you can call it that," the young woman said with a grimace as she sat down and planted her feet squarely on the floor in front of her, her back not even touching the chair. "I'm supposed to find out from the duty sergeant this morning exactly what my assignment is going to be while we get this all sorted out."

"Desk duty, you said?"

A scowl and a curt nod was all she got in response.

"What's your regular assignment?"

"Most of the time, I'm walking a beat. Sometimes, I patrol in a cruiser."

"Alone?"

The young cop hesitated briefly. "I'm usually by myself, yes."

"Is that normal? Don't officers usually have a...partner?"

Catherine couldn't help but notice her patient's reluctance to confide specific details about her job. That was obviously going to pose a problem, since it was a job-related issue that had brought the officer to her. Nevertheless, she was content to let the young woman tell her story at her own pace. She was just as interested in what she *wasn't* saying.

"Some cops work in pairs. It depends on how the assignments shake out."

"I see." Although she didn't really. She knew that Rebecca usually worked with a partner, but perhaps it was different for uniform officers. It was a point she would have to come back to in the future. "I still don't have your paperwork, so I need you to tell me the details of why you're here—in your own words. Assume I know nothing." She smiled. "In this case, it's true."

"I've been taken off street duty because a complaint of excessive force has been lodged against me."

The delivery was flat and unemotional. Catherine's tone remained conversational. "Is that the same thing as being suspended?"

"Not exactly. I still get paid, and it doesn't go down in my file as a disciplinary action—yet. But, for all intents and purposes…"

"Yes?"

"It's still a black mark. It's going to hurt me. I wanted to make detective, but now…"

Her voice was bitter, and it wasn't difficult for Catherine to imagine how devastating something like this could be for someone who was so obviously committed to her job. "What happened?"

"In the process of apprehending a suspect, I used bodily force to subdue him. His attorney is claiming police brutality."

"Is this the same altercation that led to those contusions on your face and neck?" Catherine asked quietly. She rarely took notes during a session. In this instance, she wouldn't need to because the look in the young woman's eyes was unforgettable. Although the information was delivered in a detached, clinical tone and cloaked in the dry vocabulary so typical of police jargon, the officer's eyes betrayed her. Whatever had happened had left its mark on her, and it was something far more indelible than the bruises that still marred her fresh, clear features. "Did he do that?"

"He got…physical. Yes."

"And you protected yourself?"

"I hit him with the butt of my service weapon. Twice."

"Can you tell me all of it, from the very beginning, just as it happened?" This was the moment. The trust would come now, or never. Some leap of faith, some need to believe that someone was listening—if they were to have any connection that would make a difference, it would begin here.

"It will be in the report."

"I know. But will *you* tell me?"

Seconds passed as the young woman searched Catherine's face. Catherine held the piercing gaze steadily, allowing her concern and compassion to show. Finally, the officer relaxed infinitesimally, and Catherine felt a small thrill of victory. *A beginning.*

"It was five nights ago. Just after midnight. I was working the night shift like usual, in the Tenderloin—that's my regular sector." She stopped without realizing it, thinking back to that night. It had been raining, and it was a cold miserable rain. She was wearing a slicker and her cap was covered with a protective plastic case. Her hands were cold. She wasn't wearing gloves. Every minute seemed like an hour. She'd been over it so many times in her mind—what she should've done, what she did, what she *wanted* to do.

"Officer?" Catherine's voice was calm and gentle. The woman seated across from her gave a small start of surprise and then smiled in embarrassment.

"Sorry."

"No. That's all right."

"I had just come out of the diner. I'd stopped for coffee. It was so damn cold. I heard noises coming from an alley nearby, one of the blind ones with nothing but dumpsters and derelicts in them. The streetlights were all broken, and it was dark. I couldn't see a damn thing." She paused for a heartbeat. She was cold, like she'd been then. She was shivering, too, but she didn't know it.

"I started down the alley as quietly as I could. I didn't want to turn on my Maglite because I was afraid that would make me a target. I wasn't even certain that I'd heard anything at all. I remember thinking it was probably going to be a big rat. I'd almost convinced myself that it was my imagination when I heard someone scream...or what I thought was a scream. It was just a short sharp sound, and then it was quiet again."

She looked at Catherine, and her eyes were bleak. "The facts are in the report."

"Yes, I know." Catherine leaned forward, her hands in front of her on the desk, her fingers loosely clasped, never taking her eyes off the young woman's face. "It sounds very frightening."

"I didn't feel it then."

"And now?"

"I remember."

Now Catherine shivered, although she knew it didn't show. It was a finger of ice trailing down her spine. She acknowledged it, then ignored it. This wasn't about her, and in this room for these fifty minutes, her feelings didn't matter. But unlike the young officer, who struggled so valiantly to separate her feelings from her experience, Catherine's work required that she let the emotion in, even if it stirred her own pain. She knew what it was to remember fear. It was a subtle enemy; it returned in the dark of night or on the unguarded edge of weariness, a reminder of weakness and vulnerability.

Focusing, listening to the words beneath the silence, she asked, "But you kept going? You walked down the alley?"

"Yes." The officer's voice was stronger now. "I could hear sounds of a struggle more clearly by then. I radioed for backup, and I drew my weapon. I was in the narrow space between two apartment buildings, and there was light from one of the windows high up. The fourth floor, I think. Enough so I could see a little. I could make out a man and a smaller figure—a woman, I thought. He was holding her against the side of the building, and she was fighting him."

"A robbery?"

"I didn't know. It could have been anything—a domestic dispute, a robbery, a rape."

"You were still alone?" It was hard to imagine anyone, man or woman, facing such uncertainty and danger on a daily basis. No amount of training or experience could possibly prepare a person for that. What did it take, and what did it cost, to face that every day?

"Yes." Again, the hesitation, and this time she averted her gaze. "I hadn't heard any response to my call for backup, so I assumed that no one was coming."

"Is that usual?"

The officer's hands were fisted tightly around the ends of the leather chair arms. Her pupils were dilated, but she maintained her rigid posture. Her tone was flat, empty. "It can happen. On a busy night, there might not be anyone in the immediate vicinity. Depending on the nature of the call, something like that might be low down on the list of priorities."

Might be? Catherine knew there had to be more to it, but this was not the time to explore that. Right now, this was about one young woman alone in the dark. "I see. So you confronted him by yourself?"

"Yes. By myself."

❖

"You back in the saddle?" Watts asked, looking over Rebecca's shoulder as she poured a cup of coffee at the long narrow table in the rear of the squad room. "Sarge?"

"What are you doing, Watts?"

"What? You mean now?"

"Yeah."

"Shuffling folders. Why?"

She sipped the coffee. Terrible—bitter, thick, and suspiciously filmy. She sighed contentedly as another piece of her life slipped back into place. "Let's go to the range."

"And shoot?" His surprise showed in the sudden rise of his voice.

"Yes, Watts. To shoot. Jesus."

As usual, she didn't wait, and he found himself hurrying to keep up. Just like old times.

"What did the cap say?" he ventured to ask as he lowered his butt into the contoured front seat of the Vette. Man, he'd missed that car. She was silent for so long, he risked a sidelong glance in her direction. "What did—"

"I heard you." She spun the wheel, pressed hard on the pedal, and rocketed onto the on-ramp of the expressway that ran through the center of the city. The firing range was at the police training academy, which was now housed at One Police Plaza, a newly built complex of administrative offices and classrooms. Although it was inconvenient for working cops to drive there for their semi-annual qualification exercises, no one complained. It was worth the twenty minutes to have the brass tucked away in some out-of-the-way place where they couldn't interfere too much with the real work of policing. "He assigned me to a task force the feds are setting up to chase down kiddie porn peddlers and chicken hawks."

"Huh." Watts shifted in his seat and tried to find someplace to stick his knees. He didn't see how the sarge managed to fit behind the wheel, her being so tall. "What's that mean?"

"Nothing good."

"What about me?"

Slowly, she turned her head and looked at him.

He stared back. "Us being partners and all."

"We're not..." She stopped herself, remembering that something in the man, something that rarely showed but that she sensed nonetheless, had made her trust Catherine's life to him. He would never be Jeff, and it would never be the same. But then, what was? "I'm supposed to be the desk jockey. I'll need legs."

"Yeah, sure. I can think of worse things than driving around talking to whores and pimps and perverts." He fumbled in the inside pocket of his shapeless sports jacket for his cigarettes, then caught himself. She wouldn't let him smoke in her ride. Shit.

"Look. I can get a uniform. I wouldn't want you to actually have to work—"

"No way. I'm getting a hard-on just thinking about it."

Rebecca's hands tightened on the wheel as she suddenly recalled all the reasons she couldn't stand him. "Just forget it."

"Hey," Watts said quickly. "Joke. That was a joke. It takes a lot more than that to give me a—"

"I don't need to know about that, Watts," she assured him as she smoothly changed lanes to avoid a slower driver. "I'll fill you in when I've met with the suits from DC. If there's something I can use you on, I'll let you know."

"Good enough." He sat back, glad to be out of the squad room, happy to contemplate some real work. Even if it was with a bunch of bureaucratic assholes who didn't know dick about police work. The sarge could handle them. He'd give her a week before she was back on the street. *Frye, a desk jockey. Sure. And I've got a ten-inch pecker.*

Staring straight ahead through the windshield, she added, "I never thanked you for that night we nailed Blake. I counted on you to save Catherine's life. You came through for me. I owe you."

"Nah, you don't. We both hit him." He shrugged. "Besides, I couldn't let him waste the doc. Guess I got a soft spot for dames. But you know, Sarge, you can't let yourself take 'em too seriously. You're finished if you do."

Rebecca smiled to herself, deciding not to be offended. "Catherine is special."

"Oh, man," Watts moaned, shaking his head in mock sadness. "You're already a goner." He cleared his throat. "But I wouldn't mind if you didn't make yourself a target like that too often. The IA investigation after that shooting went down really busted my balls."

She turned her head again and regarded him unblinkingly. "You're breaking my heart, Watts."

Then she ignored him for the rest of the trip as she piloted the sleek car through the streets. He just sat grinning happily to himself. Frye was back. Things were looking up.

Five hours later, Rebecca sat with the Vette idling at the curb on a narrow street in Old City, a mixed neighborhood of historic landmarks and renovated factories turned upscale condos, surveying the address that the anonymous female voice had given her when she'd called the office of Avery Clark, U.S. Department of Justice, Computer Crime and Intellectual Property Section. CCIPS.

Alphabet soup—initials and acronyms. Frigging feds just love them.

The four-story, brick-fronted warehouse looked nothing like a government building, and Rebecca was certain it wasn't. What she wasn't sure of was what it *was,* and why the task force was going to be run out of there instead of One Police Plaza or the Federal Building at 6th and Walnut. This looked private. But that couldn't be. There just wasn't any precedent for a public/private coalition on an active investigation, and certainly not when the feds were involved.

She shut off the engine. She wouldn't find out what was going on in there by sitting outside in the street waiting for a clue. Besides, as bad as this was going to be, there was the possibility that it could lead her places. Places she wasn't going to have easy access to any other way. Hopefully, this task force would open some doors that would bring her closer to understanding what the hell had gone wrong with Jimmy Hogan and Jeff.

The wide reinforced door to the ground floor was locked, and she pushed the bell next to an intercom. A disembodied genderless voice requested, "ID."

Slowly, she opened the fold-over leather case displaying her badge on one side and a police photo ID opposite and held it up to a small camera mounted in the corner of a narrow recess above the entrance. The door lock clicked open, and she pushed through into a surprisingly well lit garage that occupied the entire ground floor. A sleek black Porsche Carrera convertible sat in the center of the large room. At the rear, she could make out a freight elevator with yet another intercom and no visible access panel. Probably remote controlled.

"Third floor," a voice instructed as she approached the lift, and several more cameras swiveled to follow her progress across the room. The whole setup made her skin itch, but she never even twitched. She did, however, unbutton her blazer as she stepped into the double-wide elevator car to allow access to her weapon. That at least was something that had gone well. An hour on the range with Watts to get her groove back, and then she'd nailed every one of the recertification targets. She had her badge and her gun. She was back.

The elevator moved soundlessly upward and opened onto another huge space, this one lit by sunlight from the floor-to-ceiling windows on the wall opposite her as well as rows of overhead tracks. Through the windows, she had an unimpeded view of the waterfront and the river beyond. Prime Old City real estate. Definitely *not* city property.

Rebecca took her time getting her bearings. Lots of computers, lots of other assorted electronic paraphernalia, and lots of communication equipment. It looked like a government operation from the scope and probable cost of the hardware. The government always went big on the technical stuff and skimped on the manpower.

"Detective Sergeant Frye?"

Rebecca turned slightly to her left and surveyed the woman who approached across the highly polished wood floor, right hand extended.

Five-ten, one-forty, muscular build. Black hair, deep violet eyes, about thirty. White T-shirt, leather blazer, jeans. Heavy platinum band on the left hand ring finger.

"That's right," Rebecca replied, taking the outstretched hand. The grip was cool and firm but not overpowering. Confident, like the stance and the voice. Clearly not Avery Clark, but someone used to being in charge.

"J. T. Sloan." She indicated a slender blond man, who looked like he could have been a Ralph Lauren model, seated at one of the computer consoles. "My associate, Jason McBride."

Nodding to him, Rebecca said, "I was supposed to meet Clark from Justice."

"He called," Sloan said, her expression carefully neutral. "Said he'd been detained at the Federal Building. There's a meeting set for here—0730 tomorrow."

Rebecca frowned. It was starting already. The inevitable meetings and lousy communications that usually ended up wasting more time than anything else. "With whom?"

"Him, someone from Customs, you, and us."

"What department are you with?" Rebecca asked, feeling the beginnings of an enormous headache gathering behind her eyes. She was tired, and that added to her annoyance. Christ, she'd only been on her feet half a day. She shouldn't be tired.

"We're private."

The words came as a surprise, although they shouldn't have. Rebecca looked around the state-of-the-art room and thought about Jeff the last morning she'd seen him alive, two-finger pecking a report out on an ancient electric typewriter. This show was too elaborate for the police department, and somehow too sleekly efficient for the feds. "Your place?"

"That's right." Sloan nodded, watching the detective who had slipped both hands into the pockets of her trousers, hands which Sloan was pretty certain were clenched into fists. *This is one unhappy cop. Wonder whose shit list she got on to pull this assignment?*

"There's supposed to be a uniform assigned here," Rebecca remarked, trying to decide whether she should ask about the operation or wait for the guy from Justice. She had no idea what these two were doing on the task force, and she didn't want to advertise her own ignorance of the situation. "Our department's paper chaser."

"Haven't seen anyone," Sloan observed noncommittally. "Anyone else on your team?"

"Another detective," Rebecca replied carefully, wondering why she'd asked. Damn, she hated coming in cold on an operation, and the file Henry had given her had been very light on details. "You?"

"Just us."

Rebecca made no comment. *Looks like this is going to be a very small group, which means someone, somewhere, wants to keep whatever we find under tight control. Usually when the government is involved, there are so many management-level types in on the action that they're falling all over one another. This seems just the opposite. Interesting.*

Jason had turned on his swivel chair and was watching the two of them, his head moving imperceptibly back and forth with the stops and starts of the staccato conversation. The two women regarded each other steadily in the loud silence—Sloan, darkly good looking and unconcernedly casual, Frye starkly handsome and tautly reserved. *Lots of room for fireworks here.*

Sloan considered the upcoming operation and assessed the complexity of alliances and allegiances likely to be a factor. The past history with Justice was much further from her mind now than it had been a year ago, but some memories never fade completely, despite apologies and retractions and concessions. Avery Clark had never been an enemy, but neither was he a friend. He'd called her because he needed her, and she didn't owe him anything except her expertise. She owed this detective, who was most likely going to end up with the dirty part of the job, even less. She studied the blue eyes studying her.

"Why don't we grab some coffee, and I'll fill you in on what I know."

❖

Rebecca glanced at her wristwatch, a functional unadorned timepiece with a broad leather band and solid gold face. She wore it every day, just as her father had until the day he'd died. 4:59 p.m. She stretched her long frame in the uncomfortable straight-backed chair in the small, windowless room and thought about the spacious waiting room outside Catherine's office. *Thick oriental rug, shaded floor lamps, a coffee table with up-to-date magazines. Professional, but human. Warm and welcoming. Like Catherine.*

She remembered that first night—her own impatience, the pressure of a horrendous case, Catherine's calm, firm resistance to being questioned. A stalemate that had eventually led to something far different. Just a few months ago, two very dissimilar women finding—

"Sergeant?" a male voice asked as the door across the tiny anteroom opened with a creak. The plain entrance to the inner office carried no identifying label or occupant name.

"Yes." She stood, her face carefully blank.

A middle-aged man with thick, unruly brown hair and a linebacker's build dressed in a plain white shirt and dark trousers, sleeves rolled to mid-forearm, extended his hand and stepped toward her. "Rand Whitaker."

She shook his hand and followed him into another bland room crammed with an institutional-appearing desk, a wall of mismatched bookcases, and two generic armchairs after he said, "Come on in." Fluorescent lights in a drop ceiling and wall-to-wall dark gray carpet completed the impersonal space.

"Have you done this before?" he asked as he settled behind the desk in a swivel chair that squeaked in protest.

"No." She eyed the plain manila folder that lay closed in front of him. The label was obscured, but she knew what it was. Her jacket. Everything the department had accumulated on her during her twelve years of service. To her knowledge, there were no reprimands, no inquiries, no investigative reports in that file. There were two citations.

"You understand this is routine after an officer-involved shooting or a serious injury to an officer in the line of duty. In your case…" He regarded her intently, then continued, "It's both."

I understand I won't be able to get back to work until you say I can. I understand that you're supposed to be here to help the rank and file, but you're not one of us. And I understand that cops aren't allowed

to have problems, at least not the kind of problems that you deal with.
She met his gaze directly. "Yes, I understand."

"Any problems with that?"

"Not a one."

"Okay. Good." He leaned back in his chair, seemingly undisturbed
by the ominous sounds produced by any movement. "You're Special
Crimes, right?"

"That's right."

"Like it?"

"Yes."

"Why?"

"It's my job."

He smiled. "Have you ever been shot at before, Sergeant?"

"Yes, once." She knew it must be in the file—it had been a domestic
dispute, like the one in which her father had been killed. Like him,
she'd responded to a call from a concerned neighbor who had heard
screams from the apartment next door; and as with him, when she and
her partner had announced themselves as police officers, the husband
had opened fire. Unlike her father, she had been lucky.

"You weren't hit that first time, were you?"

"No."

"Did it frighten you?"

"Not really," Rebecca replied, wondering where he was going.
"It happened quickly, and then it was over. We fired over his head, he
threw out the gun, and we were on him in a second. There was nothing
to be afraid of."

"Did you think about it later?"

"No."

"Dream about it?"

"No."

"What about this time?"

It had been different this time. She'd known it was coming. She'd
been prepared for it from the second that she'd stepped into the dark,
cavernous room. She'd been looking right at Raymond Blake while
he held a gun to Catherine's temple. She could see him now as clearly
as she had that night. He'd been twitchy, raving, and she knew there
wasn't much time. She wanted him to focus on her; he had to be angry
at her; he had to move the weapon from Catherine's head and put it on

her. She knew exactly what would happen, exactly what was coming, as she goaded and taunted him into turning the semiautomatic on her.

"No."

"What do you remember about it?"

"Not much," she answered, sitting relaxed in the chair, one ankle crossed over the opposite knee. "It was only a minute or two."

He opened the file, shuffled a few papers, glanced down for a few seconds as if reading, then regarded her neutrally. "The report from Detective Watts says that you and the suspect—Blake—exchanged words, but your partner stated that he couldn't hear what you said."

Rebecca waited. He hadn't asked a question.

"What did the two of you talk about?"

"I identified myself as a police officer and ordered him to drop the weapon."

"That's all?"

"There wasn't time for anything else."

"You were alone at the time?"

"No," Rebecca replied evenly. "Detective Watts was behind me."

"Outside the building."

"Yes—with a clear sightline to the subject."

The psychologist was silent for another few seconds. "I'm not IAD."

She waited again. He might not be Internal Affairs, but she didn't doubt that her confidential psych eval would be available to them for the asking. She was not about to say anything that they could use against her, now or the next time something like this happened.

"I'm not inquiring because I'm faulting your procedures, Sergeant," he continued. "I'm wondering why a seasoned detective would walk into a situation where the risk was so high."

"I felt that the hostage was in immediate danger of execution."

"Dr. Rawlings."

"Yes." *Catherine. The bastard had struck her, torn her blouse open, bound her wrists. He had put his* hands *on her. He hadn't had enough time yet to do anything else to her, but I knew what he intended to do. I remembered his voice on the tape, describing it in detail, and I wanted to kill him then. I can still hear his voice.* Sitting there now, recalling his smooth, intimate tone as he'd talked about fucking her lover, she had to concentrate not to clench her fists.

"Detective," Rand Whitaker asked softly, "did you walk into that room intending to trade yourself for the hostage?"

Rebecca met his eyes, her cool blue eyes unwavering. Very clearly she replied, "No."

CHAPTER FIVE

A t 9:40 p.m., Catherine stepped out onto the sidewalk in front of a building that had once been a gracious Victorian before it had been purchased by the university and converted to offices. It was dark, the night was cool; summer was dying. A shadow moved from beneath a tree nearby, and she stiffened.

"It's me. I'm sorry—didn't mean to scare you."

"Rebecca," Catherine said with a soft sigh. She held out her hand. "How long have you been here?"

"Not long—fifteen minutes, maybe. Joyce said that you had an 8:30, so I figured you'd be done about now." She linked the fingers of her left hand through Catherine's. She was right-handed and needed to keep her gun hand free on the street.

"You could have waited inside."

"I didn't want to run into a patient. Besides, it's nice out here." They began to walk. "Drive you home?"

"Mmm, yes. My car's in the parking garage. I can leave it if you bring me in tomorrow. Can you stay tonight?" Needing to ask was hard, but this was new territory for both of them. She didn't want to make assumptions.

"I have to go in early. There's a meeting in the morning."

"Ah, so you've seen your captain." *I see you're already wearing your gun again. I knew it would be soon, but did it have to be this fast? Of course, there are some things that you police always do quickly. You work nonstop when a case is new and the blood is still fresh; you interrogate people before the tears have dried and they're emotionally the most vulnerable; you bury your dead and move on before the ground is cold. You ignore your own pain, at least you try to, until something inside you breaks or turns to stone.*

Catherine thought about her new patient, the young officer who was trying so hard not to acknowledge the pain and terror and abandonment she must have felt walking down that dark alley with no one at her back. Her heart twisted, but her voice was steady. "You're working again, then?"

Rebecca leaned down to unlock the Vette. "Not quite. He put me on a desk. Have you eaten?"

"Uh…lunch." She was relieved at the idea of a desk assignment and then reminded herself that the reprieve was temporary at best. "Doing what?"

"Feel like Thai?" Rebecca pulled away from the curb and reached for her cell phone at Catherine's affirming nod. "There's a menu in the door. Just call out what you want," she added, punching in numbers from memory. She relayed the order, then drove in silence, watching the traffic, the people on the sidewalks, the city teeming with life.

Catherine rested her hand on Rebecca's thigh and, when it became apparent that Rebecca wasn't going to answer, asked again, "What kind of desk assignment?"

"I got a half-assed briefing of sorts this afternoon." Her jaw tight, Rebecca replayed the conversation with Sloan in her mind. Finally, she continued grimly, "I'm not entirely sure *what* I'm supposed to be doing. I'll find out in the morning—at *another* briefing. Bare bones—it's a task force to ferret out the important players in a porn ring. One that uses kids, apparently. There's some kind of Internet angle and that's what got the feds involved. I don't have the details yet. It's the usual federal need-to-know bullshit, which means that probably no one knows anything."

"Why a task force?"

"To make the job twice as complicated and three times slower." Rebecca shrugged. "The feds are involved, but they can't really operate effectively on a local level—not one-on-one. They're bureaucrats—they don't have any street contacts."

"But you do," Catherine said slowly. *No wonder she's not more upset.*

"Yes." Rebecca smiled for the first time. "I do."

"How come I get the feeling that this isn't such a desk job after all?"

Rebecca pulled to the curb and turned in the seat, stretching her arm behind Catherine's shoulders, her fingertips resting on the bare skin at the base of her neck. "It's the fastest way for me to get back to work, and the captain didn't give me much choice. And I *do* know this territory. Four months ago, Jeff and I busted two prostitution houses that were dealing children. We bagged a handful of pushers and pimps, but we knew at the time it was just the tip of the iceberg. We were never able to figure a way inside the network. Everything we tried dried up— nothing but dead ends. Then the Blake thing sidetracked us. Maybe this Internet investigation will give us a break."

Catherine listened to Rebecca talk about her partner Jeff Cruz as if he were still alive. Of course, he had only been dead a few days before Rebecca herself had been shot, and the two intervening months had an aura of unreality about them. Time and events had been suspended while the detective struggled to survive and then to heal. It was no wonder that Rebecca hadn't really assimilated the hard truth of his death. *What in God's name is the police psychologist thinking to let her work? She's barely recovered physically, and she hasn't even begun to deal with everything that's happened emotionally.*

"What Internet angle?" Catherine asked, trying unsuccessfully to quell her anger. She couldn't believe that Rebecca's superiors didn't know that this was a tacit approval for her to go back to street duty.

"The feds brought a couple of civilian computer hotshots on board, at least that's what I think they are. They're going to try to contact some of these characters on the Internet."

"Why civilians? That seems unusual."

"It would be if this was any other kind of case, but we sure don't have anyone with the technical know-how of these people." Sloan had shed a little light on the situation, but she knew damn well there was more that the woman hadn't told her. "Apparently, there are so many problems with hackers on the national level with corporate and even military break-ins that the feds are stretched thin enough to see through in computers crimes investigations. They're recruiting college kids to fill in the gaps."

Rebecca pushed open the car door and caught her breath as a sharp twinge knifed down her left arm. "Let me run in and get dinner."

Carefully, she slid the rest of the way out and straightened up. The pain was gone.

Catherine watched her cross the sidewalk, wondering if the detective really thought she hadn't noticed that quickly suppressed grimace of pain. When Rebecca returned, by unspoken agreement they avoided further talk of her new assignment, letting casual conversation and easy silences dissipate the vestiges of tension.

"I'll get plates," Catherine said as she dropped her briefcase by the door, and Rebecca carried the takeout toward the coffee table in front of the sofa. Walking into the kitchen, she called, "Want soda?"

"Just water is fine," Rebecca answered, settling wearily on the couch. She glanced at her watch, amazed to see that it was only 10:20. Leaning back, she closed her eyes and absently rubbed the ache in her chest.

A minute later, Catherine returned, balancing plates, silverware, and napkins. She stopped a few feet from the sofa and quietly set the items on the table. Carefully, she lifted a light throw she kept on the back of the nearby chair and spread it over the slumbering woman. She could wake her, but Rebecca was already deeply asleep. If she awakened before dawn, she would come to bed. If she didn't, Catherine would sleep well knowing that for tonight at least, her lover was safe. That thought comforted her, but there was a dull ache of loneliness in her heart as she turned off the light and made her way by the dim light of the moon through the quiet apartment toward the bedroom.

❖

Across town, J. T. Sloan leaned against the window's edge in the large darkened loft, staring into a night only faintly illuminated by the glow from ships moving slowly on the wide expanse of river a few hundred yards below. Off to the left, the huge steel bridge arched over the water, its towering arches outlined with rows of small blue lights. She'd stood in the same spot countless times before, but the melancholy that had once been her companion was gone.

The muted sounds of the elevator ascending in the background brought a smile to her lips. The reason for her present contentment had just arrived. She walked to the long barlike counter that separated the loft living space from a sleek, efficient modern kitchen, turned on a few recessed track lights, and poured from a bottle of Merlot she had opened earlier to allow it to breathe. On her way to the door, she set the wine glasses and a cutting board with crackers and cheese on the low stone coffee table that fronted a leather sofa in the sitting area. She slid the heavy double door back on soundless tracks just as the blond in the hallway outside approached.

"Hello, love," Michael said, her full mouth curving into a soft smile. She set her bags down, regarding the woman in the doorway. Sloan's expressive eyes were one of the first things Michael had noticed the day they'd met nearly a year before. Those eyes were now a deep purple, a sure sign her lover had something on her mind.

"Hey, baby." Stepping forward, Sloan slid her arm around the slender woman's waist and pulled her close for a kiss. She'd only intended to say hello, but the touch of her, the faint hint of her perfume, settled the lingering uneasiness in Sloan's stomach that had been plaguing her all afternoon. She brought her other hand under the hair at the back of Michael's neck, caressing the smooth skin while she explored her mouth. Finally, she lifted her lips a whisper and murmured, "Welcome home."

"Yes," Michael said softly. "It certainly is." She leaned back in Sloan's arms and studied her intently. "Are you all right?"

Sloan smiled ruefully. When had she gotten so easy to read? "Just missing you."

"Uh-huh. And as smooth as ever." Michael reached for her hand and gave it a tug. "Come on, let's take this inside."

Sloan grabbed one of the suitcases and followed. Inside the door, Michael kicked off her heels, shed her suit jacket to the back of a chrome-and-leather Breuer chair, and pulled her silk blouse from the waistband of her skirt.

"Tired?" Sloan asked, resting her palm against the small of Michael's back, under the fabric, on her skin. It was always like this when Michael had been gone. She had to keep touching her, just to be sure—that she was back, that she wasn't a dream.

"A bit," Michel replied. She found Sloan's hand again and drew her around to the sofa. When they were settled, she with her legs tucked beneath her, Sloan sprawled by her side, she reached for the wine. "This is wonderful. Just one of the many reasons that I love you."

"How was Detroit?"

"Hot and smoky." Michael groaned. "Four days felt like a month."

"And the meetings?"

"They went well." Michael sipped the full-bodied red wine and sighed. "A decade ago, the catch word was *image*. *Image* was everything. Now, thank God, *innovation* is everything. DaimlerChrysler has a new team of design consultants, and I have a lot of work to do."

"Congratulations. I know you wanted this one."

Michael smiled. "Thanks."

"Are you going to have to go back?" Sloan tried to keep her tone casual, but she hated it when Michael traveled, which as head of her own company, Innova Design Consultants, she did frequently. Sloan just plain old missed her. Nothing felt quite right, no matter how busy her days might be, when at the end of the night Michael wasn't beside her in bed.

"Not often," Michael answered, glancing at Sloan quickly as she heard what Sloan wasn't saying. She lifted a hand, ran her fingers lightly along the edge of her lover's jaw. "Danny will do that. He likes to travel. I don't." Michael hooked her fingers inside the collar of Sloan's T-shirt and pulled until the other woman was leaning toward her, then kissed her. "I don't like being away from you either."

"I know that. Sorry. Just missing you still, I guess."

"I like it when you miss me—just not when you worry. Don't ever forget that I can't do without you." Then, patting her lap with her free hand, Michael said, "Now stretch out, put your head down here, and tell me what's going on."

Sloan considered protesting, but she knew it would do no good. Michael knew her too well. Besides, she *wanted* to talk. She just hadn't quite gotten used to doing it, even after a year of never being disappointed. With a grateful sigh, she turned and laid her head in Michael's lap and closed her eyes.

"So," Michael pronounced, running strands of thick dark hair through her fingers, "talk. You're edgy and something is not right."

"I took that job with Justice."

Michael stiffened, her hand stilling on Sloan's cheek. "When?"

"Two days ago." Sloan opened her eyes, reached into the back pocket of her jeans, and removed a thin black leather case. She held it up, allowing it to fall open. "See? I'm an official civilian consultant, ID badge and all."

"Why didn't you tell me before?"

"I wasn't sure even after I said yes that I wouldn't change my mind," Sloan said quietly. "And I didn't want to tell you on the phone."

"I would have come back."

Sloan reached for her hand, threaded her fingers through Michael's. "I know, but I didn't want you to. It's okay."

"What about Jason?"

"Him, too."

Michael considered the night a year before when Sloan had first shared the story of her past, a story almost no one else knew. They'd been sitting on this very couch, and she'd listened to Sloan's tale of the Department of Justice and the injustices done to her in the name of patriotism, honor, and national security. She remembered every anguished word and recalled every tremor of pain in Sloan's body. Now her own anger at the memory of how her lover had been hurt threatened to make her voice harsh. *And that won't help her.*

Tenderly, still stroking the sculpted face, Michael took a deep breath and asked quietly, "What about everything that happened before?"

"They made nice; all is forgiven." Sloan said it lightly, but her shoulders were tight against Michael's thigh.

"I don't care about them. I care about you. Are *you* all right to work with them again?"

Sloan turned her face and pressed her cheek against Michael's breasts, brushing her lips over the swell of flesh beneath the sheer fabric. "I'm okay with it. Clark seems like a straight shooter, and I don't have any history with him. It feels a little weird right now, but it's just another job."

"Is it dangerous?"

"No." Sloan laughed. "I'll just be doing some Net trolling, looking for sites that are clearinghouses for the hard-core porn sites, and trying to find any that are actually making the stuff. Especially the videos. Jason is going to play Net bait and see if he can make contact with anyone that way. The police will be doing the search and seizure part of it…if we ever get that far."

"You're sure?" Michael leaned over and kissed her again. This time her kiss was hungry. "I don't want you hurt."

Raising one hand and encircling Michael's neck, Sloan pulled her down, shifting on the couch until they were lying side by side. As she slid her hand beneath the edge of Michael's skirt, finding warm soft skin awaiting her, she whispered huskily, "Don't worry. I'm a cybersleuth. Safest job in the world."

Michael worked a hand between them, deftly opening the buttons on the denim fly. Moving her hand inside, smiling when she was swiftly rewarded by Sloan's soft groan and the subtle lift of her hips, she brought her lips to Sloan's ear. "It had better be. Your services are required right here at home, and I need you all in one piece."

Sloan meant to answer with something clever, but Michael's fingers found her and she was lost. It was nearly dawn before she caught her breath again.

Chapter Six

At 7:24 a.m., Rebecca held up her identification to the impersonal eye of the video surveillance camera again and motioned to Watts to do the same.

"What is this, Mission Impossible?" he grumbled. Looking over his shoulder, he caught sight of a figure rapidly approaching on foot from the direction of Arch Street. "Uh-oh. Looks like we have a baby-sitting assignment on top of everything else."

"That's not *we*," Rebecca reminded him, turning her back to the camera as she followed his gaze. Lowering her voice to avoid being overheard by the audio she felt sure was connected to the camera, she whispered, "You're just here as an invited guest, remember? Try not to say anything when we get upstairs. If I know the feds, it will all be taped."

"Hey! Come on, Sarge—give me a little credit." He tried to look offended, but he was aware that Frye was stepping outside of channels to bring him in on this, and he was grateful. He wasn't foolish enough to think it was because she felt any special friendship for him, but the mere fact that she let him ride along was enough for him.

"Just keep a sock in it, Watts."

A young uniformed officer approached, her smooth unlined face set in a determined expression. She looked as if she were about to salute when she came to a smart stop in front of them. "Detective Sergeant Frye?" At Rebecca's nod, she continued, "I'm Dellon Mitchell from the one-eight. The duty sergeant told me I was to report to you here."

"Did he say why?" Rebecca asked, trying not to allow her annoyance to show while giving the slim, dark-haired officer a quick once-over. She absolutely did not have time to keep an eye out for a rookie, even though the uniform looked a little older than the usual recent Academy graduate. In fact, something about the younger woman looked familiar.

"He just said…" Mitchell hesitated, looking uncomfortable for the first time. Then she squared her shoulders and replied, "He said you would need a clerk, ma'am."

"Ouch—sounds like you've been sat down," Watts observed with a chuckle. "What did you do, kid? Forget to shine your shoes?"

"No, sir. I—"

"Never mind that, Mitchell," Rebecca interrupted curtly. "If this is where you've been assigned, that's good enough for now."

She turned back to the video camera and said in a firm tone, "Philadelphia PD. Three to come up."

Without the slightest hint of crackle or electronic interference, a male voice said from the invisible speaker, "Good morning, Sergeant. Please come ahead, and welcome aboard."

❖

They were silent on the ride up, although Watts snorted derisively at the elaborate security measures throughout the building, muttering colorfully about spy games and cop wannabes as he peered about. As they exited the elevator directly into a brightly lit, wide-open room that was sectioned off by partial walls of glass and steel and filled with surveillance equipment and computers, he asked, "What the hell is this place?"

From their left, a man said, "This is the tech center for Sloan Security Services." Nodding to the group and giving no sign that he was perplexed by the unexpected presence of Watts, he stretched out a hand toward Rebecca. "Avery Clark. Justice."

"Rebecca Frye," she replied, assessing him quickly. Standard government issue—somewhere between thirty-five and forty, brown hair, dark steel-framed glasses, conservative haircut, well-tailored but conventional suit, dark tie, white shirt. Wedding ring, hip holster, sharp eyes. And he'd been briefed. He didn't make the mistake of thinking that Watts was in charge but had addressed himself to Rebecca. She gestured to the others with her. "Detective Watts and Officer Mitchell."

"Detective, Officer," he added as he shook both their hands. He turned back to Rebecca. "The briefing's down the hall. Coffee and such there, too."

"Very fancy," Watts observed dryly.

Rebecca said nothing. It was Clark's show.

❖

The conference room was in the corner of the third floor, walled on two sides in floor-to-ceiling glass and outfitted with sleek Bauhaus furniture. The occupants who awaited them looked right at home in the high-tech urban surroundings. Rebecca nodded to the two civilians she'd met the day before.

As previously, Sloan appeared deceptively casual at first glance, in jeans again, this time with a white oxford shirt, sleeves rolled up, and ankle-high leather boots. But her eyes were lasers, scanning everything, on high alert. The amazingly handsome man at her side gave off a lazy aura of insouciance, but Rebecca had no doubt that he was just as sharp. *Interesting pair.*

Watts gave them both a suspicious nod when introduced but kept silent while Mitchell shook each offered hand with rigid formality. They all then filed past a counter in the corner for drinks and food, eventually migrating to seats around the granite-topped table.

Clark walked to the head of the table and set a cup of coffee on the smooth surface. Smiling, he looked at the group. "Everybody get coffee, something to eat?"

There were a few grunts and one clear *Yes, sir.* Watts gave Mitchell a look that suggested she needn't be so polite.

"So." He sipped his coffee. Suddenly, his smile disappeared. "This is what we know. Six weeks ago, an international Web-monitoring group called the Action Coalition Against the Exploitation of Children, whose members surf the Internet looking for child pornography activity of any kind, alerted us to a number of references concerning a real-time child sex ring operating, and apparently broadcasting, from this area."

"How'd the watchdog group pick up on it?" Sloan asked.

"Chat rooms. Unfortunately, nothing too specific—just enough for them to realize there was a live feed somewhere in the Northeast. As you may know, most of the organized distribution of sex material on the Internet occurs through private bulletin boards, and they're all carefully screened, password controlled, and often encrypted. If you aren't a member, you don't have access."

"Whoa," Watts interrupted, ignoring the swift look from Rebecca implying that he shut up. "You want to translate that? I still can't figure out how to put the paper in the fax machine."

Clark regarded him expressionlessly. He'd had plenty of experience dealing with local law enforcement, and he was used to the obstacles, resistance, and outright obstructionism that was almost ritual. This guy had the look of old-school hard-ass written all over him. "There are two kinds of Internet pornography activity. The most widespread is the kind of stuff that anyone can find easily—chat rooms, mostly. People meet there, connect for sex, and sometimes even try to set up an f-to-f."

"Huh?" Watts asked, looking dazed. This time it wasn't an act.

"Face-to-face," Jason remarked quietly. "In person."

"Right...sorry," Clark added. "Real-life assignations—dates for sex. Nothing wrong with that, unless it happens to be an adult looking to hook up with a minor. That's where we come in." He glanced at the expressions of the individuals seated around the table. Everyone was alert, watching him, waiting with more than a hint of reservation. He was used to being viewed with suspicion by the locals—hell, not even just the locals always; sometimes by other federal agents.

Unperturbed, he continued, "At any rate, those kinds of open channels usually prevent file trading, so guys who want pics, and most serious pedophiles do, usually trade privately after they initially connect in a chat room. Until the last ten years, kiddie porn was pretty much limited to still pics and homemade videos. Distribution was via the good old U.S. mail, and it was geographically restricted to interstate distribution as opposed to international. Getting tapes through Customs is tricky, although a lot easier in Europe than here."

"I thought we were expecting someone from Customs," Rebecca commented quietly when he paused. The young officer, Mitchell, who was sitting to her right, was taking notes on one of a stack of pads that had been scattered over the wide stone surface. Sloan and McBride looked quietly intent, but she had a feeling that none of this was news to them. It shouldn't be, if the Internet was their street and they were any good at what they did.

"I told them we'd keep them informed if it looked as if we were going to move into their territory," Clark replied casually. "They've got their hands full with the terrorists."

Politics, Rebecca thought, but she merely nodded.

"Anyhow," the Justice agent went on, "with new digital technology, the game has changed. High-quality images can be uploaded and transmitted anywhere almost instantaneously. That's the venue of the *other* form of trafficking in child pornography—image production and procurement. It's a much more covert, highly organized, and sophisticated operation. There are bulletin boards that screen members, authenticate identities—or at least aliases, which most subjects use— and limit access to only those with passwords or electronic keys." He paused a half-beat, expecting more questions from the rumpled cop, but got nothing but a stare.

"This is where most of the image exchange occurs. And this is where we'll find a way to break into this network. The Internet is a superhighway running directly from one bedroom to the next." He looked pointedly at Sloan. "Internet law enforcement is way behind the perps in terms of expertise. The private sector has a head start on us in terms of the ability to find and infiltrate these sites, but if anyone repeats that, I'll deny I ever said it."

Sloan, Rebecca noticed, smiled, but her blue eyes were dark with something unrequited. Old scores, still unsettled? She'd run a check on both the security consultant and her associate, McBride, the previous afternoon because she was certain that the Justice Department hadn't hired them without cause. Interestingly, she'd drawn blanks on most of her inquiries. Not blanks, exactly. Gaps. Erasures. Missing data. Sloan Security Services had filed taxes for the last four years; Sloan and McBride were registered to vote; their credit records were clean; their driver licenses un-besmirched; and their pasts a complete cipher. They might have been born four years ago. And that had the smell of ex-Agency all over it. If she had to guess, she'd guess Justice. Because both of them looked like the type of whiz kids the government hired right out of college to do the kinds of things the old guard wasn't equipped to do. Just like what they were doing now.

Rebecca was curious—because she was a cop, because she would be working with them, and because she needed to know who she could trust. Sloan had given her some intel the day before, and she hadn't had to. That was a point for her, but it was too soon to tell how far that cooperation would extend. Traditionally, local and federal officers didn't mesh well. And now Sloan was technically neither. Rebecca flicked her gaze back to Clark.

"Why involve us at this stage?" she asked. "It could take months before you get a solid lead." *Unless there's something you're not telling us. And there always is.*

Clark nodded. "Because we want to cover every contingency. I don't need to tell you that child prostitution and child pornography go hand in hand. Once someone has access to kids for sale, they usually take the next step toward photographing the sex and selling that, too. You busted up a couple of kiddie rackets not long ago, didn't you?"

"Small-time houses—no big connections. At least none that we could find then."

"We're betting that they're there. It's another place to look. With those cases and the info from the watchdog groups that I'll be giving to Sloan and McBride, we've already narrowed the search and cut out weeks of Web trolling. If you dig around in the background of the guys you busted, talk to your contacts—" He stopped suddenly and grinned disarmingly. "Sorry. You know what to do without me spelling it out."

"Sure," Rebecca replied dryly while across from her Watts huffed. She shot him another look.

"Let me wrap this up then," Clark added smoothly, ignoring Watts. "A few big busts have been made in the last five years. Two international clubs—the Wonderland Club and the Orchid Club, each a network with members in the United States, Australia, Canada, and Europe—were infiltrated by members of various police agencies. There were several hundred arrests and thousands of images and videos confiscated. The problem with this approach is that it's hit or miss, and even when you make an arrest, it's only hitting the bottom of the food chain—pedophiles watching porn in the safety of their own homes. If it weren't for the fact that the material featured kids, it probably wouldn't even be illegal."

His expression became starkly predatory, and for the first time, his charming mask slipped. "We're not after the guy looking at dirty pictures in his bathroom. We're after the businessmen who are sitting around a boardroom just like this one right now planning on how to make even more money off the sale of children. What we want to know is who's behind it, how they're getting the kids, and from where they're broadcasting their real-time images."

Businessmen. A nice word for organized crime, Rebecca thought. *So why am I here and not someone from the OC division? This doesn't add up.* She knew better, however, than to voice her reservations. Like lawyers who never asked a question to which they didn't already know the answer, cops learned early never to let on that there was something they *didn't* know.

"Technically, any information that leads to an arrest needs to be documented and a chain of evidence recorded. The detectives should make out contact reports recording any intel from confidential informants, per usual. Officer Mitchell can take care of organizing that. In addition, a log of all Internet activity, any leads generated by that route, and any street follow-up instituted needs to be charted."

Jason spoke up. "That's not really possible." *And definitely not even desirable.* "Some avenues of investigation are too…uh…fluid to document."

Sloan smiled. *Fluid.* Only Jason could come up with that term to describe the fact that in a few hours they'd be hacking their brains out, breaking into anything and everything they could, including government databases and private systems.

"I'm sure you'll give her the salient details," Clark concluded easily.

Sure, Sloan thought. *And we'll take the heat for anything construed later as illegal. Which explains why Justice isn't using their own people, even if they do have someone who could do the job. Surprise. So nice to know the Agency hasn't changed. Disavow all knowledge…and on and on and on.*

"Since this is a joint venture with the Philadelphia PD and our department, I'll leave the day-to-day decisions up to Detective Sergeant Frye. Keep me informed of any major developments. We'll brief every few days. More often if things start rolling." He glanced at his watch. "I've got another appointment. Any questions?"

"Yeah," Watts replied. "I missed the part you said about what you'll be doing in this operation."

"If the trail leads across state lines, it becomes federal, so it seemed prudent for us to be in on the investigation from the start."

Rebecca met Watts's gaze for the first time. His expression was blank but his eyes spoke for him. He knew as well as she did that Clark knew much more than he was revealing.

The five of them left at the table when Clark walked out remained in silence for a moment. Clark had implied that Rebecca was in charge of the nuts-and-bolts aspects of the operation, yet there they all sat in the middle of Sloan's territory. Rebecca and Sloan looked at one another across the expanse of smooth black stone. Watts and Jason watched them. Officer Mitchell stared straight ahead, her eyes fixed somewhere over the Delaware River.

"What's your plan?" Rebecca asked finally. There was no point in drawing lines in the sand over false issues. She and Watts couldn't do what Sloan and McBride could. Chances were they'd never even get to the point of arresting anyone. Clark was after something with this fishing expedition, she had no doubt of that, but there was more smoke in the room now than before the briefing.

"This kind of Internet surveillance op isn't new," Sloan said with a shrug. "And like Clark said, it usually involves a huge number of man-hours for something that often produces short-lived results."

"Like busting hookers," Watts remarked. "No percentage in it."

"Exactly."

"So why hasn't he given you a dozen people to sit here and surf the Internet—flood the system and maximize his returns?" Rebecca persisted.

"Can't say. It's costly; there aren't that many computer-savvy agents readily available; or…" She considered her words carefully, because she didn't know the blond cop at all. She was bothered by that fact as well, had been since the first phone call had come from Washington asking her to head up the computer side of the investigation. "He wants to limit the number of people exposed to the operation."

Rebecca nodded. That played with her sense that there was a hidden agenda beneath the stated objectives of the investigation. And there was nothing to do but do the job and keep her eyes open. "Did he give you anything specific to work with?"

"Actually, yes," Sloan affirmed. "There are probably 100,000 sites that supply child sex images worldwide. Many of them link to credit card transactions and on-line billing sites that take Visa, MasterCard, and AmEx. When you trace them through their domain registry, they turn out to be in the Balkans or Bali or some other even more remote locale."

"Untouchable," Jason commented.

"Right," Sloan agreed. "A more profitable place to search is the Web-hosting companies. Most porn sites are explicit about their content when they register with a server—you know, clever names like underagenymphos.net and lolitaland.com. Justice's Child Exploitation and Obscenity Section has given us a prescreened list of potential U.S.-based companies that specialize in porn sites. I'll start there, looking for intersecting references to anything in the Northeast corridor as points of origin. If there is a big supplier, particularly a live feed somewhere local, we'll get a whiff of it eventually."

"Sounds simple," Watts commented dryly. "What's the catch?"

"There's an international network of Web resellers who buy and sell space on hosting frames. They can cloak the site content so it's not so conspicuous to broad searches."

"And that's what we're looking for, right?" Rebecca asked. "A central clearinghouse."

Sloan nodded, an appreciative glint in her eye at Rebecca's quick assessment. "Yes. That's very high up on our list of desirable intel. While I do the broad sweeps, Jason will try for individual contacts."

Watts regarded the only other man in the room sympathetically, feeling an instant kinship with him based on that fact alone. "Jeez, you're gonna pretend to be a perv?" he asked.

"Sometimes," Jason replied flatly. "The rest of the time I'm going to pretend to be a girl."

"We're going to go at this from every angle we can," Sloan affirmed, shooting Jason an amused smile that no one else noticed. Somehow she didn't think the time was right to explain to their new associates why that particular role would not be all that difficult for her friend.

Rebecca stood. "Is there someplace here where Mitchell can set up shop for us?" She didn't add that she wanted a place where she could discuss the street side of things with Watts privately, but she didn't imagine she needed to. Sloan was too sharp not to know that no one shares everything, ever.

"I'll show you," Jason offered. "There's another meeting room like this at the other end of this floor you can have. It's smaller, but the coffee machine works."

"It'll be fine," Rebecca acknowledged. "Thanks." She glanced at Sloan. "The first time you get a hint of anything that even vaguely connects to here, let me know."

"No problem."

❖

When Jason left the three cops in a conference room that made anything at the one-eight look like a slum, Rebecca said, "Mitchell, take ten. We'll discuss your assignment when you get back."

"Yes, ma'am. I'll be back in ten. Bring you anything?"

"No, thanks. How many open cases do you have?" Rebecca asked Watts when the uniform left. "Because officially, you aren't even on this case."

"Nothing pressing. A few follow-up interviews, two coming to trial, and those cold files I've been slugging through." He hiked a hip up onto the corner of another sleek tabletop, the fabric of his shiny brown suit stretching over his ample middle. "I thought we...uh...you were just supposed to be the contact person when these eggheads find something. *If* they find something."

"That's what Henry said," Rebecca agreed. "For my dime, I think we're all going fishing for Avery Clark, and I don't like that too much. Let's poke around and see if we can find out what he really wants us to catch."

"You think it could be Zamora?" Watts asked flatly, watching her carefully. Gregor Zamora was the head of the local organized crime syndicate, and he had been amazingly successful at avoiding prosecution. So successful that most cops believed he had friends in high places.

"I don't think anything," Rebecca replied steadily.

"Wouldn't it be a bite in the ass if Zamora goes down for selling dirty pictures after all the times we've tried to nail him for drugs and racketeering? Justice is a funny thing sometimes." His expression was one of happy expectation.

"Don't jump to conclusions, and don't talk this up at the squad," she warned sharply. *I don't want another...partner...winding up dead.*

"Wouldn't think of it," he replied. "Especially if chasing around for you keeps me from hunting down weenie waggers in the park. Can you get me some slack with the cap?"

She considered her options, and they were slim. Officially, this was a desk job for her. Talking to the feds, coordinating with the computer cops, and sitting on her ass until something happened. Which might be never. "I could probably justify some time for you on this by telling him I need you to run down the guys Jeff and I put away in that kiddie prostitution bust last spring. Find out if any of them are out of jail yet. Shake them down for some names. Go through the paperwork—you might even dig something up that would give us a lead."

"Good enough for me," Watts said. "I don't suppose whatever we're about to be doing is going into the rookie's log book."

She just looked at him.

"Right. I'm ready," he said more seriously. "Just give me the word."

"Go ahead and start on it," she said as a discreet cough from the doorway to the conference room announced the uniform's return. "I'll call you later."

"What're you gonna be doing?" he asked as he ambled toward the door.

She didn't answer. He hadn't expected her to. It would be a long time—maybe never—before she confided in him. Some cops never accepted another partner after one was killed. Didn't want to take the risk of losing another, or as was most likely in her case, they could only form that kind of attachment once in a lifetime. He put his hands in his pockets, walked to the elevator, and tried not to be bothered by her secrets.

❖

"Come in, Mitchell," Rebecca said as she slid open a drawer under the counter that held an automatic coffee machine and discovered prepackaged coffee packets of a better than average brand. She didn't speak again until she had poured water into the coffeepot from the cooler in the corner of the room. Then she turned to face the officer who was standing just inside the room, shoulders back, hands straight down at her sides. It was a posture that most young officers assumed when dealing with superiors, but on her it looked a lot more natural.

"What did you do before you were a cop?" Rebecca asked, walking to the windows and glancing at the view. Breathtaking. For an instant she thought of Catherine and wondered what she was doing at that moment. She looked away from the pristine sky and glistening water.

"I was in the Army, ma'am."

"Enlisted?"

"No, ma'am. Second Lieutenant."

"West Point?"

"Yes, ma'am."

"Serve long?"

A tightening of the muscles along her jaw that might have gone unnoticed, but Rebecca was looking for it. "No, ma'am. Just over a year."

Rebecca studied her, noting the faint bruise on her left cheek that was more obvious in the sunlight coming through the windows than it had been previously. Another untold story.

"How long have you been on the force?"

"Eight months."

Allowing for her time in the Academy, she was probably in her mid-twenties, which was about how old she looked. Rebecca poured herself a cup of coffee. "Have some coffee, Mitchell."

Mitchell glanced at her, surprised. "Thank you, ma—"

"And you can relax. Save the sirs and all that for the brass. They like it. The rest of us are just cops, okay?"

"Yes, ma'am."

"So. Want to tell me what your situation is?" She could find out, and eventually she'd take a look at the kid's file, but she wanted to hear it from her. You could tell a lot about a person by the way they explained their problems.

"I've been taken off street duty while the review board investigates a complaint against me," Mitchell answered immediately.

Which probably means someone in the department is covering their ass instead of supporting one of our own. If Mitchell has done anything even remotely prosecutable, they'd have suspended her, not just reassigned her. "Justifiable?"

"I subdued a suspect with force. He's complaining."

Well, that explains the bruise. Very smart answer, too. She isn't excusing herself, and she isn't admitting guilt. If she survives this inquiry, she's got a future in the department. Rebecca sipped her coffee. "Okay. This assignment will probably be deadly boring, but it's what you've drawn. For the moment, you'll be based here. If Sloan and McBride need you to do anything for them, go ahead. You can run backgrounds at the one-eight if there's something they can't find out for themselves."

"I doubt they'll need *that*," Mitchell remarked. "They're hackers."

"Yeah, that's what I figured, too. But just the same, if they need something that could later be construed as chain of evidence, try to make it look official. Go through channels and keep some kind of log so we know what the hell we have to work with if we ever need to get a warrant."

"Roger."

"I'll be in and out. Page me if something comes up."

"Yes, ma'am." For the first time Mitchell looked uneasy. "I have to report for my psych eval three times a week until I'm cleared. I'll advise you of—"

"Just go, Mitchell," Rebecca said brusquely. *I know all about it. With any luck we won't run into each other in Whitaker's waiting room.*

Mitchell stiffened at the change in the detective's tone. "Yes, ma'am. Understood."

"Hopefully, we'll all be off this duty in a week or so. Be here at 0730 tomorrow." She tossed her cup in the trash and walked out, leaving Mitchell to stare after her. She had three hours to kill before her appointment with the psychologist. It was too early in the day to find the people she wanted to talk to, and she admitted to herself as she rode down on the silent elevator that the only person she really wanted to see at the moment had nothing to do with the investigation.

❖

Catherine Rawlings stepped away from the group of residents with whom she had been discussing the preferred management of acute schizophrenia and looked at the readout on her pager. Then she walked to a wall phone and dialed the number.

"This is Doctor Rawlings."

"Any chance you're free for lunch?"

Smiling, she turned her back to the hallway and lowered her voice. "Where are you?"

"In the lobby."

Her heart beat faster, and she was aware of a faint stirring within. The fact that the mere sound of Rebecca's voice could do that to her was astounding. And a little frightening, too. The newness of anyone affecting her quite so much would take some getting used to. "Damn. I can't. I scheduled an extra patient session right before I have to go to the outpatient clinic. I'm sorry."

"That's okay. I was just in the neighborhood," Rebecca replied quickly. She glanced around the lobby and rolled her shoulders, trying to shake out some of the tension.

The frustration she'd felt upon awakening that morning on Catherine's couch just as dawn had begun to cast the room in a gray pall lingered still. She'd opened her eyes, struggled to remember where she was and how she'd gotten there, and finally realized that yet again she had fallen asleep, leaving Catherine hanging. By the time she'd stumbled, still stiff and groggy, to the bedroom, Catherine's alarm went off, and they'd barely had time to say good morning before rushing to shower, dress, and head off to work. She missed her, and worse than that, she had the uneasy feeling she was letting down her end of... things. Again. *Fuck.*

"Dinner?" Catherine asked into the silence, wanting to ask if Rebecca was working, and what she was doing, and how she was feeling, but resisted, determined not to burden this spontaneous moment with her own uncertainty and unease.

"Sure. Page me when you're finished tonight."

"I have patients, and then an appointment. Is 9:00 too late?"

"It's fine." The detective hesitated, then added, "About last night, I won't make a habit of crashing before the appetizers—"

"No, really," Catherine interjected, glancing at her watch. "It's all right. Hell, I have to go..."

"Right. I'll see you later then."

"Yes."

Five floors apart, they each stood still for a moment, holding a phone with only a dial tone, considering the things they had left unsaid.

CHAPTER SEVEN

CSI Chief Dee Flanagan didn't look up at the sound of footsteps approaching across the tile floor of her lab. Carefully, she pipetted an aliquot of fluid containing an emulsion of the material scraped off the bottom of a murder suspect's shoe into a centrifuge tube. If she was right, there'd be trace amounts of a very specific high-grade motor oil in the supernatant that would match the composition of the brand in the victim's Ferrari. Footprints at the crime scene indicated that the murderer had stepped in the oil puddle when he'd crossed the garage on his way to crushing the back of the victim's skull with a tire iron. Not a very inventive means of dispatching his neighbor—a fellow who was apparently spending the afternoons in bed with his wife—but then murder was so rarely clever. The gas chromatography analysis would confirm the match, placing the suspect at the scene. Not enough for an arrest in and of itself, but another link in the chain. Another piece in the puzzle fit neatly into place.

Dropping the tube into the centrifuge cradle, still without turning toward the intruder, she said into the quiet room, "I don't have anything for you yet, and I won't for another two hours. If you keep bugging me, it's going to be tomorrow. And don't touch anything."

"I haven't been gone that long," Rebecca remarked dryly, standing as she always did when in Flanagan's lab—with her hands safely in her pockets. "I know the drill."

Flanagan, the forty-year-old forensic chief, small, wiry, and a head shorter than Rebecca, known to be notoriously short-tempered, turned toward her visitor with undisguised delight. "I'll be damned. Frye." She held out her hand. "Maggie said she saw you at the gym. You're really back, huh?"

Rebecca took her hand, grinning. "Looks like."

"Good. Maybe those monkeys in your division will get some cases solved for a change."

"Thanks—I think."

"Come on into the office." Flanagan gestured toward a small cubicle adjoining the sparkling, equipment-filled room. "I know you didn't drop by just to be sociable."

Rebecca followed her. "I need to catch up on a few things. I figured you'd be the one to ask."

Flanagan gave her a wary glance as she settled behind her surprisingly messy desk. In sharp contrast to the rest of her domain, which was obsessively organized, her private office was apparent chaos. She knew, however, precisely where every piece of paper, dental model, and crime scene mock-up resided, and woe to the unwary cleaning person who dared move anything a micrometer.

"What do you want to know?"

"I never saw the final reports on Hogan and Cruz."

Flanagan grimaced. "You're going to start poking around in things again, aren't you?"

"Just getting up to speed," Rebecca replied neutrally. She eyed the one chair piled with copies of the *Journal of Forensic Pathology* and concluded it would be safest to remain standing.

"Bullshit. In the two months you've been away, Frye, I haven't gone senile." She looked thoughtful for a moment, then continued, "It's technically still an open case, but it's been written off by pretty much everyone as a contract hit, and unsolvable. And more importantly, it's a case I think someone, or *several* someones, would like to see forgotten."

"Two dead cops," Rebecca said softly, her expression darkening. "Jimmy Hogan and Jeff Cruz. I have to ask myself, why hasn't the department been turning the city upside down to find out who killed them? Every day, while I lay up there in that hospital bed, I expected someone to come and talk to me about it. I got old waiting for one of the Homicide dicks to question me, to fill me in, or to ask me about Jeff's cases. Nothing."

Flanagan nodded as she leaned back in her chair and regarded the tall cop steadily. "I know that Cruz was your partner, but maybe you didn't know him as well as you think."

"Don't play games with me, Flanagan. If you've got something to say, spit it out." Rebecca's tone was lethally cold. She respected the CSI chief, and over the years had grown to like her, but Jeff Cruz had been her partner. No one came before him in her allegiance—no one except Catherine.

"I'm not the enemy here, Frye," Flanagan pointed out in what was for her a reasonable tone. "You may not realize it, but those homicides are open cases on *my* books, too. Even if they weren't cops, I'd want to find the perp." When Rebecca didn't reply, but merely regarded her with a flat opaque gaze, she exhaled slowly and continued. "There's been some not so quiet speculation that Jimmy Hogan was dirty. He'd been working underground in the Zamora organization a long time. He had no family, no real friends, and even his bosses didn't always know what he was doing. His files are so thin you can see through them."

"Yeah. He was a perfect undercover agent. For that he gets this from us in return?" Rebecca commented bitterly, expecting no reply. *Where is the famous solidarity of the Thin Blue Line now? Bastards.*

"But he *did* call Jeff Cruz. More than once."

"Hogan was Jeff's training partner for a while when Jeff got out of the Academy. Then Jimmy transferred to Narco and Jeff to Vice. But they had history. It makes sense that Hogan would contact Jeff with intel if he found something that was in our territory."

"That may be it, Frye. I'm just telling you what I've heard."

"So what's the theory?" Rebecca asked tiredly. "That Jimmy went bad, enticed Jeff with—what? Money? Jeff and Shelly lived in a starter home, for Christ's sake. He drove a ten-year-old Mustang."

"Did you ever get anything solid from Hogan's intel?" Flanagan asked, ignoring the questions no one could answer.

"Not much," Rebecca admitted. "Supposedly, he had gotten on to something involving the chicken trade. He was going to feed us some names. He never got the chance."

"Or there wasn't anything there to report, and Jeff's meetings with him were a front."

"If that were the case, why would Jeff have even bothered to tell me he was meeting Hogan?" Rebecca countered. "He could have done it all under the table."

"Maybe Jeff was hedging his bets and covering all the bases. Maybe he figured if things went south with Hogan, he could always claim he was working Hogan for information and just pretended to be rolling over."

"That's bullshit."

"Yeah. I agree with you." Flanagan had the uneasy feeling that Frye was about to fold. Her face was unusually pale, even considering her normally light Nordic coloring; there were faint beads of sweat on her forehead, and her breathing was a bit jerky. In fact, she looked like hell. The criminalist got up and moved around to the front of her desk where she might have a prayer of catching the detective if she dropped. Suggesting that the cop sit down wasn't an option. You didn't tell Frye to take it easy.

"Look, Frye. All I'm saying is that there's a lot going on around their deaths that none of us understand. As far as I can tell, Homicide has backed way off it, and the brass aren't going to be real happy about anyone stirring it up. So—be careful who you talk to, and don't trust anyone."

Rebecca leaned a shoulder against the doorframe, wondering if it had suddenly gotten warmer in the small space. A river of sweat ran between her shoulder blades, and she had to blink several times to clear her vision. "I want to see the autopsy reports and your crime scene files."

"I can't give them to you."

"Damn it, Dee." She pushed away from the wall so quickly, Flanagan actually held out a hand to ward off a blow.

"Jesus, take it easy," Flanagan breathed when Rebecca halted a few inches from her. "I don't have them. The whole file was pulled."

"Who has it?"

Flanagan shrugged. "It says Homicide on my log-out sheets, for all that's worth. *I* suspect it's IAD. You know they'd be looking into any officer-related death. That's SOP."

"You *gave* them your file?" Her tone was incredulous. No one got a hand on Flanagan's files. Impatiently, she swiped moisture from her

IN PURSUIT OF JUSTICE

forehead and considered taking off her jacket. She moved back a step, putting distance between them, searching for some air.

"Fuck, no," Flanagan said, her composure cracking at last. "The bastards raided my files. I don't know how, but the whole folder is gone."

"Don't you...keep copies, or something?"

"My reports are all computerized, Frye. Supposedly, the system backs up automatically. Except it didn't, or someone is lying to me. All I know is that I can't find them, and the idiots in the technical division who are supposed to know something about this can't tell me jack shit."

Rebecca looked around the office. Motioning with her head toward a computer nearly buried by stacks of folders and reports, she asked, "Is that where you input all your final data?"

"Not only there; also substations in the various lab divisions. Serology, Toxicology, Prints—they all enter their findings under the case file number and it gets stored that way."

"But one way or another, it's all generated down here in your section?"

"Yes." Flanagan could see the wheels turning. "Why? You any good with this kind of thing? I tried but nothing worked."

"Not me," Rebecca said with a short mirthless laugh. "But I *might* know someone. I'll let you know."

"There wasn't much in the file anyhow. There was precious little evidence from the scene. I've got a few of my handwritten notes from the first walk-through. You're welcome to see them, and I'll tell you anything I can."

"Why get involved?" Rebecca asked, her tone not critical, merely curious.

"Because it's my job."

Their eyes met in a moment of perfect understanding, and for the first time, Rebecca smiled. "Thanks, Flanagan."

"Don't mention it. Oh, and Frye?"

Rebecca raised an eyebrow. "Yeah?"

"Watch your back."

"Yeah. I'll do that."

❖

Catherine unlocked the door that opened into her office from a hallway off the main corridor and crossed the room to her desk. Normally, her patients exited through this door so they did not have to go out through the waiting room and run into other patients who were scheduled to follow. It also allowed *her* to come and go without seeing her patients before or after the session. She glanced at the clock on the opposite wall and saw that it was 5:28 p.m. With a tired sigh, she settled into the high-backed leather chair behind her desk and picked up the phone. After dialing the extension for her secretary, she closed her eyes briefly.

"Yes?" Joyce responded.

"Is my 5:30 here yet?"

"Yes." *Right on time and looking like she's about to face a firing squad.* Joyce smiled faintly at the serious-faced young woman sitting across from her and was rewarded by a brief lift of her surprisingly full lips in return.

"Good. Give me a minute, and then tell her to come in."

"Anything I can get you? I put fresh coffee on."

"No, thanks. I'll grab a cup between this one and the last one."

"Very well."

A moment later, Catherine's door from her waiting room opened, and her 5:30 appointment walked in. "Good evening, Officer."

"Hi." Mitchell settled into her customary spot, the right-hand leather chair of the pair that faced the psychiatrist's desk. As she sat, she plucked at the thighs of her sharply creased trousers to minimize the wrinkling. Her back did not touch the upright portion of the chair.

"I see you're in uniform, so you're still working, I take it?"

"More or less," Mitchell acknowledged. "I'm getting paid. No street duty though. It's a desk job, more or less."

"And I assume you find that frustrating?"

"Well, until this morning, I would have said so, yes."

"Really?" Catherine raised a surprised eyebrow. "I had the impression you considered anything other than a street assignment almost a disciplinary action."

Mitchell smiled. "Most cops like to think of themselves as street cops. After all, that's where the action is. That's where you make your stripes. The only ones who don't want street duty are the ones who come to law enforcement with the intent to be administrators. They're the MBAs who want to be commissioner someday and the lawyers who can't find jobs and hope that a year or two of police work will give them a step up into the prosecutor's office. They only put in enough street time to fulfill their basic requirements before angling for something that will get them an administrative position."

"So most officers would find your present duty undesirable?"

"Well…" She still wasn't entirely certain how much she should reveal to the psychiatrist. She felt a lot safer talking to her then she would have to the regular departmental shrink, but there was no telling how much of what they discussed would make its way back to her division commander or into her personnel file. Still, it felt good to be able to talk to someone.

Carefully, she continued. "The duty sergeant gave me an assignment that I'm sure he thought would just take me off the streets and put me somewhere where everyone could forget about me. Usually when they want to bury someone, they move them to the property room, which is an assignment that most people get when they've been disciplined but can't be fired or where older uniformed officers who are approaching retirement and want something easy to do get posted. He probably figured if he stuck me in property, it would have been a little obvious. Then if I complained to my union rep, it would have made things touchy. So he posted me to what he *thought* would be a dead-end duty, but I think he figured wrong."

Catherine laughed. "You're going to have to do some translating for me here, Officer. The intricacies of police politics still escape me."

Amused, Mitchell relaxed enough to lean back in her seat. "Me too, although I'm learning quickly. He put me on this new task force that's just getting under way, probably figuring it would be nothing but a bureaucratic nightmare and all I would be doing is filing paperwork. Probably all I *will* be doing is filing paperwork, but the detective in charge is someone who almost anyone in uniform would give an arm or a leg to work with."

"I think I understand," Catherine remarked. "So you believe there might be an advantage to this assignment that no one appreciated, is that it?"

"Maybe. First of all, it's an interesting assignment. Plus, several federal agencies are involved, so there's a chance it could turn into something really big. If I can contribute something, maybe I can show that I'm not a screw-up."

Catherine didn't reply, and her face did not show her consternation. There was probably more than one task force running at any given time. This didn't necessarily have to be something connected to Rebecca's assignment. In an attempt to redirect the conversation away from the specifics, she asked, "Do I understand correctly, then, that you're not displeased with your current work situation?"

"That's right, not at all. The fastest way for someone to get promoted out of the ranks into the detective division is by assisting a detective with their case. And the detective in charge is Rebecca Frye. You know her, of course, because you were involved with her during the Blake thing. If I can manage to make any kind of positive impression on her, this assignment could actually end up helping my career."

"Yes. Of course." Catherine had known that her involvement in the serial murderer/rape case might come up with any of her patients, especially the police officers. It was unrealistic to think that anyone on the city payroll wouldn't have closely followed that case and its dramatic outcome. She never discussed her personal life with patients, but this situation, unfortunately, had been heavily publicized, and the vivid conclusion covered by the television and print media. Despite her attempts to downplay her involvement, her photograph had been displayed on national television and in local newspapers and magazines. Nevertheless, anticipating that it would come up in session and actually having it presented to her were two different things. Still careful to keep her expression neutral, she continued, "I'm glad this new assignment hasn't turned out to be a punishment."

"Are you kidding? As soon as I get a better idea of how she's going to run the street end of things, I'm hoping I can make myself useful. I've been working the Tenderloin for more than half a year. It could be I know some people who might give us some leads. But no matter how it turns out, any uniformed officer would pay money to work with her."

I don't doubt it. Except this is supposed to be desk duty for her. But I can't very well bring that up, can I? Mentally turning that thought aside, Catherine concentrated on her new patient. Mitchell's entire demeanor had changed from one of quiet resignation to enthusiasm. It was clear how important her work was to her emotional state. And it was time to get back to that.

"Our last session ended before you were able to tell me what happened in the alley that night. We need to go through it, and talk about what happened after, before I can sign off on my evaluation."

"I know." Mitchell's expression became serious as she met Catherine's eyes. She was ready to get it over with. Perfunctorily, she stated flatly, "There isn't very much more to tell. I went down the alley—"

"Wait," Catherine interrupted softly. She didn't want a recitation; she wanted the remembrances. "Picture it for a minute. It was dark, and you were alone, and your backup hadn't arrived. There were sounds of a struggle, and you went to investigate, correct?"

Mitchell's eyes darkened as Catherine's quiet voice brought her back to the moment that was still as clear in her memory as the instant it had happened. She nodded.

"I had my weapon out. My heart was beating so fast it was like a drum beating in my ears. I pressed my back flat against the brick wall, and I could feel the uneven surface of the stones catching on the back of my shirt as I eased my way down the alley. I didn't want him to know I was coming until I was close enough to subdue him, because I didn't know if he had a weapon. It's impossible to subdue a suspect hand to hand if you're not within arm's reach. If he has a gun and you can't physically reach him, you're dead."

She paused as she eased down the alley in her memory. "It was hard not to stumble over bits of trash and broken glass and rocks. I was certain I was announcing my presence with every step I took. The gun barrel was angled up—I was holding it beside my face in a two-handed grip—and I was looking past it toward the shapes that were just shadows moving in the little bit of light that filtered down from the windows high up above me." She worked to quell a surge of adrenaline, just as she had that night. She couldn't afford to have her gun hand shake. "As I got closer, I could hear him grunting, and she was..." Mitchell swallowed, trying not to remember the sound of a skull being slammed hard against a stone wall and the soft moan of pain.

"She had been screaming before—shouting, I think—for him to stop. Now she was...whimpering. I was afraid he was going to kill her."

Without realizing it, she had clutched the arms of the chair, her hands white-knuckled with the force of her grip. "I could see them more clearly now. He was big—linebacker kind of big. He had one hand around her throat and the other under her skirt. Her thighs were bare, pale, ghostly in the moonlight. I saw her face for the first time then. There was blood on her face…"

From across the desk, Catherine could see the sweat bead on the young woman's forehead and knew that although her eyes were open, she wasn't seeing anything except those moments replaying as real as if they were happening now. She didn't have to imagine the feeling. She *knew* the feeling. "Go on," she said very gently.

Mitchell jerked slightly at the sound of the voice that seemed to be coming from very far away. "I announced myself…I think I yelled 'Police! Put your hands up where I can see them.' God, he was fast. It was almost as if he knew I was coming, or at least he wasn't surprised to find me there. He let her go, and she slumped to the ground. My eyes followed her for just a second, but it was enough time for him to swing around with his hands locked together and catch me in the side of the face. Stupid move on my part."

She hesitated again, remembering the helpless feeling as she went down, thinking she might never get up. "Then I was on my knees, and he followed up the punch with a kick. At least I saw *that* coming and managed to roll away from most of it. His foot connected with my hip but it wasn't that bad. I was still between him and the street, and the alley wasn't that wide. I knew I had to get up or he would just jump over me and be gone. As I got to my feet, he grabbed my shirt and punched me low, below the bottom of my vest. And that's when I hit him with the butt of my service revolver."

"He hurt you." It was a statement, because the facts spoke for themselves. "Do you remember hitting him?"

Mitchell blinked as if awakening from a dream. She could still smell his sweat, and the coppery odor of blood, and the acrid stench of her own fear. She felt the ache between her thighs where his fist had landed, and she saw with perfect clarity the battered face of the woman lying on the ground.

She stared at Catherine for so long that Catherine began to wonder if she would answer. Finally, Catherine asked again, "Officer, do you remember striking him?"

Mitchell wasn't certain what she should say. She didn't know how her words would be used against her. She met the warm green eyes that held such tenderness, an acceptance that eased some part of the terrible pain, and she answered hoarsely, "No."

CHAPTER EIGHT

"S orry I'm late," Catherine said breathlessly. "Traffic."

"That's all right. How are you? I haven't seen you at all the last few days except at conferences." Hazel Holcomb settled into her chair and regarded her colleague with a speculative expression.

Catherine shrugged wearily as she dropped her briefcase by the sofa, then smiled deprecatingly. "I could plead workload, but…I think I've been avoiding you."

"Aha." Hazel sipped her coffee and pulled an ottoman over in front of her chair with her toe. Propping both feet up, she raised her cup slightly. "Coffee?"

"Tonight, I think I'll take you up on it." Catherine walked to the antique credenza against one wall in Hazel's home office/study and poured the aromatic brew into a delicate china cup. "I'm surprised that you even use these except for special occasions," she remarked absently as she sat down across from Hazel. "They're so beautiful."

"Too lovely to keep behind glass. Now, let's get back to that therapeutically laden statement about avoiding me."

"You said I should see you regularly, and I didn't want you to remind me about that."

"Why not?"

"Probably because there's something I don't want to talk about."

"Only *one* thing?" Hazel asked in mock seriousness. "How fortunate. We should be able to clear that up tonight then."

Catherine laughed. "All right. *Several* things."

"And yet *you* called me for the appointment this afternoon."

"Yes," Catherine admitted. "I know enough to recognize avoidance, and I know that's not the answer. So, here I am."

"How are you sleeping?"

"Better."

"And the dreams?"

Catherine shook her head. "Not for the last couple of nights."

"Good." She didn't need to add that it might be temporary. The younger psychiatrist knew that, of course. "Then what's troubling you?"

"I suddenly realized that I don't know very much about being in a relationship."

"Interesting, isn't it, how we never appreciate that fact until we're actually faced with it," the older woman mused. "What's happened to make you think that now?"

"Rebecca has gone back to work, and I don't know how to...react to it."

Hazel emptied her cup and leaned over to place it on the end table next to her chair. "Reactions aren't something you think about, they're something you feel. How do you feel, Catherine?"

"A little insecure. I'm not certain where I fit in her life anymore." She hesitated, then added, "Or where she fits in mine."

"Do you love her?"

"Yes." That was something she didn't even need to think about.

"And her? Does she love you?"

"Ah," Catherine said softly. "How do you do that?"

"What?" Hazel asked quietly.

"Ask the right question."

"Part of it is practice, as you very well know. And part of it is my knowing you. And part of it is knowing what we all fear—that our love may not be returned. So...why are you insecure about her feelings for you?"

"She's so damn self-sufficient," Catherine replied, surprised at the anger she heard in her own voice.

"And?" Hazel prompted.

"I'm afraid that all she really needs is her work."

"Some people would say that about me. Or you."

"Yes," Catherine countered, her tone still sharp. "But *my* work won't get me killed…"

"And hers might," Hazel finished softly.

"And that's the real issue, isn't it?" Catherine leaned back into the cushions and closed her eyes. Finally she said, "I'm supposed to meet her for dinner after this." She opened her eyes and sat forward. "Would you mind very much if we cut this session short? I just need to see her."

"It's your time, Catherine. I'm certain you know how best to use it. Go see her and let her remind you of what it was that first touched you about her."

"Thank you."

"And Catherine," Hazel added as her colleague gathered her things to leave. "Give yourself a little time. She wasn't the only one struck by that bullet."

❖

Catherine waited until she reached the expressway before calling Rebecca. She drove with one eye on the traffic, preparing herself for disappointment as she half-expected that the detective would not be home. When the phone was answered on the second ring, she realized she'd been holding her breath. Hurriedly, she said, "Hi. I'm done early and I was wondering—"

"Terrific. Would you like to go out or—"

"No," Catherine said quickly, "let's stay in. We can watch a movie. I can cook—"

"Don't bother—I'll take care of that," Rebecca said swiftly, then broke into laughter. "Maybe if we stop interrupting each other, we'll be able to figure out what we're doing. Is thirty minutes all right?"

"Anytime," Catherine said, her voice suddenly husky. God, she'd never thought she could miss someone so much after just a day apart.

"I'll be right there," Rebecca replied in a tone filled with promise.

In fact, by the time Catherine found a parking place and walked the half-block to her brownstone, Rebecca had arrived and was waiting on her front steps, leaning a shoulder against the doorframe, hands in her pockets, and eyes fixed on Catherine's face. The sight of her, all long lines and lean strength, produced a storm of anticipation in Catherine's stomach.

"Have you been waiting long?" Catherine asked as she hurried up the stairs, searching in her briefcase with one hand for her keys.

"Only a minute."

The four marble stairs bracketed by wrought-iron railings that led to Catherine's front door were not very wide, and as she reached past the taller woman to fit her key into the lock, their bodies brushed lightly together. Absurdly, her hands began to shake. It was moments like this that made her wonder how she had ever believed that she understood anything about life or human relationships. How could she, when she had never experienced anything like this before? Of course, there was no understanding it, as it made absolutely no sense that the mere presence of this woman could reduce her to nothing more than raw nerve endings and mindless desire.

"You're trembling," Rebecca murmured. "Are you all right?"

"No," Catherine said as she pushed the door open and entered hurriedly.

Rebecca followed with a paper bag filled with groceries tucked under her right arm. She set it down on the telephone table just inside the door and stood still, regarding Catherine intently as she dropped her briefcase. "What's wrong? Has something happened?"

"No. Everything is fine." Hesitating, Catherine wondered how much to say and then, at a loss for logic, simply said, "It's just that… these last few weeks, I was so used to coming home and you would be here. We'd have dinner; we'd talk; we'd sleep together. I miss you."

For an instant, Rebecca was stunned. She still wasn't used to the fact that Catherine, so accomplished and intelligent…and so damn wonderful, could even *want* to spend any time with her, let alone miss her when they were apart. It was fantastic and terrifying, and she expected at any moment for it all to disappear. But there Catherine stood, three feet away, looking at her with something close to sadness in her eyes, and the thought of Catherine hurting in any way tore through Rebecca more sharply than any bullet ever could.

Propelled by concern, she swiftly crossed the distance between them and pulled the other woman close, whispering fervently, "I'm sorry. I'm sorry about last night. I wanted to be with you."

Threading her arms around Rebecca's neck, Catherine pressed tightly against her, content for the moment to forego words and simply feel. Besides, there were no words to describe the sensation of everything suddenly being made right by a simple embrace. She didn't understand it, but the veracity of it was undeniable. Rebecca's hands moving softly over her back felt more essential to her being than the air she was breathing. "I love you."

Rebecca closed her eyes and pressed her cheek against the silky softness of Catherine's hair. "I love you."

"Is there food in that bag?" Catherine asked after her breathing had steadied, leaning back slightly in the circle of Rebecca's arms and letting her eyes play over that strong face.

"There is," Rebecca replied, but it wasn't food that she hungered for. Deftly, she lifted the blouse from beneath the band of Catherine's slacks and slid her hand onto the warm skin at the base of Catherine's spine. Circling her fingers over the hollow just above her lover's hips, she pressed her own hips forward, drawing a gasp from the woman in her arms. "But it will keep."

Their lips met, and for a time they merely swayed together in the midst of the gathering darkness, hands claiming flesh and lips pledging promises with kisses that grew more abandoned with each passing second. Catherine finally pulled back when she thought she was in danger of falling, her legs shook so badly. Gasping, she asked, "Does this go away? This feeling of never being able to get close enough?"

"I don't know," Rebecca answered, desperate for air, her chest heaving. "I've never felt it before."

"It doesn't really matter," Catherine murmured almost to herself as she worked the buttons free on Rebecca's shirt, pulling it from the trousers as she did. She pushed the constraining fabric aside and slid her palms over firm muscles, capturing the soft swell of breasts in her palms. "It's beyond my control."

"Good...don't stop then..." Rebecca groaned, her knees nearly buckling as pinpoints of pleasure streaked from beneath knowing fingers. She shrugged her shirt off onto the floor and pressed her pelvis hard into Catherine's, needing more—more contact, more connection, more sweet torture. Arching her back, she closed her eyes and tried to steady herself with her hands on Catherine's shoulders. When she felt Catherine's teeth on her neck, she thought her head would explode.

She'd never had a woman take her this way, and she'd never even known before how much she'd wanted it. But she did. More than wanted it—she craved it. The feeling of surrendering to Catherine's passion was more freeing than anything she had ever experienced. "Just don't stop…"

"Can't," Catherine moaned, her head throbbing and her vision nearly gone. Some small working part of her brain reminded her that they were standing in the middle of her living room, and she grasped Rebecca's hand and pulled her urgently toward the sofa. "Sit down," she commanded as she yanked down the zipper on Rebecca's trousers.

The backs of Rebecca's knees hit the edge of the sofa, and she had no choice but to comply, feeling the rest of her clothes stripped from her thighs as she went down. She found herself nearly naked, Catherine in her lap, their mouths dancing over one another's skin again. When fingers slid between her thighs, finding her unerringly, all she could do was drop her head against the back of the couch and moan. It had been like this that first night, her need rising so fast she'd never had a chance to contain it, but this time she didn't resist the aching surge of pleasure. She welcomed the fire that burned through her blood, purging the wounds far deeper than flesh.

"Please," she begged.

Catherine slipped to her knees between Rebecca's legs and then leaned forward to take her with tender hands and demanding lips. No thought, no insecurity now. This—this splendor, this wonder, this indescribable beauty—this was hers for the taking, and take her she did. With certainty of touch and surety of heart, she lifted her lover on the wings of her own breathless desire to a place far beyond words.

❖

Watching moonlight flicker on the ceiling, Rebecca sifted strands of thick auburn hair through her nearly lifeless fingers, unable to muster enough strength to lift her head from the cushions of the couch. Her thighs still trembled, and her stomach rippled with aftershocks. "Catherine?" she murmured hoarsely.

"Mm…"

"I'm wasted."

"Me, too."

"If you help me up, we can probably make it into the bedroom. You must be uncomfortable." With effort, she slipped her palm beneath Catherine's chin, raising her lover's head from where it rested against her own inner thigh, and managed to focus on the deep green eyes. "If you give me a few minutes, I might be able to reciprocate, too."

"I'm fine." Catherine smiled. "Something else about being with you that surprises me—making love to you seems to set me off."

"You amaze me, too." She was tired, and her chest ached, and the lassitude that lingered after her climax had nearly lulled her into sleep, but she needed Catherine to know how much she wanted her. She needed to show her. "Still, I have plans for you."

"Hold that thought," Catherine said warmly as she pushed herself upright and extended one hand to Rebecca. "Let's have dinner first. We both need to eat."

"All right. Food first, but don't think I'm forgetting."

"Oh, believe me, I won't let you forget."

As it turned out, time slipped away. It was close to midnight by the time Rebecca stir-fried the vegetables and noodles she'd picked up earlier in the evening, and even later by the time they finished eating and piled the dishes into the dishwasher.

"Come on," Catherine announced, grasping Rebecca's still-untucked shirttail and tugging her away from the sink. "Bed. I'm fading and—"

"I need to go out, and it's already later than I thought."

Catherine stopped moving abruptly, letting the material fall from her fingers. "What?"

Exhaling softly, Rebecca turned and rested her hips against the counter. She didn't want to see what was in Catherine's eyes—she was afraid it would be that combination of hurt and resentment that had so often been in Jill's—but she forced herself to meet the other woman's gaze. There were questions in the depths of those green eyes, and confusion, but they hadn't grown cold. Not yet. Drawing a deep breath, she steeled herself for the pain that was sure to come when Catherine turned from her in anger, and pushed herself to answer.

"I've been away from the job a long time. I want to get a leg up on this new case, and there are some people I need to see."

Catherine stared at her, struggling to absorb the words and place them into some context she could deal with. There wasn't any. "Tonight? In the middle of the night—alone?"

It was Rebecca's turn to be confused. "Catherine, I'm a cop."

"Of course, I *know* that, Rebecca," Catherine snapped, rubbing the bridge of her nose and pacing the length of the kitchen. "I thought this first assignment was desk duty for you. A paper chase."

"It is—well, it is and it isn't. It's a real investigation, and a lot of it will be done through computer searches and whatever the hell else it is that those eggheads are going to do, but there's real police work to be done, too. Someone out there knows *something* about this racket, and I need to find out what."

"What about Watts?" Catherine heard the edge in her own voice, realized that she was still pacing, and forced herself to slow down. Screaming would not help, and the very fact that she *wanted* to scream was upsetting enough. She'd been involved with other women before— nice, interesting, attractive women. None of them had ever turned her upside down this way. "I thought *he* was going to do the street work?"

"He is," Rebecca affirmed. She took a chance and walked the few feet to her lover, tentatively taking her hand. The slight contact eased some of the tension in her stomach, although Catherine's response was guarded. "But he can't talk to my contacts. It took me years to cultivate them, and they don't talk to just anyone. I'll just be talking. I swear."

Catherine took a step away, but she kept her hand in the detective's. She couldn't think clearly when they were so close. "Why didn't you tell me this earlier? When you got here…or on the phone when I called you from the car?"

The cop was silent.

"Rebecca?"

"I was…" She ran a hand through her hair, shrugged her tight shoulders. "I thought you'd be angry. I thought you wouldn't want to see me."

"Angry," Catherine said softly, incredulously. The desire to scream had returned. So had the desire to hold her, because the detective's uncertainty, her expectation of loss, was so plain in her voice. "Did you not think that I might be worried? That I might be concerned that you've barely been out of bed a week and you're already working fifteen-hour days? God, Rebecca…"

Dropping Rebecca's hand, Catherine walked over and sat wearily at the small kitchen table, motioning to the adjoining chair with one hand. "Sit down. You look tired."

Rebecca sat. "I meant to tell you, but when we got here—"

"I didn't give you much opportunity to talk then, did I?" Catherine finished, a faint smile relaxing her troubled expression. "I barely gave you a chance to say hello."

"I wanted you, too. All day. Badly." Rebecca took her hand again, and this time Catherine's fingers laced comfortingly between hers. "When you touch me, everything just...falls into place. Everything makes sense."

"I know." She brushed her fingers over the detective's cheek. "For me, too. Our nonverbal skills are just fine—outstanding, as a matter of fact. But we need to do a little better on the verbal parts."

"I'm bad at that," Rebecca said honestly. "Talking wasn't big around my house. My father was a cop; *his* father was a cop. The job came first. My father never explained; my mother never complained. But I know there were a lot of nights he didn't come home. And then... well, then one night he went to work, and he never came home again, and we never talked about that either. It's a cop's life."

Catherine's heart thudded painfully, but she just nodded. Rebecca's expression was distant, and she doubted that the detective really saw her. There'd be time enough to think about what this meant for her—for them—in the hours after Rebecca left.

"I grew up with silence. That's the way most cops are with everyone, about everything," Rebecca finally said. The blue eyes she lifted to Catherine's swirled with anguish. "I've never even said these things out loud before."

"And that's exactly why I love you," Catherine whispered. "Because you're saying them now."

CHAPTER NINE

In the hours after midnight, the streets in Catherine's sedate neighborhood were eerily quiet. But as Rebecca approached the Tenderloin in the heart of the downtown area, foot and vehicular activity picked up. Here on the neon-lit sidewalks and in innumerable run-down bars, strip joints, and cheap hotels, life teemed with restless energy. She pulled to the curb not far from an all-night diner that was a local hangout for the area's denizens—mostly prostitutes taking a break between johns, panhandlers who had been lucky enough to scrounge the price of a cup of coffee, and bar goers who *hadn't* been lucky enough to find company for the late lonely hours.

Stepping from the Vette into the night for the first time in nearly two months, Rebecca felt oddly at peace. On these streets, she knew exactly who she was, and exactly what was expected of her. A strange comfort, but a familiar one. Her blood hummed with the faint stirring of anticipation that being out here, hunting, always produced. She wasn't hunting a person, not tonight, but the information she gathered—the odd comment, the offhand observation, the bit of gossip bandied about—might someday lead her to her prey.

She'd almost reached a brightly lit spot on the sidewalk in front of the diner when she caught sight of a familiar figure pushing through the revolving door on the way out of the establishment. Quickly, she stepped into the darkened overhang of a boarded-up video store and waited for the person to pass. She only had a fleeting glimpse of the leather-jacketed, blue-jeaned form as the woman strode quickly by, but the sharp, clear features beneath midnight black hair were impossible to mistake. Dellon Mitchell was out very late in a very dicey part of town.

Rebecca decided to wait a few minutes before checking out the diner. The minute she walked in, she'd be obvious to everyone. Those who didn't know her would still be able to tell she was a cop. Even though she'd stopped home to change into jeans and a T-shirt and wore a light windbreaker to cover her holster, her eyes screamed cop. Usually, she didn't mind. Visibility could be a form of power, especially if it intimidated informants into telling her what she needed to know quickly with a minimum of pressure. But she didn't know who might be inside, and Mitchell's presence here, for no reason that Rebecca could imagine, worried her. Maybe it was coincidence, but any cop could tell you that there was no such thing. Ignoring the smell of urine and rotting wood, she leaned against the moldy wall of the tiny dank alcove and watched the diner.

She didn't have to wait long. Less than five minutes later, three young women came out and headed her way, walking close together as they laughed and talked. It didn't require a detective's skills to determine their occupation. Too-short skirts and body-hugging, scooped-neck tops, along with too much make-up and cheap accessories, spelled hooker. Rebecca fell into step next to a slender blond with spiked hair who might have been anywhere from twelve to twenty.

"Hiya, Sandy," she said quietly.

"Christ!" the young woman exclaimed. Glancing quickly at her companions, who were staring at her curiously, she grabbed Rebecca's arm and pulled her into the shadows under an awning. "Go ahead, you guys. I'll catch up." When they'd moved away, she hissed, "God damn it, Frye. When are you going to leave me alone?"

"I did. Two whole months."

"Well, it seems like yesterday. What do you want?"

"Let's go somewhere we can talk," Rebecca offered. She knew that being seen with her could be a problem for the young prostitute, although she didn't care if she ruined her business for the night. She *did* care, however, if she put her in physical danger. Anyone in that part of town appearing too friendly with the police would make enemies quickly. "I want to catch up on old times. Have you eaten? I'll buy you breakfast."

"It's 4:00 a.m."

"Okay—dinner then."

Sandy snorted in disgust. "Fine. Chen's. Come on."

They moved quickly through back streets that were so narrow they might have been alleys except for the historic townhouses lining them. The residents of Society Hill, as the area was called, issued constant complaints to City Hall regarding the adjacent Tenderloin and its undesirable activity. Unfortunately, the seedy part of town bordered some of the most expensive real estate in Center City. Every six months, the police swept the area nightly for a week or two, an attempt to reduce the nightlife, but it always returned.

Rebecca kept a careful eye out for anyone following them or lurking in the shadows as they hurried along. Ten minutes later, they emerged on South Street, another pocket of late-night activity, although here the crowd was younger and the excitement centered more on alcohol and drugs than sex. Chen's House of Jade was a hole-in-the-wall restaurant that looked like a Board of Health citation waiting to be served, but the food was good and the proprietor discreet.

Rebecca and Sandy took a booth in the back beneath flickering fluorescents. A smiling waitress materialized with a pot of steaming tea and a bowl of crisp noodles before their butts had hit the cracked vinyl seats. She moved to hand them menus, but Rebecca shook her head, and Sandy said, "Moo shu pork with extra pancakes. And a Tsing Tao."

Then they were alone, staring at each other across the stained Formica surface. Automatically, Rebecca took inventory, her eyes flickering over the blond's face and then down to her bare arms. The pretty young woman's eyes were clear and her arms bore no track marks. The detective was glad. She liked the spunky kid.

"What happened to your head?" Rebecca asked.

Sandy shrugged and lightly traced the fresh red scar on her forehead. The suture marks still showed along the edges of the cut. "I fell."

"Did someone help you fall?" Rebecca asked casually, plucking a twisted crispy fried noodle from the bowl. There were a dozen reasons why a woman in Sandy's position could end up dead—turf issues from veteran prostitutes who didn't want younger, more desirable competition moving in on their corners; angry pimps who didn't think the nightly returns were high enough; a trick gone bad. But Sandy was Rebecca's informant, and the cop protected her own. It was one reason why Sandy helped her, although not always happily, with street intel.

"I already said. Accident." She studied the cop, noting the shadows under her eyes. Her normal leanness bordered on gaunt. "I didn't think you'd be back."

Rebecca was silent.

"I heard—well, everyone heard—about what happened to you the day after Anna Marie got...killed." The last time Sandy and the tall cop had seen one another, Sandy'd been crying on Frye's shoulder and her best friend had been lying dead—murdered—upstairs in a rat-hole hotel. She could still feel the safe, solid feel of the cop's arms around her. Shaking her head to dispel the memory, she added, "I'm glad you blew that fucker away."

"So am I."

Sandy looked at her in surprise, her skin prickling at the cold hard flatness of the cop's voice. She was starting to wonder if she hadn't been wrong about a lot of things about cops. Frye wasn't like those prick bastards who hassled her and her friends for sex in exchange for not running them in on prostitution charges that they all knew wouldn't stick past night court. Frye was different; she cared, just like—

The waitress interrupted her musings as she deposited an enormous platter of steaming moo shu on the table between them along with pancakes and sauce.

"More beer?" the waitress asked Sandy, who shook her head no. Looking at Rebecca, she asked, "How about you?" The word *detective* hung in the air.

"No, I'm good."

As Rebecca watched her companion pile food on her plate, she remarked, "I'm looking for somebody selling young stuff."

"Everybody sells young stuff. That's what sells. Or haven't you noticed?"

"I'm talking about the real thing, not the eighteen-year-olds pretending to be thirteen."

"Don't know anything about it." Sandy rolled another pancake and sipped her beer, keeping her eyes on her plate.

"This is probably a big, well-run operation, not some pimp

selling chickens out of an apartment in the slums," Rebecca continued unperturbed. "Maybe a well-*organized* operation. "

Sandy raised her gaze to Rebecca's. Their blue eyes met, but try as she might, she knew that she couldn't match the hard stillness of the cop's cold stare. Sandy blinked, then said softly, "Are you fucking nuts? I don't know anything about that, and I don't *want* to know anything about it. If this is *organized,* then asking about it gets you dead. Look at what happened to your cop friends last spring."

Rebecca's expression became granite. "What did you hear?"

"Just that they were poking around where they shouldn't have been poking—in somebody *important's* business. And that somebody shut them up."

"You get this important person's name?"

Sandy shook her head. "Uh-uh."

"Who did you hear this from?"

"Can't recall."

"Try."

"Are you looking to get offed, too?" Sandy hissed, leaning forward across the small tabletop. Fuck, why did she even care? But she remembered the ache in her chest when she'd heard that Frye had been shot, bad shot. God damn her for coming around again. "What is it with you?"

For some reason, Rebecca answered. "One of them was my partner."

"Well, now he's dead. End of story."

"No," Rebecca said quietly as she pulled her wallet from her back pocket. "Not yet." She laid four twenties on the table. "Ask around. Be careful, though."

"Yeah, right. Thanks." Her tone was not grateful. "Listen," she said quickly as Rebecca slid across the seat and stood up.

"What?"

"A friend of mine is in a jam. An undercover guy busted her tonight—not before she finished the hand job, I might add, although of course *he* denies that—and I know she doesn't have the bail. She's been picked up before. She could go away for this."

"What's her name?" Rebecca asked, glancing at her watch. "If the paperwork's not processed yet, I'll see what I can do."

"Rita. Rita Balducci."

"I'll see you soon."

"Can't wait," Sandy grumbled, watching the cop walk quickly through the narrow aisle between the rickety tables and out into the night. A part of her felt better knowing Frye was back on the streets.

❖

"Oh, God, I need a shower. I need *two* showers." Jason McBride pushed away from the computer terminal and rubbed his face with both hands. "I always heard it, but I never really *knew* how many sickos there were out there."

Sloan swiveled in her chair and faced him from the console where she had been working. The clock on the far wall said 4:42 a.m. The last time she could remember checking it had been 8:30 the previous evening. Jason's hair was uncharacteristically disheveled, and his shirt was actually untucked. Intentionally. That was highly unusual for her fastidious friend. It was the hollow-eyed expression on his face that caught her attention, though. It wasn't fatigue—they'd worked forty hours or more without stopping when they'd had major system failures to repair or massive viral infestations to cleanse. This was something else.

"I guess you've been successful?"

He winced. "If you can call almost having sex with a dozen perverts *successful*, then yes—wildly so."

"Who are you tonight?"

"QtGrl13. She was a big hit."

"Where have you been trolling?"

"The Hot4U message boards. As soon as I showed up and announced that I was a new girl in town, I had three offers to move off to a private room to get acquainted. I was in and out of the chat rooms all night after that."

"Anything look promising?"

He shrugged, then sighed. "Too soon to tell. The patter is pretty sophisticated for the most part, except for the high school boys who are the same the world over whether it's cyberspace or the junior prom. They just want to get laid, and they're not too subtle about it. But I have a feeling that the real pedophiles are being very careful not to expose themselves. They're probably pretending to be kids until they feel safe enough in a relationship to cop to their real age. There were one or two who sounded as if they might be angling for more than a quickie, but I'll have to go back on again a few more times to see. If I move too fast, it will spook them."

"All right. As soon as you have a possible, let me know and we'll start a back-door trace. And we need to narrow down geographic locations. There are literally thousands of people using these boards, and we have to search for a local hit."

"Got it."

"Try to bring the conversations around to pics, especially current ones or anything with videos."

"I'm doing that when I go on as BigMac10; that's where I've just been—swimming with the scum who are looking to trade files. I'm posing as a guy who's interested in twelve- or thirteen-year-old girls. But I haven't been real specific yet. These guys aren't stupid, and the people we're looking for are going to be very savvy. I can't just ask to see some guy's etchings."

He sighed and stood. "I'm going home. Sarah got in from that alternative medicine conference in Santa Fe tonight...last night... whatever. Somehow, being with her always makes me feel normal."

"Yeah, she has that effect on me, too," Sloan replied, thinking of her best friend, current training partner, and—light-years ago—one-time colleague. They'd both been stationed in Southeast Asia when they'd been young and still believed that their government had the best intentions of its people at heart.

"That's a stretch for you," he said good-naturedly.

Sloan just laughed. "Say hi for me, and tell her she owes me a workout."

"Will do. You should quit for the night, too. Michael home?"

"Yes."

"Then go."

Sloan glanced at the screen, considering the credit card clearinghouses she still needed to trace, then thought of the woman upstairs asleep. The case was already getting ugly, and it was likely to get even uglier before it was done. She stood and stretched. "Excellent advice. I'm gone."

She locked the office doors and set the security alarms as Jason descended in the silent elevator, then walked the length of the dimly lit hall to the rear stairwell and climbed the one flight to her fourth-floor loft apartment. As quietly as possible, she keyed in the lock codes and slid the large double doors apart, closing and bolting them behind her. Making her way through the darkened space by memory, she shed her clothes along the way and crossed to the bathroom on the far side of the partitioned sleeping area. She left the light off so as not to awaken Michael, but as she reached into the shower to turn on the water, there was a soft sound behind her. Turning, she was startled as a warm, naked body pressed into her arms.

Nuzzling Sloan's neck, Michael murmured sleepily, "Is it morning?"

"Not yet." She kissed her gently. "Go back to bed. I'll be in as soon as I shower."

"Mmm. Want company?"

"Now that is by far the best offer I've had all night."

"Oh?" Michael asked, sounding much more awake. "And have you had many offers this evening?"

"None worth mentioning," Sloan reassured her. Unfortunately, she had a feeling that that circumstance was about to change, given their current undertaking. Pushing aside thoughts of predators and innocent victims, she drew her lover into the shower and let the warm water and Michael's embrace wash the unwelcome images from her mind.

❖

When the alarm went off, Michael made a quick grab for it in an attempt to silence the insistent buzzing before it awakened Sloan.

"What time is it?" came a husky whisper from the darkness.

"6:15."

"You have a meeting this morning, don't you?" Sloan asked, clearing her throat and trying to dispel the cobwebs from her brain.

"Yes. Development and Marketing are meeting to discuss agendas."

Sloan rolled over and watched Michael sit up in bed, appreciating the way the sheets cascaded down her lover's body, leaving her breasts bare. Suddenly, she forgot the fact that she'd only had an hour of sleep. They hadn't been able to have dinner together the evening before, because by the time Michael had returned from a late meeting with a new client, Sloan and Jason had been deep into another night on the job. Internet traffic was high between 4:00 p.m. and 2:00 a.m., when kids were home from school. That's when adults looking for a contact would be trolling. With effort, she pushed aside those thoughts.

Running a hand down Michael's arm, she said, "I missed you last night."

"Me, too." Michael sighed. "I hate to leave so early, but I need to be there to referee. You know those two groups can never agree as to whose timetable should take priority. And of course, both division directors are total hotheads, and usually one or the other or *both* of them threatens to quit after every meeting. I figured I'd save myself some time by being there to put out any fires."

"They'll play nice if you're there. And you could always threaten to can them before they have a chance to quit."

"Maybe. If they weren't so good in their areas, I'd do it." Michael laughed and leaned down to kiss her. "Go back to sleep."

"Mmm. I will," Sloan murmured languorously, her arms encircling Michael's waist. Pulling the other woman down into her arms, she added, "In just a few minutes."

Surprised, Michael emitted a short peal of laughter that turned to a muffled moan as her body met Sloan's, and her skin hummed with the familiar pulse of desire. Her brain said *go to work,* but her body called the next shot, and before she knew it, she was straddling Sloan's thigh and devouring her lover's mouth, suddenly ravenous for the taste of her. While she was lost in the kiss, Sloan lifted her hips, rolled Michael over, and then settled possessively upon her. The hum became a roar.

Unwillingly, Michael pulled her mouth away from the kiss, gasping, "No time."

"I'll be quick," Sloan growled, her lips against Michael's neck, her hand brushing the length of Michael's side to her hips.

"Liar. You're never quick." But she wasn't moving away.

Sloan pushed herself up and in one fluid motion slid down the bed until her breasts nestled between Michael's thighs and her cheek was pressed to Michael's stomach. Nipping at the sensitive skin around her lover's navel, she trailed her fingers lightly up the inside of Michael's left thigh, then danced them back and forth over the tender places between her legs.

"Tease me like that for very long and it *will* be quick," Michael warned, arching her hips under Sloan's clever fingers.

"I know."

Still, Sloan took her time, drawing her fingertips along the sensitive folds, dipping into welcoming heat, then pressing the length of Michael's clitoris only to move away quickly, eliciting sighs and faint cries from her lover. Only when Michael's long delicate fingers fluttered over her cheek in mute appeal did she lower her head and take her gently between her lips. At Michael's sharp cry, she pulled her in more deeply, her tongue stroking counterpoint to the pulse that hammered through swollen tissues. Careful not to increase the pressure enough to snap the threads of Michael's control, Sloan kept her quivering on the edge for long moments. Not until Michael began to thrust erratically against her, impossibly hard now and clearly on the verge of exploding, did she relent and increase the cadence of her strokes.

Instantly, she was rewarded by the rigid stillness in Michael's legs that signaled she was close, followed by a wrenching gasp and a quiet sob of surrender. Sloan closed her eyes, savoring every tremor that spiraled beneath her lips and moved outward through her lover's body. Then she lay quietly, one hand extended, her fingers intertwined with Michael's, completely satisfied.

Sloan was almost asleep again as Michael whispered in her ear, "I've set the alarm. Be careful today. I love you."

❖

Catherine turned off the alarm twenty minutes before it was set to ring. She'd been awake for a long time, listening to the silence in the still house punctuated occasionally by the distant sound of a car door opening, an engine starting, and someone leaving for an early day. It had taken her a long time to fall asleep after Rebecca had left the night before, too. It was impossible not to wonder where she was going, to whom she would be talking, and with whom she would be spending the last dark hours of the night. She had hoped that Rebecca would return when her work was done, to come quietly through the door to rest at her side. Once she had even awakened, heart beating fast with anxious anticipation, thinking she had heard her—only to realize it had been the wind blowing branches against her window that had called to her.

Wearily, she swung her legs from beneath the covers and stood, reaching for her robe as she straightened. She was tired, not from lack of sleep, although that endeavor had certainly been fitful, but from something deeper that tugged at her heart. As if standing at a distance, dispassionately watching a scene played out on stage, she studied the feeling, finally recognizing it as a combination of loneliness and fear. The loneliness did not surprise her. She missed Rebecca, which was only natural. The fear would take some time to understand, but part of it was simple enough. She was afraid because her love for the other woman made her vulnerable—susceptible not only to her own fate but also to Rebecca's. Their paths had crossed, their lives had intersected, and now their futures were entwined. It was entirely possible that the road ahead would be paved with disappointment and sorrow, but she could not help but travel onward. Leaving Rebecca was unthinkable.

How many times had she counseled others that there were no guarantees in life and that only through living was there any chance of fulfillment? Smiling to herself, she made her way toward the shower, thinking how easy it was to give advice and how hard, sometimes, to heed it.

CHAPTER TEN

Rebecca parked illegally in a bus stop and left her flashers on. She jogged up the block, glancing at her watch and searching for Catherine's car. She didn't see it, but she told herself that Catherine had returned late the previous night and probably hadn't been able to find a place on her own block. Her breath was a little tight, and she was aware of a faint stabbing pain deep in her chest that pulsed with each footfall. Chalking it up to a still-healing wound, she ignored it. Nevertheless, as she pressed Catherine's doorbell, she had to work to suppress the sound of her own breath wheezing in and out. *What I really don't need now is to give Catherine something else to worry about.*

After a minute, she pressed the doorbell again, but even as she did, she knew that she had missed her. When they'd parted the previous evening, they had been careful with one another, trying not to ignite the fires of anger that still smoldered dangerously. She hadn't thought to ask Catherine what her morning schedule was. *Another fuck-up, Frye.*

Turning away, she walked more slowly now down the marble stairs to the sidewalk and toward her car. There was a place inside of her that still hurt, and it had nothing to do with her injuries. It was that part of her that always felt empty when they were apart, and now she knew it was going to ache all day. Cursing softly, she slid into her Vette, gunned the engine, and roared away into the morning.

❖

Rebecca's temper hadn't improved any by the time she reached the station house, and it wasn't soothed by the thought of her 7:30 a.m.

appointment. Rand Whitaker opened the door to his office precisely on time.

"Come on in, Sergeant," he said with a welcoming smile.

Rebecca followed him, carrying a cardboard cup of coffee she had picked up from the vending room on her way to his office. She settled into the straight-backed chair and balanced the cup on her knee.

"So you've been back on the job a few days now, isn't that right?" He jotted the date and time on a yellow legal pad as he sipped from his own mug of coffee.

"Not precisely," Rebecca corrected in an even tone. The one place you didn't want to appear disgruntled was in this room. "My normal assignment is working active Special Cmes cases—detective work. For the time being, I've been assigned as an intermediary between the police department and a federal agency that's running a multijurisdictional task force."

"That sounds like a desk job."

"More or less," she conceded, not seeing the necessity of offering anything further. The less he knew, the less he could report to someone else.

"You okay with that?"

"It's not what I'm trained to do, and it wouldn't be my choice of assignments. I'm assuming it will be temporary, and as soon as you sign off on my evaluation, I expect my captain to pull me off and put me back on regular duty." Hopefully, he'd get the hint and do what everyone knew he was going to do anyhow, which was certify her fit for duty. *Christ, I'm the one who got shot. You'd think that would earn me some slack.*

He eased back in his chair, nodding as if he agreed with what she was thinking. "I'm curious, Sergeant. Why didn't you wait for backup that night with Blake? Wouldn't that have been standard operating procedure?"

"As I told you before, I felt that the hostage was in imminent danger and that any delay would put her at risk."

"Your partner stated in his report that she had not been harmed up to that point. What made you think the situation was so serious?"

"Detective Watts stated in his report that Dr. Rawlings had apparently not been *sexually assaulted* up to that point, but he confirmed that she was physically restrained and in immediate peril." *Jesus, doesn't he know that I would have read Watts's report by now? I know what he said in it. Whitaker is clearly no detective.*

"The reason I'm asking is that if someone were to look at this from the outside, your actions could be construed as taking the law into your own hands. You saved the hostage—true, but you also executed the perpetrator."

Rebecca almost smiled. Now he was trying to provoke her into saying more than she intended to reveal. Another interrogation technique that he wasn't employing very well.

"Dr. Whitaker, I did not execute the suspect. I used appropriate force to subdue a violent criminal who gave every indication that he was about to inflict severe bodily harm on a civilian and who gave verbal confirmation that he intended to kill her as well as me."

"Let's cut to the chase, Detective Sergeant."

"That would be nice."

"Given the same situation, would you do the same thing again?"

"Yes," Rebecca answered without hesitation. Her eyes met his, and whatever he saw in her steel gaze made him blink.

"Would you risk your life for *any* hostage, or only one you were personally involved with?" he asked softly.

She leaned forward, never taking her eyes from his, and her voice was flint. "Meaning what?"

"You knew the hostage personally, didn't you?"

"I met her during the course of the investigation, yes."

He gave no sign that she hadn't precisely answered his question, but merely continued. "Did the fact that you...knew her...influence your reaction to the situation?"

"No." She didn't see any need to tell him that she'd been almost out of her mind with fear and anger only a short time before she'd finally found Blake and Catherine. No need because her mind had been crystal clear when she'd stepped into the room with them. She'd been in perfect control.

"So," he said with soft finality. "What you're saying is that you would risk your life...no, *forfeit* your life...for anyone in the same situation."

"I'm a cop, Whitaker," Rebecca remarked sharply, at last allowing her impatience to show. "In case you haven't noticed, that's what we do. I'm not a loose cannon; I'm not a danger to society. I'm not a risk to anyone."

"Except yourself."

Standing, she asked quietly, "Are we done here?"

"For today, yes. I'd like to see you one more time, which is my standard operating procedure." As she turned to leave, he added, "You might consider, Sergeant, that you would be much more effective if you valued yourself as much as those you are sworn to protect."

She didn't answer but closed the door gently behind her.

❖

When Rebecca stepped out into the hallway after leaving Whitaker's office, she turned right and almost walked into Watts, who was leaning against the wall smoking a cigarette under a big bright red *No Smoking* sign. She stared at him. "What are you doing here?"

"I saw you pull into the parking lot this morning."

"And what? You didn't have anything better to do for an hour than hang around out here?"

"Well," he said unhurriedly, taking the last drag on his cigarette, dropping it onto the stained tile floor, and crushing it beneath his scuffed wingtips, "Now that you mention it, I do have something better to do, and I thought you might like something better to do, too."

"What have you got?" She was curious despite her irritation at finding him outside the psychologist's office.

It wasn't exactly a secret what she was doing there, but she still didn't like being reminded that her colleagues were aware of the fact that she was undergoing evaluation. Even though she was not under any kind of suspicion, the process still made her feel as if she was not on firm ground within her own province. As much as she intellectually accepted the need for police officers, with their steady diet of stress and physical danger, to have the support of psychologists who understood the pressures of the job, it was still something of a stigma to actually *see* one.

Before Watts could speak, she snapped, "Let's get out of here."

As the two of them walked toward the stairwell at the end of the hallway, Watts replied, "I've tracked down a guest of the state, conveniently staying at the correctional institution at Graterford, who might be willing to provide a bit of information for a little something from us in return. You know the drill—these cons will roll on their own mothers for extra privileges or a shot at an earlier parole hearing."

"Who is he?" Rebecca asked, her pulse quickening at the thought of any kind of hard lead. It wasn't in her nature to sit by and wait for other departments, or in this case federal agents, to point her in the right direction on a case. If Sloan and McBride turned up something with their Internet searches, all the better, but she wasn't holding her breath.

"A guy by the name of Alonso Richards. He's doing six to ten for possession with the intent to sell."

"Huh," Rebecca said disappointedly. "Drugs. What makes you think he can help us?"

"Because when they raided the house where he was holed up with his stash of crack cocaine, they also found some very interesting videotapes. Tapes with a whole bunch of teenage girls and a couple of… uh…mature men frolicking in the nude in a variety of combinations. And they weren't commercial tapes—these were home movies."

"Do you have the tapes?"

Watts shook his head disgustedly. "Nope. I checked with the evidence room last night. Mysteriously, the tapes have disappeared."

"So we don't know who was on them?"

"No such luck. There was no mention as to whether the men were ever ID'd or not."

Rebecca stopped at the bottom of the stairwell and stared at Watts. "How did you find this? And how come we're just hearing about it now?"

Watts shrugged, but his expression was wary. "Something doesn't smell right, but I can't figure out where the smell is coming from. Since we're Vice, someone from Narco should have tipped us off about it when they turned up the tapes during the raid. But it was buried in the arrest report, and the only reason I found it at all is because I pulled the files on the busts you and Cruz made when you closed down that chicken coop last spring."

They pushed through the exit door into the parking lot, where Watts promptly lit another cigarette. Rebecca regarded him impatiently.

"And?"

Hastily taking a drag, he continued. "I was looking to find some connection with the guys running that deal, hoping we'd find someone still working the streets. Didn't find anything, so I cross-referenced the names of the guys you sent away for known associates. Then I ran the names of *those* guys looking for recent activity and out popped this Richards."

Police vans, cruisers, and unmarked vehicles were interspersed with civilian cars in the broad lot. As the two of them wove between the haphazardly parked automobiles toward Rebecca's Corvette, she remarked, "You must have spent a lot of time humping that computer. Nice job."

He didn't reply, but a smile flickered across his face and was just as quickly gone. "I think we need to hunt down the Narc dicks who made the bust and find out why we never heard about the pornography tie-in. I've called and left messages, but no callbacks. Anything to do with prostitution and kids should have automatically been kicked over to someone in our division, and I couldn't find a record of it."

As Rebecca opened the door and slid into the seat, she grumbled, "There seem to be a lot of things that we should have been informed of that we haven't been. Come to think of it, Cruz and I were lucky to have made that initial arrest. We were tipped off to the place by a junkie we were bracing about something entirely unrelated, and he gave up the location hoping we'd leave him alone. Now I wonder if we hadn't moved on it so quickly whether there would have been anyone there at all when we showed up."

When Watts had settled in beside her, she swiveled in her seat and said to him, "How come you didn't tell me about the rumors that Jeff Cruz was dirty?"

Watts merely regarded her with his bland, laid-back to the point of stupor expression. "Because it's bullshit. And if I had any idea who started that talk, I'd wait for them some night after dark out here in the parking lot and kick the crap out of them. Cruz was a cop who died in the line of duty, and you don't tarnish a cop's badge unless you've got evidence carved in stone."

Rebecca started the engine and pulled out of the parking lot. There wasn't any reason to comment. For once, she and Watts were in perfect agreement.

❖

Three hours later, Rebecca dropped Watts off in front of the one-eight. "I need to stop around to Sloan's office and put in an appearance," she said. "You want to write this up and run those names through the computer?"

"Sure," Watts said, considering it wise not to mention that *she* was supposed to be on desk duty and *he* was supposed to be the leg man. Whoever thought they could put Frye behind a desk didn't know her very well, or knew her well enough to know that it would be a sit-down job in name only. "Hey, Sarge," he added as if in afterthought, "if you're going to poke around in other departments, you might not want to spread around why."

Rebecca studied him thoughtfully. Not counting the period of her recovery, she and Watts had really only worked together a few weeks. She had absolutely no reason to trust him, but she reluctantly had to admit to herself that she did.

"What are you saying, Watts?"

"I'm not saying anything," he intoned innocently. He looked as if he was about to scratch his balls, and then thought better of it, putting his hand in his pocket instead. "I just think it would pay to be careful until we know what happened to Hogan and Cruz."

"You think we have a leak in the department?"

"Don't you?" His expression didn't change, but his eyes grew hard.

She looked away for a second, thinking of all the inconsistencies that had surfaced in just a few days. Homicide had apparently dropped the investigation of two dead detectives; files were missing from the crime scene lab concerning the deaths of the same two cops; arrest reports containing information that might have pointed toward a local child prostitution network had been buried; and, finally, she had been quietly assigned to an investigation that was being run from outside the department but which seemed to have connections to local organized crime figures. She was beginning to wonder exactly who Avery Clark was investigating.

"Yeah, Watts, I do. That or something worse. So you watch your back, too, okay?"

"You don't have to worry about me, Sarge. I don't intend to make waves." Whistling, he turned and walked away.

She watched him for a minute, wondering how many people he had fooled with his blasé facade. Watts was a good cop, and that was one department secret she was happy to have uncovered. Just as she was about to pull away, her beeper went off, and she recognized the University Hospital's number. She fished her cell phone from her pocket and punched in the number even as she headed across town toward University City.

"This is Frye," she said when the call was picked up.

"It's Catherine, Rebecca."

Rebecca's heart skipped a beat. "Hey. I'm just on my way over. Can I see you?"

"I'm in my office."

"Is everything okay?" There was an odd formality to Catherine's tone that made Rebecca uneasy.

"Everything's fine. I just wanted to talk to you for a minute."

"Okay," Rebecca replied suspiciously. It hadn't been her experience that when a woman wanted to talk to her that it was something minor. Especially not when she and that woman had parted on less than perfect terms the night before.

Catherine laughed, picking up on Rebecca's uncertainty. "And I wanted to tell you that I miss you."

"I miss you, too."

"Good. Drive carefully."

❖

An instant after Rebecca knocked, Catherine answered the door.

"Hi," Rebecca said, hesitating on the threshold, still feeling uncertain about her welcome.

"Hi." Catherine took her detective's hand and pulled the unresisting woman into the waiting room that adjoined her office, closing the door resolutely. "Joyce is at lunch, and I don't have a session for an hour. What about you?"

"My schedule is my own. I'm still on light duty, remember?"

"Yes, I know that's what it's called," Catherine said dryly. "Come on back to my office."

Catherine locked her inner office door and motioned Rebecca to the couch, then settled beside her. Before she could speak, Rebecca slipped an arm around her waist and kissed her. It was more than a simple hello kiss. There was an edge to it, an underlying pulse of hunger that immediately left Catherine aroused. She kissed her in return, for longer than she should have, but she liked knowing that she stirred this desire in her. Finally, she broke away, palms against Rebecca's chest.

"Enough. I'm working," she reminded her lover regretfully. "I have to see patients in less than an hour. I can't sit here all afternoon in a state of sexual frustration."

"I could fix that in just a few minutes."

Catherine laughed. "I have no doubt that you could. But I think I'd rather anticipate now and be satisfied later at a slightly more leisurely pace."

"Then that's what you shall have," Rebecca promised, lifting Catherine's hand from her chest and kissing her palm. Serious now, she asked, "What did you need to see me about?"

Catherine appeared uncharacteristically tentative as she glanced away, then met Rebecca's gaze squarely. Taking a deep breath, she said quietly, "I was contacted by Agent Clark this morning. He requested my services as a consultant to a task force he's running."

Rebecca stiffened, and her eyes grew cold. "Son of a bitch," she said softly. "How did he get your name?"

"I'm on the list of departmental consultants," Catherine said. "He also mentioned Captain Henry."

Rebecca got up and quickly crossed the room to the window that fronted the street. She'd stood there once before, the first night she'd met Catherine, but it had been dark then. She watched university students come and go outside the window, carefree and confident. It was a beautiful early September day.

Without turning, she asked, "What did you say?"

"I said I would get back to him. This is your task force, isn't it?"

"No," Rebecca said sharply, her back still to the room. "It's *Clark's* task force."

"You know what I mean."

There was no anger or accusation in Catherine's voice, and Rebecca realized that Catherine had not instigated the situation. Her lover didn't deserve her wrath. Turning to face her, she tried to figure out why she felt like punching something. "I'm sorry. You caught me off guard. Yes, it's the task force I'm involved with—the pornography prostitution investigation."

"I work with the police fairly frequently, Rebecca. It's quite likely that you and I will come into professional contact from time to time."

"I know. Why didn't you give Clark your answer earlier?" She tried and failed to keep the resentment from her voice.

"Because this is the first time something like this has come up for us," Catherine said gently. "I wanted to see how you felt about it."

"Does that matter?"

"Yes, it does." Catherine heard the anger, but she saw something else in the troubled blue gaze. Worry. Gently, she said, "You matter. And *we* matter very much to me."

"The last time you and I worked together," Rebecca pointed out darkly, "it ended badly."

"But this isn't the same thing, though, is it?" When Rebecca was silent, Catherine rose and crossed to her, worried now herself. "*Is* it, Rebecca? You said this was more or less an administrative assignment for you. That it wasn't dangerous. Is there more to it than that?"

"No," Rebecca said, deciding that there was no point in bringing up her suspicions and speculations about something going on behind the scenes in the department. She didn't really have any facts, and there was no point in worrying her lover for nothing. Still, she didn't like the idea of Catherine being anywhere near an investigation that felt as off as this one did. "I only wonder why Clark isn't bringing in his own people. If there's one thing the feds have plenty of, it's profilers."

"I asked him the same thing," Catherine said. "He pointed out that we're not profiling an individual but just a general pathologic type, and that I probably have as much experience with it as anyone. He also suggested that it would be helpful to have someone local so that… he mentioned two people, Sloan and McBride…so they would have someone immediately available if they got a hit."

"That makes sense," Rebecca agreed reluctantly.

"Rebecca," Catherine said, taking the other woman's hand. "This is what I do, and it's something I love to do. If it's going to be a problem working this closely with me—"

"No," Rebecca interrupted swiftly, finally getting her emotions under control. "It's not. When you first mentioned it, I thought about Blake. That's all."

"It's not the same thing." Catherine moved closer, gently threading her arms around Rebecca's waist. "I will never do anything like that again. I would never put you in danger."

Rebecca stared at her uncomprehendingly. "What are you talking about?"

"I insisted on being involved in the Blake investigation, and it resulted in you being shot. Nearly killed." Her voice broke on the last word.

"That wasn't your fault."

"Yes, it was." There were tears in her voice, although her face was calm.

"Jesus, Catherine. Is that what you think? You blame yourself?" She pulled her tightly into her arms, resting her cheek against Catherine's hair. She thought back to the nights that Catherine had lain beside her, tossing fitfully and awakening in terror. *Christ, how could I have been so blind?*

"Is *that* what the dreams are about?"

When Catherine didn't answer, Rebecca leaned back, cupping Catherine's chin in her palm. Looking into her deep green eyes, she saw the pain swimming close to the surface. "No. It wasn't your fault. What happened—that was *my* decision. I thought of Blake just now because I don't want you anywhere near an investigation that might be dangerous. I can't stand the thought of anything happening to you. I can still see him with that fucking gun against your head."

Suddenly, they were both trembling, each of them remembering that moment, each fearing for the other. Quietly, Catherine said, "I love you."

Rebecca pressed her lips to Catherine's temple, her fingers curved possessively on the back of her neck. "And I love you." Sighing, she asked, "When are you briefing with us?"

"Tomorrow at 7:00 a.m." Her cheek was still nestled against Rebecca's shoulder. "Will you come to me tonight?"

"It might be late," Rebecca answered reluctantly.

"I don't care."

"I want to. I miss you so much."

Eyes closed, listening to Rebecca's heartbeat, Catherine said softly, "Then don't stay away."

Chapter Eleven

Rebecca knew that what she should do was go home and catch some sleep, but she was too restless for that. Watts was following up on the scant help they'd gotten from Alonso Richards, the inmate at the State Correctional Institution at Graterford, in exchange for a promise to get him moved to another cell block far away from a particular prisoner who wanted to kill him for reasons Richards couldn't imagine. He'd reluctantly given them a couple of names of some of his old running buddies who *might* know somebody who *possibly* knew somebody who *maybe* had once helped make some sex movies. But he swore he didn't know who or where or for whom—all he knew was that it was someplace in the city and the chicks were young.

Maybe Watts would pull another rabbit out of his hat, but she'd pretty much resigned herself to the fact that, for the moment, unless Sloan came up with something, or an informant gave her a lead, she had nothing to chase. But Jeff's murder was still open, and she wanted to be able to tell Shelly Cruz that justice had been done when she went to see her. She'd been putting off visiting Jeff's wife because she was embarrassed that the department—that *she*—had nothing substantial to offer the young widow in terms of consolation.

Taking a shot in the dark, she drove back to the station house and took the elevator to the second floor where the Homicide division was housed. She usually walked up, but she was beat. A couple of detectives she knew nodded hello, one of them remarking as she passed, "Good to see you back, Frye."

She muttered her thanks but didn't stop to talk. She found the person she was looking for in the break room, jacket off, feet propped on a wastepaper basket, multitasking with an open murder book propped next to her brown-bag lunch.

"Sorry to bother you," Rebecca said to the woman in the dark blue suit as she closed the door to the small stuffy space. There was a window with a view of the river, but it was grimy and looked to be nailed shut. "Got a minute?"

Trish Marks glanced up from the case file she was reviewing, startled but too experienced to show it. "Frye. How are you doing?"

"I'm not bad. You?"

"Different day, same old shit. Crime might be down, but murder still has a way of happening."

Rebecca nodded. "I know what you mean. Sex still sells, too."

Trish closed the thick file and pushed it aside, draining her Coke can and tossing it into a nearby wastebasket. Leaning back in her chair, she fixed Frye with a steady look. "What's on your mind?"

"Jeff Cruz and Jimmy Hogan."

"Why aren't I surprised," Marks said to herself, and it wasn't meant to be a question. She got up and stretched, then walked to the coffee machine and poured a cup. She glanced inquiringly at Rebecca, who shook her head no. When she had added two sugars and enough fake cream to give herself brain cancer, she walked back to the table and sat down again. "What have you heard?"

Rebecca wondered how much to reveal. Trish Marks had a rep as a solid cop, and whenever Rebecca had interacted with her in the past, everything had seemed to confirm that. On the other hand, Marks was one of the detectives responsible for solving Jeff's murder, and she hadn't done that. Rebecca had to question why she had dropped the ball.

For a moment, the two women simply assessed one another in the silence. At first glance, they didn't seem all that similar, even though Marks was about Rebecca's age. She was dark where Rebecca was light, short where Rebecca was tall, mildly curvaceous where Rebecca was lean, but the look in their eyes was a matched set—tough, competent, and wary.

Rebecca could almost see it when Marks reached a decision, and she just waited, giving the Homicide detective a chance to gather her thoughts. There were allegiances to be considered, and cops were loath to give out information on their cases, even to other cops.

"We didn't get anything from the crime scene," Marks said, carefully choosing her words, "which is about what you'd expect. Flanagan worked it hard, but there just wasn't anything to find."

"Contract hit, right?"

Trish nodded. "Despite how fucked up this case got, I still think that's the truth. There was absolutely nothing at the scene to go on. And no rumors on the street to say differently—no talk of personal beefs, nothing to suggest it was a drug buy gone bad. Everything about it spelled hit." She stopped, wondering without much hope if Frye would let it go at that.

"What about Jimmy Hogan's files? What about his supervisors? Somebody somewhere knew what he was into. The last time I spoke with you and your partner, you hadn't had a chance to go through Jimmy's cases. Since that was over two months ago, I'll ask again. What did you turn up there?"

Marks's eyes narrowed. "Nothing."

"Now, see, that's where I start to get confused," Rebecca said tonelessly, her eyes boring into the woman across from her. "What did his captain say? What about his contact man in Narco? He must have been reporting to someone."

"Yeah, maybe he was." Marks shrugged. "But I've got a feeling it wasn't anybody in Narcotics." She watched Frye stiffen in surprise, the first sign of any unguarded emotion the blond detective had shown since she'd walked into the room, and Marks hastened to add, "And that stays in this room."

"Are you telling me you don't think Hogan was undercover for Narcotics?" Unconsciously, Rebecca reached under the left side of her jacket and rubbed her chest, trying to work the tightness out of the scar. When she realized what she was doing, she placed her palms flat on her thighs. *Never let on you're tired; never let on you're hurt; never let on you're scared.* Where'd she learn that—the Academy, or home? She concentrated on Trish Marks and forgot about the pain.

"What I'm saying is, no one in Narcotics is willing to cop to being Jimmy's contact. No one admits to having received any significant intel from him in months. And the more I asked about it, the bigger the wall got. Finally, I couldn't get anybody over there to talk to me at all."

"You think they were shut down by someone higher up?"

"Probably, but I can't get a line on who that somebody might be."

Rebecca's mind was racing furiously. There was a strange sort of logic to what Marks had told her. If Jimmy Hogan was undercover, he could be gathering information on anything—for anyone—not necessarily simply on drug traffic for Narco division. The problem was, if he wasn't Narcotics, then who was he? Or more importantly, *what* was he? She was beginning to see how people thought Hogan might have turned bad, and that kind of suspicion naturally tainted anyone who was associated with him, including her partner.

"Has anyone specific told you to back off the case?" she asked Marks.

For the first time, Marks looked like she was contemplating an evasion. "Look, Frye, I don't think that this homicide is solvable. You know as well as I do that finding a contract killer is almost impossible. Someone hires an out-of-towner who is only here for an afternoon, and there's absolutely no way to trace him. He flies in; he rents a car along with a thousand other businessmen at the airport; he drives to a location that someone else has already set up; he identifies Hogan—probably from a faxed photo—and, unfortunately, Cruz is with him. He needs to take Hogan out and anybody with him that could identify him. Bang, bang, two dead cops. He turns around, he drives back to the airport, and he goes back to wherever he lives. End of story."

"You know, Marks, when you're talking to another cop, it's pretty obvious when there's something you don't want to say. I can tell when you're trying to blow me off." Rebecca waited.

"Fuck." Marks strafed her short thick dark hair in frustration. "All I know is one morning a few days after you got taken down during that Blake thing, the chief of detectives was in a closed-door meeting with your captain and my captain. An hour later, Horton and I got the word to back off the case. They gave us some bullshit about IAD following up on it." She snorted derisively. "Like that was supposed to make us happy."

It was Rebecca's turn to look startled. "Captain Henry was in on this?"

"Yeah, he was there," Marks admitted, nodding uncomfortably. "Look, I didn't hear the conversation, Frye. Give me a break. But I got the distinct feeling that if I ever wanted to make detective-three, I'd better toe the line. The case wasn't going anywhere, so that's what I did. Sorry, Frye, but he wasn't my partner. Maybe if he had been..."

Rebecca stood and extended her hand. "Thanks, Marks. I know you didn't have to give me anything. And as far as I'm concerned, if anybody asks, you didn't."

❖

Her first impulse had been to storm into Captain John Henry's office and demand to know what the fuck was going on. Fortunately, it was one floor up and an entire city block away, and by the time she was halfway there, she realized that if she was going to confront anyone about the situation, she needed to have a little bit more than just a hunch under her belt. What she needed to do was dig a little bit more into Jimmy Hogan's background, and for that she was going to need to talk to some people at the Academy as well as the narcotics detectives he'd worked with. There were things she could get from a computer search, too, but she didn't want to do that in the middle of the squad room in the middle of the afternoon.

She believed Marks' story that someone high up in the chain of command had shut down the homicide investigation, and that could mean any number of things. It could mean there were things that the bureaucrats who really ran the police department did not want made public, like the fact that Jimmy Hogan was dirty. That was certainly one explanation. It could also mean that the people in charge who were *supposed* to know what was happening didn't have a clue as to what was really happening, and the best way to protect your own ass was to limit the flow of information.

Taking that line, she could almost believe that IAD had taken over the investigation, which as far as she was concerned was equivalent to flushing it down the toilet. IAD had never solved anything that she was aware of, but they did answer directly to the chief and the commissioner, so they would be the logical choices to take over the investigation if the brass wanted the findings kept quiet. That would fit with what Flanagan said about IAD raiding her files.

And then there was the possibility that Jimmy Hogan was exactly what he appeared to be—an undercover narcotics detective who had done his job so well that someone in the Zamora organization had seen him as competition and simply had him eliminated. Jeff was there by mistake and just got caught in the crossfire. She probably would have believed that, if so many roadblocks hadn't been thrown up around the case.

By the time she pulled up in front of Sloan's building, her headache was raging and her temper was ready to snap. Maybe concentrating on this investigation was the best thing she could do for the moment. As she stepped from her car, she thought fleetingly of the few moments she had spent with Catherine earlier that afternoon. It occurred to her that the best thing she could really do would be to meet Catherine after work, take her somewhere for dinner, forget about prostitution and pornography and dead partners, and simply enjoy the company of a beautiful, intelligent woman who loved her.

Why was it, she wondered, that she wasn't going to do just that?

❖

Mitchell jumped to her feet when Rebecca unexpectedly walked into the room. A muscle twitched at the corner of Rebecca's mouth, but she managed not to smile.

"Status report, Mitchell?" She could see that Mitchell had been working at a computer terminal next to those occupied by Sloan and McBride. It looked as if she was updating some kind of data sheet. Clearly, the young officer was a good choice for the post, even though Rebecca doubted that that had been the intention of the duty sergeant when he had assigned her to the task force. Women didn't get accepted to West Point unless they were tough, sharp, and dedicated. Mitchell must have once been among the brightest of the bright, and now some idiot at the one-eight was trying to bury her. Nothing of Rebecca's disgust at that thought showed in her face. "Bring me up to speed."

"I've been logging in potential on-line suspects as Mr. McBride has initiated contact, ma'am. It's too early to tell you the specifics such as location or level of activity, but I should be able to begin cross-referencing within a day or two and generate possible lines of follow-up from that."

Rebecca glanced at Sloan, her eyebrow elevating slightly in question. That hadn't been part of Mitchell's job description. The kid had initiative as well as brains, apparently.

Sloan nodded, as if reading her thoughts. "Officer Mitchell has been making herself very useful. She's freed me up to focus on large-scale Web-hosting sites that seem to have concentrated activities in this area. Anyone receiving live video feeds will need high-speed access, and they're going to be paying hefty user fees. I'm trying to get in the back door by starting with the customer databases and looking for common-user time frames."

"How about grabbing a cup of coffee, Sloan?" Rebecca chose not to comment on Sloan's information until they were alone. You didn't discuss strategy in front of the ranks.

"Sure," Sloan replied. The two of them walked in silence to the conference room where they had first been briefed by Clark, helped themselves to coffee, and settled across from one another at the conference table.

"How close are you to narrowing this search down to real people and not just Internet aliases?" Rebecca asked.

"Closer than anyone would have expected a week ago. We caught a break—the FBI has been running a national sting operation over the last eighteen months called Operation Avalanche. They've already identified and collated a tremendous number of potential Internet sites that are marketing porn, and they've prescreened hundreds of e-mail accounts, specifically of users frequenting porn chat rooms aimed at those with a taste for kids. A lot of those accounts have already been traced and filed geographically."

"Did Clark get you that information from the FBI?"

"Nope," Sloan answered immediately.

"Are you going to tell him you have it?"

"Nope."

Rebecca sipped her coffee, considering Sloan's openness in answering questions, her seeming lack of concern about the repercussions of her hacking into federal law enforcement databases, and her obvious skill. The woman had all the earmarks of a rogue agent, but Rebecca didn't think she was. Rogue agents were always wary, suspicious, and afraid of being caught. Sloan was just untouchable. And you only got that way if you'd already had everything done to hurt you that *could* be done.

"What about Mitchell? She's just a rookie, and I don't want her getting in the middle of anything."

"Mitchell may be young, but she's savvy. I'll give her the info when we have some local leads to chase electronically. Everything she touches will be clean and accountable." Sloan eased back in her chair, astutely watching the blond detective. "If you want, I can just give you the bottom line and leave out how we got there, too. You'll be able to deny all knowledge then."

"I don't need your protection," Rebecca replied, her tone oddly mild. "But I appreciate the thought. I prefer to have as much information as possible during an investigation. What I'm curious about is why you are so willing to share."

"I'm willing to share with *you*, because when the time comes, I figure you're going to be the one standing in front of the door, not Avery Clark. Maybe I'm wrong to trust you, but then, I don't work for Agent Clark."

"No, you don't. Not anymore."

Sloan's eyes narrowed and her fingers tensed on the coffee cup. "I never worked for Clark."

"But you did work for the Justice Department, didn't you?" Rebecca knew she'd struck gold when the dark-haired woman across from her grew tight and still. A second later, she could see Sloan consciously relax each tense muscle in her formidably powerful shoulders. Incredible control. "Does Clark have something on you and McBride?"

"Not a thing," Sloan said amiably. "Believe it or not, I took this job because I thought it was a job worth doing. And for the record, Sergeant, I don't take *any* job unless I want to. Not even for the Department of Justice."

"Fair enough," Rebecca said with a nod. "It's been my experience that people who are blackmailed into an assignment aren't very trustworthy. And I like to know if I can trust the people I'm working with."

"I could *tell* you I'm trustworthy," Sloan said, unveiling her megawatt, devil-may-care grin, "but I don't think that would impress you."

"I don't impress very easily, Sloan." Despite herself, Rebecca grinned back. "But if you can come up with someone for me to investigate, I'll be appropriately impressed, I promise. What about McBride? Do you vouch for him, too?"

"Jason is his own man, and if you have any doubts, talk to him yourself."

"But he's your associate."

"And my friend."

Rebecca could easily imagine J. T. Sloan standing up to the Justice Department, and she had a feeling that the woman probably had. This computer expert had obviously been valuable to them once, or they wouldn't have come back to her when they needed her services. Rebecca had a feeling that they had come back with apologies in one hand while waving the flag in the other. "I'm working on a few things from my end, but at this point I don't have dick."

Sloan looked surprised at the honest admission, then said good-naturedly, "I'll never tell."

"Thanks," Rebecca said dryly, but she finally smiled. On impulse, she added, "Question. If someone pilfered files—stole them—from someone's system, could you figure out who did it?"

"Probably." Sloan's deep violet eyes sparkled with interest. "Unless they were awfully good at concealing themselves, and most hackers aren't that good."

"Compared to you, you mean."

"Yes, that's exactly what I mean."

"What would you need to do to find them?"

"I'd need the hard drive and access to the network. After that, I'd like to bring the CPU here, but I could work on the system in place if I had to." Sloan watched the detective's face. Nothing showed. "I guess we'd be doing this at night in the dark, huh?"

"No comment." Rebecca stood and rolled her shoulders. "It would be unofficial, and it would be for free. If you did it, I'd owe you."

"No, you wouldn't. I do it because it's fun."

"Deal." It never hurt to have options, and she had a feeling that the cocky computer jock could deliver on her promises. "If I can't find what I'm looking for any other way, I'll let you know."

Sloan stood with her, and as they walked back toward the work area, she said softly, "Usually people who hack computers aren't very dangerous, but you never know, Frye. You should be careful."

"I'm a cop. I don't scare easily."

"I used to be a cop, too. I didn't carry a gun, and maybe I should have."

Rebecca watched Sloan walk away, surprised to discover how much she liked her.

Chapter Twelve

Sandy opened the door and immediately considered slamming it. "I'm working. Go away."

"No, you're not. I've been watching your building for two hours, and I know you don't have anyone up here unless they've paid for the whole night."

"If you keep hanging around me, I'm going to starve to death."

"No, you won't." Rebecca lifted the brown paper bag in her hand. "I brought dinner."

Sandy rested her forehead on the edge of the door and cursed colorfully. "Whatever it is you *think* you do for me, Frye, it is *so* not enough to make up for all the trouble you could cause me."

"I know," Rebecca replied seriously. "Can I come in?"

"What did you bring?"

"Thai."

"Yeah, I suppose."

Rebecca had never been in Sandy's apartment before, although she had known for months where the young woman lived. She knew almost everything about the people in her territory who were important to her—friends, suspects, and enemies alike. She wouldn't have come to Sandy's if she'd had any other choice, but after checking all the normal places and failing to find her, she had finally staked out the apartment. When the light had come on in the front windows, she'd waited until she was certain that Sandy wasn't with a john, and then she'd come up. She took in the small efficiency in one practiced glance. It was neat, tidy, and tastefully, although economically, decorated.

"Nice place," she said, meaning it.

"Thanks," Sandy replied, eying the tall cop suspiciously. "Hey, Frye, has anyone told you lately that you look like crap?"

Rebecca didn't reply, just settled herself on the sofa without being invited and put the bag of takeout on the low, plain pine coffee table in front of her. "Go ahead and eat while we talk."

"You want something?" Sandy asked as she walked into the small, adjoining galley kitchen. "A beer?"

"Water would be fine." Her throat was scratchy and dry, and, even though it wasn't warm in the apartment, she was sweating. Briefly, she considered taking off her jacket, then thought better of it. She didn't make a habit of flashing her weapon if she could help it.

"You don't drink?" Sandy asked as she placed a pile of paper plates, silverware, a bottle of beer, and a glass of water on the table.

Rebecca hesitated, surprised by the question and even more surprised that she was considering answering. "No."

"Huh. Strange cop," Sandy mumbled, opening bags and checking out the contents of the cardboard cartons. She dished out a generous amount for herself, then gestured to Rebecca with one of the containers. "Want some?"

"No, I'm fine."

"Uh-huh. Sure," Sandy replied, not bothering to repeat that the cop looked even paler and more drawn then she had the night before. "Rita called me and said you sprung her last night. Thanks."

"You should tell her to be more careful who she pitches her lines to."

"Hey!" Sandy exclaimed indignantly. "She swore she never mentioned money to that cop. The guy was cute, and he told Rita he'd make it worth her while if she got him off. Doesn't that sound like entrapment to you?"

"It's just her word, Sandy," Rebecca pointed out quietly. The undercover Vice cop had reported that the prostitute had solicited him, but Rebecca was inclined to believe Sandy. Nevertheless, a prostitute's word against that of a cop would never hold up in court. She shook her head, not quite certain how she had allowed the topic to stray from what had brought her here. Probably the damn headache that was back again in force. "So, what have you got for me?"

"Not a thing."

"I don't have anywhere to be tonight."

"Meaning?"

"Meaning I'm not leaving until you deliver."

"God, you think because you buy me dinner a couple nights in a row that you own me?"

Rebecca smiled. "Trust me, Sandy. Owning you is the furthest thing from my mind."

Sandy took a pull on her Corona and shifted on the couch until her knees brushed Rebecca's and their eyes met. "I've heard that a couple of the girls have been making extra cash doing films."

"Films?" Rebecca asked with interest.

"Skin flicks."

"Tell me everything you know—names, dates, places. What details do you have?"

"Nothing yet," Sandy said defensively. "Only talk. But I think I can probably find out more if you give me a little room here."

"Good," Rebecca said, reaching for the water as she coughed dryly.

"Who knows, maybe I'll get into a new line of work. Do you think I would make it as a porno queen?" She frowned. "Probably my tits are too small...but then I'd fit right in if they're looking for *girls*."

"Don't even think about it," Rebecca said sharply, ignoring the pain that had started in her chest on the heels of the cough. "All I want is for you to get some information. Do *not* agree to anything else."

"Well, I could probably get a lot more information if I hired on to do one of the movies," Sandy said musingly. "The talk is they're paying mucho bucks."

"Just call me if you hear anything," Rebecca ordered as she stood, suddenly feeling like she needed some fresh air. "Don't go playing games."

"You know, you're a real pain in...Frye?...Hey!"

Rebecca was aware of Sandy's voice, but she couldn't make out the words over the roaring in her head. She could just barely hear someone saying *fuck*...it might have been her...she *thought* she was speaking. She couldn't tell for sure, and it didn't really matter. Mostly all she wanted to do was get one clean, deep breath, and she'd be fine. *Man, it hurts to breathe.*

It kept on hurting as the room swam, her legs gave out, and she went down.

❖

Catherine knocked sharply on the door to apartment 3B. Although the residential area immediately surrounding the university where she lived in a historically renovated Victorian was socioeconomic light-years away from the apartments bordering the Tenderloin, they were separated in distance only by twenty city blocks and the river that bisected the city. It had taken her less than six minutes to arrive after she had gotten the phone call. The door opened, and a young Annie Lennox look-alike in a tight, midriff-baring T-shirt and hip-hugger jeans, slung so low they barely covered the essentials, greeted her with a distinct disregard for social amenities.

"Are you Catherine? Fuck, you better be."

Catherine merely nodded and stepped hurriedly inside. "Where is she?"

"Over there. Goddamned stubborn cop moron."

Sandy jerked her head in the direction of the couch, but she needn't have bothered. Catherine could hear the labored breathing from across the small apartment. Two steps further into the room and she saw Rebecca lying on the sofa, her shoulders propped against the arm with a pillow behind her head. The top three buttons on her shirt were open, and her chest heaved spasmodically as she struggled to get air. Sweat poured from her face, and her skin had a faint bluish tint. Catherine's heart seized with fear. *God, what is this? Hemorrhage? Embolus? It looks like an MI...no...that can't be!*

"Call 911." Catherine's voice showed none of her terror, but for one second, she though she might scream.

"No," Rebecca gasped, opening her eyes at the sound of Catherine's voice. When she turned to Catherine, her eyes were swimming with pain and something else, something Catherine didn't think she had ever seen in them before—fear.

"See what I mean?" Sandy muttered, following Catherine as she hurried toward Rebecca. "You think I didn't want to? She threatened to shoot the phone if I did. I'm lucky she gave me your number. Fucking rockhead."

"Rebecca, what happened?" Catherine knelt by the sofa, noting the remains of a takeout meal and Rebecca's jacket thrown over a nearby chair. Anger was an excellent antidote to fear, but she had time for neither, so she pushed the quick surge of jealousy and confused disappointment aside.

"Don't…know. Pain…can't breathe."

"Sudden onset?" After pulling open a worn satchel that she hadn't used in more than a decade, Catherine extracted a stethoscope, which she swung around her neck with one hand while reaching for a blood pressure cuff with the other.

Rebecca gave a weak nod and closed her eyes.

"I need to get you to a hospital," she said steadily as she wrapped the cuff around Rebecca's arm.

"I…know." Rebecca made an effort to sit up, but any exertion made her light-headed. "I'll go. Just not…in an…ambulance."

Catherine tried not to think about what might be going on inside Rebecca's body as she forced herself to concentrate on the physical facts. It looked like a myocardial infarct at first glance, but Rebecca was way too young for a heart attack. Although her blood pressure was low, it wasn't critical yet. Slipping her hand under Rebecca's shirt, she moved the stethoscope back and forth over her lover's chest. Frowning, she listened for a few seconds to the right and then the left, then she glanced quickly at the distended veins in Rebecca's neck.

"Your left lung is collapsed. We need to get you out of here." Looking over her shoulder, she said again, forcefully, *"Call 911."*

"Uh, it will probably take them a few minutes to get here. This area doesn't get the fastest service. Maybe it would be quicker if you drove her?" Sandy stood close behind Catherine's shoulder, watching Rebecca's face. "She didn't look this bad when I called you."

Listening to Rebecca fight for air, Catherine had to agree with the young woman. "Can you stand?" she asked, pulling the blood pressure monitor from the detective's arm and stuffing it into her bag. "We'll help you."

"Okay…yes."

Sandy and Catherine steadied Rebecca from either side with an arm around her waist and half-carried her down the three flights of stairs to Catherine's car, which she had left in front of a hydrant a few doors down from the once elegant brownstone. By the time they got the detective into the front seat and Catherine had fumbled the seat belt around her, Rebecca was barely conscious and her respiratory distress had worsened. The ominous sound of an airway about to collapse completely filled the car.

"Rebecca," Catherine said sharply, grasping her chin, turning her lover's face toward her. "Rebecca, don't struggle. Breathe as slowly as you can. Do you understand?"

She couldn't get enough air any longer to speak, but she nodded.

Sandy bent down and whispered something to Rebecca that Catherine couldn't hear as she ran around the front of the car to the driver's side. She had the key in the ignition before she was completely settled behind the wheel, and she careened away from the curb without even a backward glance at the young woman who stood on the sidewalk watching the taillights disappear into the dark.

Thankfully, at that time of night there was almost no traffic in University City. Within a matter of minutes, she was screeching to a halt outside the emergency room at University Hospital. She ran through the double doors into the harshly lit admitting area and shouted, "I'm Dr. Catherine Rawlings. I have a critically ill patient in my car! Someone bring a gurney."

❖

Catherine glanced at the clock in the small doctors' lounge adjacent to the emergency room. Midnight. She was alone in the drab, disorganized room. A pot of hours-old coffee steeped on a water-spotted, double-burner coffee maker next to the sink, and the institutional-issue table in the center of the room held the vestiges of a half-eaten pizza. It was a desolate place to be at any time of the day. The waiting created a painful sense of déjà vu, and as the minutes dragged on, it was harder and harder for her not to think about the night that Raymond Blake had taken her hostage and had nearly taken Rebecca's life.

Forcing her thoughts from that horror, she reminded herself that Rebecca was not dying, not tonight. But being separated from her, not knowing precisely what was happening, frayed the last remnants of her nerves, and she was losing the battle to stay calm. She had too many recollections, some of them too terrifying to erase even from her dreams. Now, she had another unwelcome memory—the image of

Rebecca suffering, struggling in agony for each insufficient breath. It was tearing her apart.

"Catherine?"

She spun around, grateful for the sound of another human voice to distract her from her pain. "Jim! How is she?"

"She's stable…"

"Where is she? Can I see her? What—"

The emergency room physician smiled, raising a hand to stem the flow of words. "In a minute. She's on her way back from CAT scan."

"How serious is it?" Catherine managed in a more controlled fashion. The panic that had simmered just beneath the surface of her soul was beginning to abate.

"Well," the treating physician replied, motioning to a chair beside him as he sank heavily into a seat at the small table, "if you're interested in a new job, I'm fairly certain we could find you one down here. Your exam on the scene saved us a lot of time and her a lot of pain. She had a pneumothorax, just as you suspected. Probably an area of scar tissue had adhered to the inner surface of one of her ribs, and it tore lose tonight, collapsing her lung."

"Will it require surgery?" These things happened, she knew that as well as anyone; it was no one's fault. Then why did she feel like screaming?

"A little too soon to tell." He gave her a satisfied smile. "I put a needle in, aspirated the air, and the lung came back up. The CAT scan looks good right now. We'll have to see if the lung stays up or not."

"Thank you, Jim."

"Don't mention it. She should be back by now. Cubicle seven."

Catherine murmured her thanks once again and hurried away. To her great relief, when she opened the door to the small private treatment room, she found Rebecca sitting up on a stretcher, looking drawn but breathing easily. The relief was so intense, for a second she feared she might cry.

"Hey, there. How do you feel?" She managed to keep her voice from quivering, but something of her fragile emotional state must have shown in her face, because Rebecca's welcoming smile immediately turned to a look of concern.

"I'm okay." Reaching out a hand, the one that was not tethered to an intravenous line, Rebecca caught Catherine's and drew her closer. "If I understood what the doc told me, it was a fluke—a little bit of scar tissue acting up. Not a big deal."

Catherine was emotionally and physically exhausted—tired and still reeling from worry and her own terrifying memories. If she hadn't been so shaken, she probably would have been more circumspect, but she just didn't have enough strength to control her response. It was raw emotion, uncensored.

"Rebecca, you could have *died*. If you weren't as physically fit as you are, you probably would have. It could happen again; in fact, it often does. This was a warning, and you were lucky that your young friend was quick-witted enough to realize how ill you were."

"She's not a friend. She's a source."

"What she may be to you, I don't know," Catherine said more sharply than she intended. "But *she's* fond of you, I'll tell you that."

"What?" Rebecca had never seen Catherine quite like this before. When she had first walked into the room, it'd looked as if she was going to break down. That was so unlike her that it was alarming. During all the long weeks of Rebecca's convalescence, Catherine had been nothing but upbeat and positive. If she had cried, she had done it alone. Now, she was all over the place. First, on the verge of tears, then in the next second, angry—the shifts so sudden that Rebecca was stunned. Carefully, she replied, "What are you talking about? Sandy is an informant. I was working and—"

"You're not required to explain," Catherine interrupted, irritated with herself for even bringing up the subject of the girl. She had no idea why she had. Except there had been something uncomfortably intimate about the entire setting—the small cozy apartment, the takeout dinner, and the way the young woman had berated Rebecca with unmistakable tenderness in her voice. *You have another life that I know nothing about. A life that might mean more to you than anything we could share.*

"I'm sorry that you had to go through this," Rebecca said urgently, lifting Catherine's hand and placing a kiss against the fingers she cradled in her own. "I'm sorry I had to drag you into it at all, but I didn't want an official report—*any* kind of record—tying Sandy to me."

"Why not?"

She hesitated only a second. "Because officially Sandy and I don't *have* a relationship. It's safer for her that way."

"I'm surprised you didn't call Watts instead of me," Catherine said, and there was pain in that knowledge. "*Would* you have called me if I hadn't been a doctor?"

She hesitated longer this time. "I don't know."

"Would you even have *told* me?"

The silence between them grew so loud that Catherine slipped her fingers out of Rebecca's hand and moved a little away from the stretcher. "Rebecca?"

"I don't know. I would have told you...something. Maybe not all of it."

"I see. Why not?" Her anger was gone, replaced by an honest desire to know, and by incredible sadness. *How can we feel so much, and share so little?*

"Because I don't want you to worry. I don't want you to hate what I do," Rebecca admitted. The foot of space between them felt like a hundred miles, and it hurt so much more now than she had hurt an hour ago. She was doing this all wrong, but she couldn't think of the right way to do it. Desperately, she whispered, "Because I don't know what else to do."

"I'm sorry," Catherine said softly, withdrawing her fingers from Rebecca's grasp. "We can't do this now. You need to rest."

"Catherine—"

"Jim says your CAT scan looked good. It might be a while before they move you upstairs to a bed. You should try to sleep. I'll come by tomorrow to see how you're doing."

"Okay." Rebecca swallowed the plea for her to stay, a sinking feeling in her stomach. It was all coming apart.

Catherine turned to leave, then looked back over her shoulder. "Is there anyone you want me to call? Watts?"

"No. I'll call him."

"Sandy?"

"No. Catherine—"

"Get some sleep," she said softly as she closed the door behind her.

Chapter Thirteen

"What do you mean you don't have any record of her?" Catherine snapped into her cell phone's wireless mic while she attempted to maneuver through early rush-hour traffic. "She should have been admitted last night. I don't know—sometime after midnight. Are you spelling the last name correctly? That's Frye—with an 'e' on the end."

She listened for a few seconds, eyes searching the street for a parking place on the block with the address she had been given. Pulling to the curb, she said with uncharacteristic irritation, "Never mind. I don't have time to wait. I'll call back later."

She clicked off the cell phone, cut the ignition, and sat for a few seconds behind the wheel, waiting for the last shards of frustration to ebb. *I should have stayed at the hospital last night. It was ridiculous to think I could do this briefing now, not knowing how she is. If I were a patient, I'd say this is a very good example of self-delusion resulting from lousy conflict management and unresolved anger.*

"Well, thank you, Doctor. That's very helpful," she said out loud in disgust. Glancing at her watch, she saw that she had five minutes to find the building. "And now you can just do what you came here to do."

She locked the car and started north on Front Street, checking the building numbers as she walked. Fortunately, she had guessed right and had started searching in the appropriate direction. In less than a minute, she was standing on the steps of an unremarkable-looking warehouse, fumbling in her briefcase for her wallet and a photo ID. After the disembodied voice instructed her to enter and an electronic lock clicked open, she stepped through into the cavernous ground floor and proceeded toward the elevator as she had been directed.

As curious as she was about the place, her mind was only half on her surroundings. She had spent yet another restless night, finding it difficult to fall asleep after the adrenaline surge of emotions that had started when she had first gotten the call from Sandy and hadn't begun to abate until she had been satisfied that Rebecca was out of danger. It had been excruciatingly hard to leave her, but the evening had brought up too many conflicting feelings—fear, anger, and unexpectedly, jealousy. The conversation had been deteriorating, and she doubted either of them was equipped to deal with the aftermath of an argument in the middle of the night. Nevertheless, when she had finally slid naked beneath the sheets, she had ached for her lover, body and soul.

The elevator stopped smoothly and opened with no more than a whisper, whereupon she found herself looking out into an enormous room filled with electronic equipment. It was time to set her personal life aside and do her job. As she stepped out into the hall that ran along one side of the building opposite the warren of computer stations, she glanced right and left looking for someone who might know the whereabouts of the meeting. Almost immediately, she saw a woman approaching in jeans and an open-collared navy shirt. At first glance, the startlingly attractive dark-haired stranger didn't strike Catherine as being a law-enforcement officer of any type. Even discounting her decidedly informal appearance, she moved with a kind of casual confidence that suggested she rarely worried about protocol. There was none of the tight focus that Rebecca displayed when she was working or the self-important attitude of the typical bureaucrat. If she were asked to guess, Catherine would say this was the private consultant.

"Good morning," Catherine said as the woman drew near. "I'm Dr. Catherine Rawlings."

"J. T. Sloan, Doctor." Sloan extended her hand to the elegant, auburn-haired woman in the stylish beige suit. "We were just gathering in the conference room. I'll take you there."

"Thank you."

As they walked, Sloan explained, "Unfortunately, the full team isn't here at the moment. I know your schedule is very tight, so we'll go with what we have for now. I'll fill in the others later."

Much later, Catherine thought to herself, but she merely nodded.

She wondered, not for the first time that morning, if Rebecca would be pulled from the case. At this point, it should be evident to everyone at police headquarters that the detective wasn't ready to go back to work. In some ways, it was fortunate that the episode had occurred when it did. If it had happened when Rebecca was in the middle of an altercation, or even if she had just been out on the street alone, the outcome could have been fatal. At any rate, she was out of danger for the moment, and Catherine gratefully cleared her mind to focus on the job at hand.

As she followed Sloan into a glass-enclosed conference room, several people stood and turned in her direction. One of them she already knew, but she kept any sign of recognition from her face.

"Dr. Rawlings," Sloan gestured as she spoke, "this is my associate, Jason McBride...Agent Clark, there at the end of the table...and Officer Mitchell, who is with the Philadelphia Police Department."

Catherine shook each individual's hand in turn, saying merely, "Officer Mitchell," in a neutral tone when she got to the young woman.

It wasn't uncommon for her to run into patients in social or professional settings. And though she tried to anticipate when that might happen and discuss with the patient their feelings about the situation beforehand, it wasn't always possible to do that. She had known Mitchell was involved in a task force that might have been this one, but she hadn't really expected her to be at the briefing. As was usual when something unforeseen like this happened, they would have to deal with it later.

"Thank you for coming on such short notice, Doctor," Clark said with an appreciative smile. Looking pointedly at Sloan, he added, "Our investigation is moving a little faster than we had anticipated. Since I know that time is short, and I expect that what Ms. Sloan and Mr. McBride have to discuss will be of most use to you, let me say a few brief words and then turn it over to them."

Catherine listened while he gave her a capsule summary of the task force's purpose and some background on the results of similar operations across the nation, but she was watching the people at the table as he spoke, trying to get a sense of how the individuals fit into the team. Clark, the federal representative, alone at one end of the table, was clearly the titular head, but she had the feeling that Sloan, an arm draped over the back of her chair in an utterly relaxed pose, was the real leader. The woman projected an incredible sense of self-assurance, and as she toyed with a pencil, her eyes fixed on a spot in the center of the table, she reminded Catherine of a great, sleek predator fixing on its prey. Her associate, the remarkably handsome man by her side, was completely expressionless, but his eyes glinted with intelligence. Mitchell sat stiffly to her right, and Catherine wasn't certain if the rigid pose was due to *her* presence or just the young officer's natural intensity.

Were Rebecca present, Catherine knew, she'd be sitting across from Sloan, the two of them perfectly matched in skill and drive. Rebecca, relentlessly single-minded when in pursuit of a suspect, was every bit the hunter Sloan appeared to be. The thought of Rebecca brought a swift surge of longing, and Catherine brought her complete attention back to Clark before her mind could wander further down distracting avenues.

He was saying, "We have general information pertaining to perpetrator profiles that have been generated by other investigations. What we need, Doctor—actually, what our computers experts need— is a way to flag the contacts with the most potential to lead us into a real-life meeting. Any specific guidance you can provide would be welcome."

"Before we talk about profiling," Catherine said, turning her attention to Sloan and her colleague, "it would help if you explained how you've approached the problem. What I have to say may very well be redundant."

"It wouldn't be for me, ma'am," Mitchell said from beside Catherine, meeting her gaze unwaveringly when Catherine glanced her way.

"I agree, Doctor," Sloan added, wanting to hear what the psychiatrist had to say. She'd had enough experience with Bureau profilers to know that they were often too rigid with their composites to be of any real use in dealing with individual cases. In all fairness, that probably resulted from the necessity of using probability models. Still, a practicing clinician like Rawlings, with real-life experience, might have a different take. From the brief rundown Clark had given her, this woman was supposed to be an excellent forensic consultant, even though it wasn't her primary specialty.

"Let me tell you where we stand," Sloan elaborated. "Thus far Jason has focused on establishing an Internet presence by adopting various personae that might be attractive to someone who is interested in preteens or adolescents. I've been working to localize areas of concentrated activity by targeting intersecting or overlapping patterns of transmission, site traffic, and financial expenditures. The theory being that eventually, between the two of us, we'll have a list that can be cross-referenced using additional identifiers to produce a manageable number of individuals for actual investigation. Jason and I are close to narrowing down the search, and while we started with a broad net, we've found ourselves with more potential avenues of pursuit than we could possibly explore. Very shortly, we're going to be in one-on-one situations, and there's a real likelihood of scaring these guys away if we go about it incorrectly."

Smiling, Catherine replied, "All right then. I'll hit the highlights and then you tell me what else you need from me."

"Excellent," Sloan replied, liking the psychiatrist's composed, noncompetitive attitude. There was no evidence of the turf struggles she'd previously experienced within the agency when different departments collaborated. And there was sincerity in the woman's calm, ocean green eyes that instilled trust. Sloan caught herself short and almost grinned at her uncharacteristic reaction. She bet Catherine Rawlings was one hell of a psychiatrist. "Fire away, Doctor."

"What we're talking about here is typology," Catherine began, "profiling, if you will. Despite popular conceptions, I'm sure all of you realize that this is not hard science. We can make general assumptions, but there are always exceptions, and it pays to be flexible when assessing prospective perpetrators."

Mitchell, Catherine noticed, was taking notes. "Pedophiles are almost always men and may be heterosexual or homosexual. It's difficult to determine the percentages, because so many instances are never reported. I assume this will have some bearing on how you focus your Internet search, and since I don't know your starting point, my best advice would be to know the victims and begin there."

"As far as we can ascertain," Sloan said carefully, "the video productions we're interested in tracking primarily depict adult men with adolescent girls. Jason is trying to make contacts both as a young girl and as an adult male."

"Sounds reasonable," Catherine responded. "The Internet provides a sense of anonymity, thus making many individuals more comfortable in revealing socially unacceptable preferences that they might otherwise keep hidden for fear of exposure and reprisal. On the other hand, that may make it easier for you to pick up on the truly serious pedophiles because they will have a false sense of security—believing that the Internet provides a blind behind which they can hide."

"I'm sorry?" Mitchell asked abruptly. "Serious pedophiles as opposed to *what*?"

"Sorry. Poor choice of words. What we know is that many individuals, quite a large percentage, in fact, are content with graphic material and have no interest in instituting actual sexual contact. They will most likely never act on their fantasies."

"Collectors," Jason clarified. "The bulletin boards and newsgroups are filled with people who just want to trade image files. They look but don't touch. Then there are the chatters, the ones who probably never take their interest behind the keyboard."

"Precisely," Catherine agreed. "These men rarely show any interest in exchanging files, but *do* spend hours on-line engaging in cybersex and occasionally escalating to phone sex. Both groups are on the bottom rung of the probability ladder in terms of the likelihood of seeking real-life sexual contact. Because the problem is so widespread, both geographically and in terms of numbers, it makes sense to focus on the theoretically more dangerous class of perpetrators. These would be the travelers—men who manipulate on-line relationships with children in an attempt to institute physical contact. They often set up meetings, pay for bus fare or plane tickets or hotel rooms in advance, and then coax kids into joining them."

"How do we sort them out—or get them to expose themselves?" Sloan ignored Jason's pointed groan at her unintended pun.

"If you were to ask me how to target an individual type—a man whom you could actually track down and ultimately arrest," Catherine said by way of summary, "I'd say you need to bond with him, instill trust. And the fastest way to do that is to express the behaviors that you expect *him* to display. Instead of trying to make direct contact, which might seem suspicious, let him see you doing what he does—talk about the same kind of lust object, vocalize a desire for obtaining digital images, or, better yet, boast about a fabricated conquest. He'll come to you eventually, because he's seeking validation through sharing experience with others like himself."

"Perfect," Sloan said, giving Catherine an appreciative glance. *Yeah, she's good all right.* "Jason? Any thoughts?"

He looked pensive. "Makes sense. I can focus more on my interactions in the chat rooms and try to attract some attention."

"Mitchell?" Sloan added. "We can set up computer models to screen the chat transcripts for identifiers."

Mitchell's face lit up. "Absolutely."

Catherine turned to Avery Clark. "It seems to me that your team already has the plan well in hand. I'm not certain how I can help you."

"Agent Clark, I'd be very interested in hearing your thoughts on that, too," a voice said from the doorway.

Everyone in the room turned as Rebecca and Watts walked in.

"Sorry we're late," Rebecca said, carefully avoiding Catherine's eyes. "Traffic." She and Watts took seats at the table while everyone murmured greetings.

"Dr. Rawlings," Clark said, "this is Detective Sergeant—"

"We've met, thank you." Catherine stared at Rebecca, who had taken the seat next to her, her initial disbelief rapidly giving way to something between incredulity and outrage. The detective was wearing the same clothes in which Catherine had last seen her, and it was obvious that she had come directly from the hospital. From the nearly translucent pallor of her skin and the hollow shadows beneath her eyes, it was also apparent that that was precisely where she still should have been—in a hospital bed.

While Clark perfunctorily outlined his reasons for consulting the psychiatrist, Sloan watched the nonverbal communication between the two women curiously, aware that the temperature in the room had suddenly plummeted to below freezing. Frye, after a brief nod to the psychiatrist, stared pointedly ahead and Rawlings, appearing startled for a second, then looked away as well. Still, Sloan could have sworn the air between them vibrated, rather like the tremor in the tracks when a freight train approached. *Something very volatile going on here— professional differences, maybe? Cops rarely take to theoreticians.*

At that thought, Sloan smiled inwardly, reminded of her own theoretician and how very quickly and inextricably she had taken to *her.* Thinking about Michael in the middle of a meeting was a bad idea, because Michael, in body *or* spirit, was the only person she had ever encountered who could distract her. And she couldn't afford to be distracted—not with Clark already hinting that he'd picked up on how quickly she and Jason had developed a working list of suspects. She wanted to end the briefing as quickly as possible, before Clark could push her for the specifics of their investigation or ask just *how* they had managed to assemble a preliminary list of potentials in record time.

Clearing her throat, Sloan said into the obvious silence, "We have transcripts of dozens of on-line chats between Jason and persons who thought he was a thirteen-year-old girl. We also have a number of hits from guys using a private bulletin board who've made overt or veiled allusions to movie distribution. It would be great to nail them— all of them—but what we really want are the manufacturers. Those are the guys who have set up their computers as FTP servers and are broadcasting to a select group of subscribers. With a videocam hook-up, they can produce live feeds of child sex. And they have the kids."

"Locations?" Rebecca asked sharply. She needed a lead to chase, a case to work—something to take her mind off the hollow feeling in her chest that hurt every time she breathed. The pain had built all night in that place left barren by Catherine's absence, until finally she hadn't been able to stand it any longer, and she'd called Watts. Catherine sat next to her now, and it felt as if they were strangers. The loneliness had been so much easier to bear before—before she had known what it was to be touched. "Anything solid?" She hoped she didn't sound as desperate as she felt.

"Nothing specific, not yet," Sloan admitted. "But I'm prioritizing regional credit card activity and high-speed accounts, and Jason has been mostly working the local bulletin boards." She glanced at Catherine. "It would be very helpful if you could go through the transcripts with us and give us your take on the most likely possibles. Perhaps lend some insight as to how Jason can more effectively manipulate these likelies into committing themselves."

"And then?" Catherine asked with genuine interest, even as she listened with relief to the sound of Rebecca breathing beside her. Respirations steady, unlabored. Stable. For now.

Sloan grinned, a happy, hungry grin. "As soon as we narrow the list down to a manageable number, I can launch digger programs which will follow the sender back to his ISP address, among other things.

Then we'll cross-reference to the credit card clearinghouses, track the business sources. Then we'll have names."

"Yeah, and once you get us a name, we can start knocking on doors," Watts said with evident satisfaction. "*Real* police work."

Sloan barely managed not to snarl.

"Anything from your street sources, Sergeant?" Clark ignored Watts, looking only at Rebecca.

"Not yet." She had no intention of sharing anything with Clark at this point, and she certainly didn't want to discuss the details of the case with Catherine in the room. *Jesus, everyone is already acting as if Catherine is an official part of the team.*

"Doctor? Can you set up times with Sloan to review what they have so far?"

"My schedule is pretty full," Catherine stated, "but I should be able to spare an hour or two in the evenings—or even during the day if you absolutely need me."

Avery Clark stood, signaling the end of the meeting. "We'll try to give you as much advance notice as we can, Doctor. *Any* time you can spare would be greatly appreciated. I'll leave the details to you and Sloan to work out."

"Certainly," Catherine replied, standing as well and gathering her things.

"Sloan, may I see you outside?" Clark murmured softly as he passed behind her.

"Sure," Sloan responded, rising and following.

Jason and Mitchell left as well, leaving Catherine staring at Rebecca, who stood inches away while Watts fidgeted in the doorway, looking as if he wasn't certain whether to go or stay.

"What in God's name are you doing here?" Catherine demanded sharply. She needed so to touch her lover—it felt like days since she had—but she was so angry, the last thing she wanted was contact. Her mind was reeling from the barrage of disparate emotions.

"I knew the meeting wouldn't be long. I wanted to make it."

"How did you get discharged so quickly?"

Rebecca held Catherine's gaze. "I was never admitted."

"Jim would never have released you, not in the shape you were in last night. You signed out AMA, didn't you?" Catherine accused.

"Not exactly against medical advice. We made a deal." She said it reasonably, trying to sound confident, but Catherine's fury was so potent it was like a blow. Her hands trembled, and she stuffed them in her pockets.

"Doctors don't make deals."

"All right. I signed out AMA...on paper," Rebecca admitted reluctantly. "But I agreed to go back for a chest x-ray this morning."

"And if your lung drops right now?"

"He left a catheter in my chest. In an emergency, he said I'd be able to aspirate the air out. That I'd have plenty of time to get back to the emergency room."

"What is the *matter* with you?" Catherine slammed both palms down on the tabletop and leaned forward, her eyes blazing. "Don't you know you almost died last night? What could possibly be so important about this meeting to take the risk?"

"It's not the meeting," Rebecca said quietly, but the fear was thundering through her now. She had to stay calm. If she explained it clearly, Catherine would *have* to understand. "If I let them admit me, if I didn't show up here—if I can't *work*—Henry wouldn't just take me off the case. He'll put me on medical disability. I couldn't even have desk duty."

"You shouldn't have any kind of duty! You should be home or in the hospital." Catherine whirled in Watts's direction so quickly that he jumped. "Did you have a hand in this? After all the nights we sat by her bedside, waiting for her to live or die? After that, you could help her do *this*?"

"Uh..." He looked toward Rebecca desperately. *Christ, help me out here.*

Catherine ran a hand over her eyes and then slowly turned from one to the other. In a voice that was deadly calm, she said, "I do not understand what is important to you. All I know is that whatever it is, it's more important to you than your life. And *I* can't live with knowing that."

For a moment, it seemed as if no one even breathed. Then, Catherine quietly lifted her briefcase and walked from the room.

❖

Rebecca stood rigidly; the fingertips of her right hand, pressed against the granite tabletop, were white to the bone. She hadn't realized that her eyes were closed until they snapped open at the sound of Watts's voice. She blinked in the bright sunlight coming through the windows.

"Sarge?"

"I want to talk to Mitchell and you—alone. We need to assess where we are in this case. Five minutes, in our conference room."

"The doc is just steamed, Sarge. She'll get over it."

No, she won't. Christ, what do I do now?

"You just gotta give her ti—"

"Let it go, Watts."

"Yeah, but—"

"God damn it," she shouted, her fist connecting with stone as she pounded her hand onto the table. "Go find Mitchell and shut the—"

She started to cough, and he thought his heart would stop. "Oh, fuck. Are you—"

"I'm fine," she snapped, waving a hand as she caught her breath. "Just do it."

"Right. Okay. Just do me a fucking favor and go sit down until we get there." He didn't wait for an answer but went to find the rookie. They couldn't get back to the hospital soon enough to suit him.

❖

Sloan looked up as Watts charged by and then caught sight of Frye still in the conference room. She walked back in, poured a cup of coffee, and leaned against the counter, observing the detective, who seemed a little unsteady on her feet.

"You all right?"

Rebecca stared at her. "Yeah."

Sloan sipped her coffee. "We're making progress."

"Good." Rebecca sighed, giving in and sitting down. She rubbed her eyes, then blew out a breath. *Just work the case, Frye. That's what you do. That's what you know.* "Because *I'm* not. We ran down a couple of names that turned up from the previous kiddie prostitution bust, but we haven't been able to go anywhere with that. I've got a few feelers out, but so far, *nada*. And there's a rumor of somebody making sex movies, but right now that's weak. If I get lucky, someone will point us toward that."

"It's early, on a case like this," Sloan observed mildly, wondering how out of line it would be to ask Frye what the hell was going on. The cop didn't exactly make it easy to get friendly, but she looked as if she was hurting. And not just physically. There was desolation in her blue eyes that Sloan had never seen before.

"Is Clark on to your FBI hack?" Rebecca asked suddenly.

"You're sharp, Frye," Sloan said with an appreciative laugh. "You were here, what? Five minutes? And you picked up on a certain *tension* between us?"

"I've met the type." Rebecca shrugged and grinned weakly. "When someone says *outside* the way Clark said it, it usually implies they have a burr up their ass."

"He suspects we might have used *unorthodox* methods to acquire some of our information, but he didn't want specifics."

"They never do," Rebecca observed wearily. "Too accountable then."

"Yeah. Mostly he wanted to be certain that I understood I was on my own."

"Why are you doing this, Sloan? You could be making a lot more money doing something with a lot less potential to fuck you over."

Sloan walked to the sink and poured out the last of her coffee, surprised at the question. When she turned around, she said quietly, all hint of her usual cockiness gone, "Maybe I wanted them to see what they lost."

Rebecca rose, more surprised at herself for asking than she was by Sloan's answer. "That's a fairly fucked-up reason."

"Yeah," Sloan admitted, feeling an odd sense of relief. Suddenly the bitter memories didn't seem to matter so much anymore. Maybe the past really was dead. "It is."

"But I understand," Rebecca added as she headed out the door. "Keep me up to speed, Sloan."

"Right," Sloan called after her. She hesitated for a second, then walked to the wall phone and dialed a number. After a minute, she smiled and said, "Hey. Any chance you could meet me for lunch?…No special reason. I just love you."

Chapter Fourteen

Hazel Holcomb reached for the phone, pushing aside a pile of administrative bulletins as she did. "Yes?"

"Dr. Rawlings is on line two," her secretary informed her.

"I'll take it." She pressed the other line. "Catherine? What can I do for you?"

"Can you see me this morning?"

"Just a minute," Hazel replied, instantly alert to the flat tone of her friend's voice. She rummaged under a stack of file folders and found her weekly schedule. "I have forty-five minutes open now. If it's urgent, I could cancel a meeting later this morning."

"No—I'll come right over. I have clinic in an hour, too. That's perfect. Thank you."

Hazel buzzed her secretary and instructed, "Send Dr. Rawlings in when she arrives, and then hold my calls."

Five minutes later, a knock on the door heralded Catherine's arrival.

"I'm sorry to barge in like this," Catherine began as she took one of the upholstered chairs in front of Hazel's desk.

"It's fine," the chief of psychiatry assured her colleague as she moved around to join her in the other chair. "What's happened?"

"Is it that obvious?" Catherine asked ruefully, folding her hands in her lap to hide the trembling. "God, I'm embarrassed."

"Catherine, nothing is obvious unless one knows you. You wouldn't have called if it weren't important, and you wouldn't have that very wounded expression in your eyes if it weren't personal. So... something has happened."

"I think Rebecca and I just—I don't even know what to call it. Broke up?"

"Well," Hazel said gently, a small smile on her face. "We can start with that and worry about definitions later. What prompted this... event?"

"I'm not sure," Catherine admitted. "That's why I'm here."

"Ah, I see. Good point—spoken like a true psychiatrist. Let's hear the details, then we'll plumb for all the deeper, hidden meanings."

Catherine managed a faint laugh. "Do you talk to all your patients like this? It's very irreverent. Freud is cringing somewhere in another dimension."

"You're not a patient. You're a friend," Hazel replied softly, placing her hand briefly on Catherine's arm. "So, tell me."

Catherine closed her eyes for a few seconds, then opened them and sighed. "I got a call from a woman last night whom I'd never met, telling me that Rebecca had collapsed in her apartment and that she needed my help."

Hazel listened, her expression intent, as Catherine described the previous night and morning's events. When her friend fell silent, Hazel remarked, "Trite as it seems, I'm afraid I have to ask—how do you feel right now?"

"Hurt. Terribly angry at her and just...empty." Catherine met Hazel's eyes, tears swimming behind her lashes. "It's tearing me apart that she would risk her life like this, and that she doesn't realize what that does to me."

"Yes, I can see how much it hurts. I'm sorry."

"I thought about calling her captain, telling him what happened. Insisting that he relieve her of duty."

"Why didn't you?"

"Because," Catherine sighed again, "it would be divulging patient confidences—"

"You're not her doctor," Hazel pointed out.

"No, but I have privileged knowledge that I wouldn't otherwise have had."

Hazel made a dismissive gesture. "A technicality at best."

"All right," Catherine conceded. "Because she'd never forgive me."

"She's hurt *you*." Hazel's tone suggested that turnabout was fair play.

"She's hurt me because she's stubborn and careless with herself, but this would be such a betrayal."

"And what she's done—isn't that a betrayal? Of the connection between you? Of your love for one another?"

Catherine regarded her sharply. "It's only a betrayal if you know what you're doing—if it's a conscious act. She didn't intend to hurt me, she's just doing what's she's always done."

"But things are not the same any longer…for either of you," Hazel pointed out reasonably.

"No," Catherine said quietly. "Everything is different." She looked at Hazel in frustration. "What a mess. I keep thinking that I should be better at this."

"Why?" Hazel laughed. "Love is messy. Relationships are horrible, unpredictable things." Suddenly serious, she asked, "What do you intend to do?"

"I don't know. I can't be with her like this; I can't watch her kill herself." Her eyes darkened, and she added softly, "But I don't know if I can stand losing her this way either."

"You know, Catherine, I haven't met this detective of yours, although I'd certainly like to. She sounds fascinating, especially if you don't happen to be in love with her. But I do know that she almost died two months ago. That's a terrifying occurrence. For someone like her, the best defense against that fear is to—"

"Deny it ever happened." Catherine grimaced. "Yes, I know. Like the business executive who has an MI and insists on taking phone calls in the cardiac care unit. I *know*. It just doesn't help." She rubbed her eyes, glanced at her watch. "I have to work and so do you."

"Don't make any decisions today, or even tomorrow. It's already too late to break up. You love her, remember?"

"Yes, I do," Catherine said, wondering if that would be enough.

❖

Catherine contemplated canceling her last patient of the day. It was almost 8:00; she was tired. Beyond tired. Bone weary and just plain sad.

"It's going to be a tough session, and you want to avoid it. Because she's going to walk in here, all spit and polish, and very possibly pissed off. And she reminds you of Rebecca." She rubbed her temples. "And you've started talking out loud to yourself, which can't be good."

Joyce knocked on the door and stuck her head in. "You've got five minutes. Want anything?"

"Yes," Catherine replied. "When she gets here, tell her I need to resched…"

"What?"

"Nothing. A Coke if you're getting one."

"Will do."

A few minutes later, the door opened again to admit Dellon Mitchell.

"Hi," Catherine said as Mitchell settled into the chair. She wasn't in uniform, but she wore her dark chinos and pressed denim shirt as if they were one. Neat, tidy, precise.

"Hi."

Catherine waited a beat, and when nothing else appeared to be forthcoming, she said, "Let's talk about this morning."

"All right," Mitchell replied neutrally, but her eyes were wary.

"Sometimes it can be awkward or uncomfortable when you run into your therapist unexpectedly. Was it a problem—my being there?"

Mitchell regarded her steadily. "What we talk about in here; it's confidential, right?"

"Usually, yes," Catherine answered. Mitchell stiffened, and she quickly clarified. "Officer, you were referred for an official evaluation. I still have to do that. I don't include information that isn't relevant to my opinions, and I very rarely include specific details of what we've discussed."

"But you wouldn't…" She searched for words. "You're going to be working with the people I work with. There are things…private things…I don't want anyone to know."

"They won't learn them from me," Catherine assured her firmly. "First of all, it's my business to keep confidences. Second, I'll be there for professional purposes and on a fairly limited basis. There is absolutely no reason anyone should know that you and I have a therapeutic relationship."

"Thank you."

"Good." Catherine watched Mitchell cross one ankle over her knee and sit back a little into her chair, a pose Catherine was coming to recognize as relaxed. For Mitchell. "Now, let's talk about the incident in the alley."

"I knew her."

Catherine had many years of therapeutic experience, and she was glad of that now. Because she wanted to blurt out, *What?* Slowly, carefully, she asked, "The young woman who was being attacked? You knew her?"

"Yes."

"When did you realize that?"

"He'd been beating her, and when I announced my presence, he let her go. She fell...I saw her face in the light from the window."

There was sweat now on Mitchell's forehead that Catherine was certain she didn't know was there. Her right hand trembled where it rested on the chair arm.

"What happened when you recognized her?"

Mitchell was quiet a long time. Then, voice hoarse, she replied, "I hesitated. I thought maybe I had imagined it. That's when he hit me, knocked me down." She looked at Catherine, stricken. "There was so much blood on her face, I froze...I thought she might be dead...Jesus, there was so much blood."

So much blood. Rebecca. Catherine's stomach lurched. She took a long, slow breath—refocused. "How well do you know her?"

"She's just someone I met...on the job."

"More than a passing acquaintance?" Catherine probed softly. "A friend?"

Another pause. "Yes."

"You told me you don't remember hitting him with your gun."

"I don't." For the first time, the young woman looked scared.

"What do you remember?"

Mitchell ran a hand through her hair. "I remember...I remember her *face*—the blood. I was so fucking angry. The bastard had his hands up her...and then I was on the ground...and I heard her screaming *at him*. Screaming not to hurt *me*..." She stopped, staring at Catherine but not seeing her. "Oh, fuck. I was on the ground, and he kicked me. Kept kicking me. My head...my side...it hurt. And I could hear her screaming at him...he hit her again then, I think. I was afraid he'd kill her."

"Do you remember striking him with your gun?"

"I *don't!*" Mitchell covered her face with both hands, shoulders heaving. "I don't."

"It's okay," Catherine said gently. "It's okay."

She finally looked up, her face streaked with tears. "It isn't really, is it?"

"Oh, yes, it is," Catherine replied firmly, sitting forward, hands clasped on the desk. "You were alone, in a dangerous situation. There was the threat of deadly injury to yourself or a civilian. Suddenly, unexpectedly, the situation is personalized—this is someone you know, care about. And you were both in peril. You had a gun, Officer Mitchell...and you were facing a bigger, stronger opponent who had already hurt you. You protected yourself, instinctively, but you didn't shoot him." Catherine paused, making certain that Mitchell was listening. "You *didn't* shoot him. And you could have. You did well, Officer."

Mitchell grinned weakly, brushing impatiently at the moisture on her cheeks. "Would you mind putting that in your report?"

"I most definitely will," Catherine replied, smiling. "In my opinion, you acted appropriately under the given circumstances."

"There's a problem."

"What?"

"The part about me knowing her? It's not in my report."

"Why not?"

"Because that's nobody's business. It doesn't have any bearing on the events. I reported it exactly as it occurred."

Catherine considered the information. "I can't see that it affects the legalities involved, but," she continued as she saw Mitchell give a sigh of relief, "it is germane to the effect this has had on *you*."

"I'm okay."

"Yes, in all probability you are," Catherine answered wearily, suddenly aware of her own fatigue. "I'll take care of the report to your precinct, Officer."

Mitchell was quiet for a long moment. "Would you mind...uh, holding off for a little while? You said it might take five or six visits, right?"

"Do *you* mind telling me what brought about this sudden change of heart?"

"I don't want to get pulled off the task force."

The task force. And here I thought it was my stellar therapy techniques. "I think the situation reasonably warrants another visit or two. But then I'll have to file the report."

"Fair enough. Thank you." Mitchell stood, a smile to match the one she'd had when Sloan included her in the plans that morning breaking across her face. "Thanks a lot."

As the door shut behind Mitchell, Catherine leaned back in her chair and closed her eyes.

❖

Rebecca rolled over and opened her eyes. She lifted her wrist and squinted at the dim dial of her watch—9:00 p.m. She'd been asleep for eleven hours, ever since dragging home from the hospital too exhausted to see straight. Watts had had to help her up the stairs to her apartment. *Christ. He probably thinks I'm soft now.*

She was wearing loose cotton workout shorts and nothing else, and her body was covered with a thin film of sweat. When she brushed her palm over her chest and down her abdomen, her hand came away wet.

I need a shower. Nine o'clock. Still plenty of time to get some work done tonight.

She got up from the bed, stiff muscles protesting, and made her way slowly into the bathroom. If she was working, she wouldn't have time to think. Wouldn't have time to miss Catherine.

❖

Catherine answered the door and stared wordlessly at the woman on her porch. Finally she said, "Hi."

"Hi." Rebecca lifted the pizza box with two videotapes resting on its top. "Dinner and a movie?"

"We have a lot to talk about, you know." Catherine leaned a shoulder against the partially open door. Behind her the soft strains of jazz played in the dimly lit living room.

"I know. Would you rather I—" She stopped, looked uncertain. "What do you want me to do?"

"Are you working tonight? Is this just a drive-by visit on your way to somewhere else?"

Rebecca winced. "No. I *was* going to work. I intended to, when I got up. But...no."

"I'm too tired for this, Rebecca. I really am," Catherine said with a sigh.

The look in her eyes, the sound of her voice—sadness, disappointment, loss. It was a knife in Rebecca's heart. She lifted a hand toward her lover's face, then stopped herself. "Okay. I'll call you. Can I call you?"

"No," Catherine said with a shake of her head, and Rebecca's world tilted, then began to crumble.

"Please. Catheri—"

"I really can't talk now." She reached out, took Rebecca's hand, pulled her gently forward. "Just come inside for tonight. Just...be here."

❖

"Hey," a quiet, husky voice said from the shadows.

Sandy jumped at the sound, then peered into the dim overhang of a video store closed for the night. "Jesus, Dell. Will you not *do* that? Some night I'm going to shoot you."

Mitchell laughed. "You don't have a gun."

"I'll get one if you keep this up."

"Can we talk?" She stepped onto the sidewalk beside the young blond. A light rain had been falling since midnight, and she wiped the moisture from her eyes.

"Yeah, okay. Let's go to the diner."

"How about Chen's? It's quieter."

Sandy regarded her curiously. "Sure."

Ten minutes later they were seated at a back booth, the only customers in the place. Sandy ordered her usual, and Mitchell opted for steamed dumplings and a beer.

"So," Sandy asked, regarding the dark-haired young woman in the black jeans and T-shirt curiously, "What's up? Gonna bag out on Quiver this weekend?"

"No," Mitchell said hastily, looking surprised. "Hey, I said I wanted to go."

Sandy hadn't really expected the other woman to go through with it. She'd teasingly dared the young cop to join her at a club to hear a band down from New York City, and to her surprise, Dell had agreed. Sandy didn't even know why she'd asked the cop to come with her. They'd just been talking on the corner one night, only passing time, the way they had been now and then since they'd met. Since that night Anna Marie had died.

"You don't have to take me home. I know where I live."

"Sorry, ma'am. The detective in charge requested I see you home."

"Ma'am?" Sandy stopped dead on the sidewalk, impatiently brushing the last tears from her face. "You're kidding, right?"

Mitchell regarded her steadily. "My patrol car is right this way. If you'd follow me, please."

"Look, rookie—give it a rest. The night is young, and I've got a living to earn. So, beat it."

"I really think you should go home. You look...upset."

Sandy snorted. "You mean I look like hell? The johns don't care how you look in the dark." She turned and walked away.

"It's probably best if we don't discuss that," Mitchell remarked, falling into step beside her.

"Discuss what?" Sandy snapped.

"Your line of work."

"Why, you don't approve?"

"It's...unlawful."

"Now, there's a news flash." Sandy stopped once more, turning so quickly her breasts grazed the young cop's arm. "I don't happen to be so crazy about your job either, you know."

"So we won't talk shop," Mitchell said quietly as they began to walk on beneath flickering street lamps, stepping through pools of red and yellow, reflections from blinking neon signs. "You knew her, the dead woman?"

"Yeah, I knew her," Sandy said softly.
"I'm sorry."

Sandy hadn't said anything more, but she'd let the rookie walk her home. And after that, when she'd see the young cop walking her beat, she'd acknowledge her with a tilt of her chin as they passed. And then after a week or two, a word of hello, until, unexpectedly one night, Sandy had been eating alone in Chen's, and Mitchell, off duty and in street clothes, had slipped into the seat across from her. They'd talked easily, and now, it happened a lot. Dell would show up, and they'd have breakfast and talk about anything—everything—except the life.

"So," Sandy asked, dabbing a pancake with plum sauce and rolling the moo shu inside, "you gonna tell me?"

Mitchell hesitated, looking for the right words.

"Dell?" Sandy watched uncertainty play across the rookie's good-looking face. "It's not about what happened, is it? Are you in trouble?"

"No," Mitchell said quickly. "Everything's okay with that."

"Then how come I haven't seen you down here playing super cop since then?"

"I'm off the streets for a bit—just routine." At Sandy's quick expression of concern, she added hastily, "It's okay. Really."

"You're fucking lying, Dell," Sandy said angrily, tossing her chopsticks down and rising. "I don't need that from you. And I didn't ask you to come down the goddamned alley and get in the middle of something that wasn't any of your business."

"I was doing my *job*, Sandy," Mitchell protested, reaching out and grabbing her wrist.

"So was I," Sandy snapped, jerking her arm away.

"No, you weren't," Mitchell growled, angry now, too. She slid from the booth and blocked Sandy's path. "He was *raping* you."

Sandy stared, truly astonished by the fury in the young cop's voice. As if it mattered to Dell what happened to her. "You know what I do."

"Yes, I know," Mitchell said flatly, trying not to think about the sound of a fist striking flesh, Sandy's head meeting stone. "But that wasn't what was happening with him, was it?"

"No." Sandy sat back down. Mitchell followed. After a minute, she said quietly, "We agreed not to talk shop."

"I guess we'll have to reconsider."

Sandy looked away. She hadn't counted on this. She hadn't expected things to get so far, to the point where she cared. "Are you in trouble?"

"A little," Mitchell admitted. "But it will work out."

"Then what did you want to talk to me about?"

"Rebecca Frye."

"Never heard of her."

"Now who's lying?" Mitchell leaned across the small, chipped tabletop. "Maybe this will help you remember her—tall blond detective. The one who had her arms around you the night we first met? The one who was holding you while you cried on her shoulder?"

Sandy studied her companion and saw the hard penetrating look in her eyes. *Cop's eyes. Jesus, just like Frye's. Oh, man, I so do not need this.* Hurt, disappointed, she asked harshly, "What? You want in on this, too? Is that why you've been coming around? Do you need a snitch, Dell?"

"Oh, for fuck's sake," Mitchell cursed. "*No.* God damn it."

"Then what?"

"I wanted to tell you…" God, what *had* she wanted to do? All she knew was that she'd felt a little sick in the meeting that morning when Frye had mentioned how one of her street sources was trying to track down the porno makers. That maybe they'd get a break in the case from her.

"How good is the source?" Watts asked.

"Very good," Rebecca replied. "She's a hooker, knows everyone in the Tenderloin, and she's smart."

"She got any kind of body to go with the brain?" Watts inquired, apparently not noticing Mitchell stiffen beside him.

"What do you care, Watts? I don't think she's looking for a date."

"'Cause whoever's making the kiddie flicks is probably making other skin movies, too. Maybe she could hire out for a walk-on part." He laughed. "Well, she probably wouldn't need to do any walking— kneeling'd be more like it. They gotta be using local talent, and you know it's always runaways or whores. It'd be good if we could get somebody inside. You can't ask an undercover cop to do it, 'cause she'd have to fuck somebody, most likely. But a hooker wouldn't care."

Mitchell sat very still, her fist white around the pen in her hand.

"She suggested it, and I said no," Rebecca replied in a tone that said it wasn't negotiable. "It's dangerous, and she's not trained for it."

"What's it take to lie on her back and spread her legs? She probably does it twenty times a day."

"We're done discussing this, Watts," Rebecca said, and this time there was a hint of danger in her tone. "She's not some junkie skel like you're used to bracing in an alley. I'm not putting her at risk."

And that's when Mitchell'd realized who Frye's informant must be. Because Sandy and the detective had a history.

"I know you're her informant," Mitchell said.

"Don't know what you're talking about."

"Look," Mitchell said, trying to sound calm and reasonable. "Passing on what you hear on the street is one thing. Asking around, that's something else. People notice when you ask questions."

Sandy actually grinned. "Frye will kick your ass if she finds out you're messing with her sources."

"She could try," Mitchell responded sharply. Sandy laughed out loud, and Mitchell grinned weakly. "Okay, yeah, probably."

"Listen, rookie. *You're* the newbie here. I know my way around." Her expression softened for an instant, and she added quietly, "But thanks."

Without thinking, Mitchell reached out and traced the healing wound on Sandy's forehead with her fingers. "Just be careful, okay? One scar's enough."

"I thought it looked kinda sexy," Sandy said, her voice oddly thick.

"It does."

❖

Catherine lay with her head on Rebecca's right shoulder, tracing her fingertips in a circle around the newest wound on Rebecca's chest. Two stitches closed the puncture site where the catheter had been inserted between her third and fourth ribs to reinflate her collapsed lung.

Rebecca reached up and covered Catherine's hand with her own, stilling it. "The chest x-ray was normal this morning."

"I know. I called the ER and asked about it."

"I said I'd go back tomorrow for a repeat, just to be sure," Rebecca continued. They were in bed, naked under a light cover, their bodies touching but distance between them still. It made her insides ache to have Catherine in her arms yet feel her slipping away.

"Good."

"Catherine, I'm sor—"

"Shh," Catherine said softly, her fingers pressed to Rebecca's mouth. "Don't talk. I just want to hold you."

Rebecca pulled her closer, ran her palm down her back, over her hips. Pressing her lips to Catherine's temple, she whispered, "Please don't leave me."

Catherine Rawlings closed her eyes and listened to the steady heartbeat beneath her cheek, the most precious sound she'd ever heard.

Chapter Fifteen

Michael Lassiter lay with her head on Sloan's shoulder, waiting for the alarm to go off. She was surprised when she felt soft warm lips against her brow. "Good morning," she murmured quietly.

"You know," Sloan whispered in the rapidly graying dawn, "this is the first time we've been together *and* awake in four days. I've missed you."

"I was just thinking the same thing," Michael said with a sigh, turning her head to kiss the faint hollow just below Sloan's collarbone. "When I get home from work, you're already behind closed doors downstairs. When you come upstairs—*if* you come upstairs—to get some sleep, I've already left for work."

"What's today—Friday?" Sloan asked, trying to dispel the cobwebs from her still-fuzzy brain. "You've got that managers' meeting this morning at 11:00, then the 4:20 flight to Boston, right?"

"How do you manage to keep my schedule in your head?" After a year together, Michael was still amazed that Sloan always seemed to know exactly where she was and what she was doing, despite whatever projects absorbed either of them.

"I like to remember the important things." Sloan kissed her again. This time it was a bit more than a good-morning kiss.

"Hmm...I could move the meeting back an hour," Michael suggested, the kiss tingling all the way down her spine. "Except you should probably get some sleep. Do you think you'll be working all night again tonight?"

"Probably," Sloan admitted regretfully, caressing the smooth muscles in Michael's back. "I'm sorry. We've been pushing pretty hard on this case because, believe it or not, I think something's going to break soon. It's just a question of finding the right combination of factors and narrowing down our list of possibilities."

"None of you are going to be able to keep at this pace for much longer," Michael pointed out quietly. She'd seen Jason and Sloan work nonstop for days, including during her own business crisis when she and Sloan had first met. It happened sometimes, she knew that; there were times she was working against deadline or in the midst of some creative brainstorm when *she* didn't get home for a day or two either. Still, knowing it was part of the job never stopped her from being concerned about the toll it took on her lover. It wasn't her intent to change the way Sloan worked, as if that were even possible. All she wanted to do was interject a tiny voice of reason. "After all," she chided gently, "you wouldn't want to miss something because you were too tired to think straight. It might ruin your superstar reputation."

"Heaven forbid." Sloan laughed. Then sighing, she shifted, settling Michael more firmly in her arms. It was good—no, better than good—to be close to her like this. It was this connection to Michael that restored her and gave her the perspective she needed, a perspective that was critical now. "Not much longer, I hope. At least for this stage."

"Are you really close to getting names?"

"We've been making a lot of headway in that direction. Catherine Rawlings has been here every night all week reviewing transcripts with Jason and discussing indexing parameters with Mitchell. That's given me enough free time to narrow down locations of subscribers to the two or three Web credit card clearinghouses that the f—that other sources provided."

Michael slid her thigh across Sloan's hips and sat up, straddling the supine woman. Leaning forward slightly, she began to circle her palms over Sloan's shoulders and chest. "Believe me, I'm glad it's going well. I just want to make sure you're still functional when it's over." She lowered herself until she could find Sloan's mouth with hers, kissing her as she slowly rocked her pelvis back and forth over Sloan's stomach.

"Don't worry," Sloan murmured when Michael finally released

her. "I promise to be at least one hundred percent anytime it's required." As she spoke, she lifted her hands until she cradled the undersurface of Michael's breasts, rubbing her thumbs deliberately back and forth across the peaks of the hardened nipples.

Michael drew a sharp breath, catching her lower lip between her teeth. She arched her back, pressing her breasts harder into her lover's palms. "I think your services might be needed soon."

"Really? How soon?"

"I'll let you know." As her lids fluttered closed, Michael ran her hand slowly down her own torso until her fingers rested between her legs. Already hard and wet. "Mmm, shouldn't be long."

"Don't hurry," Sloan managed through a throat tight with desire. "You know how much I love to watch."

"I know," Michael whispered back, eyes still closed, listening to Sloan's breathing quicken, feeling the abdominal muscles beneath her thighs ripple spasmodically, sensing the hot gaze upon her skin. Very carefully, not wanting to lose control, she teased her lover as she teased herself. "Ah...God, lover."

Sloan continued to work Michael's nipples, eyes fixed on the slow indolent motion of her lover's hand as she stroked herself, loving the exquisite torture of watching Michael's passion rise. "Baby, you're so beautiful."

Michael's eyes opened, their blue depths virtually eclipsed by the dark shadows of desire. She watched Sloan watch her, nearly slipping over the edge when she saw the hunger in her face. "Do you want me to stop?" she asked haltingly, her hips thrusting into her hand of their own volition now.

"Not yet," Sloan ordered, arching her pelvis, forcing Michael's fingers to caress them both. "Just don't...come."

Michael laughed shakily, her stomach muscles tensing with the first warning contractions. "Then...I should stop...now." She thought she could hold back, barely, if she stopped soon. Very soon.

"No," Sloan growled, her voice savage, her expression wild. Knowing how close Michael was, knowing how much she must want to let go, was making her crazy. Michael was leaning hard into Sloan's hands now, nipples rock hard against her palms. Entire body shuddering, Michael whimpered softly.

"Easy."

"Sloan...love...I can't...can'tstop," Michael pleaded helplessly, her hand a blur between her thighs.

"Hold on," Sloan urged, lifting her own hips higher so that the back of Michael's fingers pressed into her clitoris. Watching Michael nearing orgasm, feeling her hand circling faster as she pleasured herself, was almost enough to get Sloan there, too. The intermittent brush of Michael's fingers over her clitoris was all she needed. Desperately close, she became the one struggling to wait. "Tell me...when."

"Oh...now. I'm comingnow..."

Sloan fought not to go off with her, raptly watching the pleasure flow through Michael's body, her own nerves melting as she began to burn from the inside out. Her arms trembled, supporting Michael's weight as she convulsed, and her legs twisted as orgasm finally thundered through her. Her shouts were lost in Michael's cries as they held to one another while pleasure raged.

Moments, eons, later, Sloan managed, "What do you think?"

"A hundred and ten percent," Michael gasped, still trembling as she lay stretched out on Sloan's body.

"Hmm," Sloan grumbled. "Maybe I *am* slipping."

Michael laughed, pushing sweat-dampened hair from her face. "Any better, lover, and I'd go up in flames." Leaning up on one arm, she regarded Sloan intently, her expression suddenly serious. "You know, I can cancel this overnight to Boston. I don't want to be away if something breaks on your case."

"No—go ahead," Sloan said, brushing her cheek against the fine hairs on Michael's arm as she smiled contentedly. "We're not that close. I'll pick you up at the airport tomorrow night like we planned."

"If something happens, will you call me? I'll come right back." Michael ran her hand along Sloan's side, feeling her stiffen. "I know you, Sloan. You'll want to be in the middle of it. And I want to be here."

"Just go sew up your deal," Sloan insisted. "You'll be back in plenty of time. Promise."

"Mmm," Michael said, curling into Sloan's body and closing her eyes. "I'll hold you to that."

❖

"Get you coffee?"

Catherine looked up at the dark-haired woman and smiled. "Not unless you want to peel me off the ceiling."

Sloan laughed as she filled her mug. "There's some left if you need a boost."

"Thanks. By the way—do you ever sleep?"

"Now and then. But Michael left town on business this afternoon, so tonight...well, I'd just as soon work."

"Michael?"

"My lover."

"Ah." *Michael. Odd, I would have bet money...*

"What about you? This is the fifth night in a row that you've been at it."

Catherine glanced at her watch. Almost 11:00 p.m. "I'll call it quits soon."

"Uh-huh." Sloan smiled, gave a half wave, and disappeared.

When the conference room door swung open again, Catherine glanced up casually, expecting to see Sloan or Jason. Then, as it never failed to do, her heart rate skyrocketed at the sight of the handsome blond in the pale blue button-down-collar shirt and faded jeans. It was unusual to see Rebecca working in anything other than a well-tailored suit, but it *was* Friday night, and Catherine supposed that when the detective worked the streets well into the early morning hours, she did it in jeans and a leather jacket. The memory of just how good Rebecca looked when dressed that way was quickly replaced by an image of Sandy's small cozy apartment, complete with the remains of a takeout meal. Impatiently, she set that thought aside. There was work to be done, and musing about Rebecca's secret life was not going to help. "Hi."

"You're working late again," Rebecca remarked, surveying the pile of computer printouts on the table. *I've missed you.*

Other than several phone calls and one hurried lunch together in the hospital cafeteria, they hadn't really had much contact the rest of the week. It was the longest they had been separated since Rebecca moved back to her own apartment, and with each passing day, Rebecca felt more at sea. They still hadn't talked about what happened at the hospital—and after—and she knew that Catherine was waiting for her to say something, or do something, but she wasn't certain what that was.

"I can't believe how much traffic there is on these sites," Catherine said, indicating the stacks of on-line chat transcripts. "And these are just the ones that Jason thought were interesting."

"You look tired. You *do* still have a day job, remember."

Catherine studied her, sensitive to the reservation in her tone. The concern was genuine; she could see it in her eyes. But Rebecca hadn't touched her when she'd walked into the room, and although she stood within arm's length now, the emotional distance between them seemed unbridgeable. Not for the first time, she wondered where Rebecca had been spending her nights. "I'm okay. Reading through these is a lot easier than doing an hour or two of therapy."

"I can only imagine." Rebecca smiled wryly. "How's it going?"

"Surprisingly, not too bad," Catherine said, pushing back in the chair with a sigh. "It occurred to me this morning while I was making rounds that we aren't the only ones profiling."

"What do you mean?" Her interest sparked, Rebecca edged a hip onto the corner of the table.

"Well, thus far, Sloan and Jason have been concentrating on finding individuals who fit a certain profile. I'm sure that the computer wizards in the other room will be able to manipulate this information and eventually come up with something concrete. Still, they've amassed a tremendous amount of data which could take a long time to analyze."

"Right," Rebecca grimaced. "If I think about it too hard, it gives me a headache."

"Actually, me, too. I think I might be able to add another piece to the puzzle and speed up the process."

"How?" Rebecca asked and crossed the room to test the heat of the coffeepot with her palm. It was warm and the coffee smelled fresh. She lifted the pot and gestured in Catherine's direction. "Want some?"

"Thanks, no," Catherine replied with a shake of her head. "Anyhow, it occurred to me that if someone is making money, presumably a lot of money, producing and selling pornographic movies, as well as broadcasting live videos of child prostitution, they have to have an audience."

"Well, that's the point, isn't it?" Rebecca moved back to Catherine's side with coffee in hand. "All of these dirtballs that Jason's been communicating with are the audience members."

"I'm not arguing that they are all purveyors of child pornography in one form or another. But only a select few—probably *very* few—would actually be in the position to subscribe to this live broadcast that Sloan's so anxious to get a lead on."

"Wait a minute," Rebecca said, an edge of excitement in her voice. "It's just like any television program—a target audience always has a particular profile. A particular demographic make-up. Is that what you mean?"

"Precisely," Catherine stated emphatically. "That's exactly what I mean. Obviously, the *viewers* are going to be men, probably between the ages of twenty-five and fifty. Secondly, they need expensive equipment and high-speed Internet access; that requires a certain income level."

"Probably single, or at least someone who has a large chunk of private time," Rebecca interjected, enthusiasm growing.

"So my theory," Catherine continued, "is that there are probably a number of middlemen recruiting potential subscribers for this…this broadcasting service, for want of a better word. And we should be able to identify them by the questions *they're* asking."

"So you're looking for someone who is trying to find out if Jason—well, the Jason persona—is a single adult male with expendable income who might be interested in something more than still pics or cybersex."

"You've got it. I'm looking for someone who appears to be profiling. What I did was give Mitchell a list of hypothetical questions that these recruiters might ask so she can screen for them. Then we'll pull the transcripts of anyone who hits fifty percent, and, with luck, I can string all of *that* individual's chats together and see if the whole picture fits."

"I don't know why Clark didn't get you in on this from the beginning," Rebecca said with a shake of her head.

A voice from the door responded, "Because we didn't know what the hell we were doing. And if you repeat that, I'll deny all knowledge." Grinning, Sloan nodded to Rebecca as she made her way to the coffeepot again. "How are you doing?"

"Fine." Rebecca glanced at the woman who entered behind Sloan. "Officer Mitchell. Putting in a little overtime?"

"No, ma'am. I'm here on my own time."

Rebecca raised an eyebrow. "Any particular reason?"

"Since Dr. Rawlings is here, I thought I could help out with logging identifiers and running probabilities. Seemed like the best use of resources."

"It's your dime, Mitchell." But she made note of it. The kid was quality.

"Any luck with street intel, Frye?" Sloan inquired.

"Maybe. I'll know better in a couple of hours." Rebecca glanced in Sloan's direction, not noticing Mitchell's body stiffen or her expression darken.

"Here's something," Catherine said almost to herself. Every eye in the room turned to her.

"What?" Sloan asked immediately.

Catherine pushed a sheet of paper into the center of the table. "Look here. These are segments of five chats with the same person over the course of the last ten days."

All conversation stopped as everyone crowded around to read the annotated transcripts.

"Sloan?" Rebecca queried, glancing at the pages. "What's the background here?"

"Let me see." She read the notations from the log, which Mitchell had generated with her indexing program, that were printed across the top of each sheet. "These are segments of conversations that took place in a private chat room reached by way of an open bulletin board. The main site is trafficked by kids and adults—no real way to tell anyone's age because, even when they say, it might not be true. Many pedophiles pretend to be teenagers until they have established a relationship with a kid and, even then, may never reveal their true age."

Sloan pointed to the headers. "At any rate, this board is known for lots of chat and a lot of invitations to go private for sex. These transcripts are from a room frequented exclusively by men who have a taste for young girls—eleven to fourteen, mostly. Invite only. You have to be sponsored to get in it."

"How did Jason get in, then?"

Sloan grinned, a predatory grin without a hint of humor. "We hacked in. Easy. Jason's persona is BigMac10."

"Creative," Rebecca said wryly.

"These guys aren't subtle."

"What do you see, Catherine?"

"I've highlighted the text I believe represents the profiling questions."

Transcript One - Excerpt
```
BigMac10: Hey, man. Saw you with KewlChic12
over on the main board. Did you score?
LongJohnXXX: Oh, yeah. Sweet
BigMac10: Wish I coulda been there
LongJohnXXX: Where were you? *Watching?*
BigMac10: LOL. Yeah. Until you went
private
LongJohnXXX: *You get off on that?*
BigMac10: Watching?
LongJohnXXX: Yeah
BigMac10: Every chance I get
```

Transcript Two - Excerpt
```
LongJohnXXX: Back again, huh, buddy?
BigMac10: Can't stay away. Such fine
company
LongJohnXXX: *Still watching?*
BigMac10: Whenever I can
LongJohnXXX: *Got flash to trade?*
BigMac10: Stills don't do it for me
LongJohnXXX: Know what you mean. I like 'em
moving. You?
BigMac10: Moving and screaming. Oh yeah
```

"Jesus," Rebecca murmured. "Jason is good."

"Yeah," Sloan said quietly. "And it doesn't come easy."

Rebecca glanced at her but said nothing. She understood standing up for your partner. She returned to reading.

Transcript Three – Excerpt

LongJohnXXX: Hey, BM10 – any action on the boards?
BigMac10: Just talk out there
LongJohnXXX: Kids stuff
BigMac10: Yeah
LongJohnXXX: How long you been lurking?
BigMac10: Few weeks here. Been around HotRods before that
LongJohnXXX: *You sharing the line?*
BigMac10: No – all mine. Home alone

Transcript Four – Excerpt

BigMac10: welcome
LongJohnXXX: Evening watchman
BigMac10: Not much to see here tonight
LongJohnXXX: Second hand pickings, huh?
BigMac10: Insufficient for a man of quality
LongJohnXXX: *Quality costs*
BigMac10: Not an object – for the right merchandise, I've got the green
LongJohnXXX: *You looking to buy?*
BigMac10: Maybe if the stuff is prime

"And then this from last night—early this morning, I should say," Catherine remarked, pointing to the last entry.

Transcript Five – Excerpt

LongJohnXXX: Yo-BM10. You lurking?
BigMac10: here
LongJohnXXX: How'd you do?
BigMac10: How so?
LongJohnXXX: Don't be a cock tease. HotChic13
BigMac10: <g> Now who's watching?

```
LongJohnXXX: yeah - so give
BigMac10: she blew me off
LongJohnXXX: Whoa - for real?
BigMac10: No, man - she went private then
backed out. Left me high and hard
LongJohnXXX: Bummer. *No sure thing in
cyberspace*
BigMac10: yeah - not like RL
LongJohnXXX: The *real thing* is sweet
BigMac10: But hard to come by
LongJohnXXX: depends on who you know
BigMac10: yeah - I'm available<g>
```

"This guy has potential," Sloan agreed. "He sounds like he's getting ready to offer Jas—uh, *BigMac* something."

"And look there," Mitchell noted, pointing to the scripts, "he's mentioned *watching* a half dozen times. Could be he's brokering the real-time feeds."

"There's a problem," Rebecca remarked with a frown.

"What?" Catherine asked in surprise. "Surely, it can't be entrapment?"

"No—trouble for Jason."

"You want to spell that out?" Sloan asked, her voice suddenly edged with flint.

Rebecca regarded Mitchell for a moment. Mitchell squared her shoulders, set her jaw, and stared back. Clearly, she was not going to leave until ordered.

"How many of Jason's chats do we have recorded, Mitchell? Logged in somewhere."

"All of them," Mitchell replied immediately. That had been part of her assignment, and she was very thorough.

"That's what I figured." Rebecca rolled her shoulders, then faced Sloan, whose eyes had grown hard. "Jason could be in trouble if he's been soliciting sex from minors on the Internet, even in the course of an investigation. Especially when these transcripts go into anything I take to the DA for a warrant."

"Soliciting sex?" Sloan's surprise was evident.

"The interaction mentioned here with HotChic13," Rebecca clarified, waving the last page. "Is that recorded somewhere also?"

"Yep." Sloan's grin reappeared. "Every red hot word."

"Well then—"

"Except," Sloan added, "I'm HotChic13."

Mitchell coughed. "Uh, and I'm PhillyFilly11—BigMac10's other cybersex partner."

Catherine laughed. Rebecca fixed Mitchell with a hard stare. "Redefining your assignment, Officer?"

"No, ma'am. Just...expanding it."

Sloan looked for a moment as if she were going to come to Mitchell's defense, then thought better of it. You didn't get between a superior officer and a subordinate. Not and keep the superior officer as an ally, or a friend.

"Just remember you're a cop, Mitchell. Accountability is part of the job."

Sloan smothered a smile. She was willing to bet that there were a dozen things a day that Frye never reported and would deny any knowledge of. But she appreciated the detective keeping her rookie on the straight path. "We'll cease using her, Sergeant, if you think it's a problem."

"No," Rebecca responded. "Go ahead as you've been doing. But she doesn't make contact with anyone else."

"Roger," Sloan said with a half-smile. "So," she continued, turning to Catherine, "you think this LongJohn guy's our best bet so far?"

"It certainly looks as if he's pumping Jason for the right kinds of information."

"Should we be a little more aggressive with him then?" Sloan asked. "Lead him a little?"

Catherine nodded thoughtfully. "Try to *run into* him tonight. I'd think it would be understandable if Ja—BigMac was curious after their last exchange and asked about real life opportunities. Shouldn't run up any red flags."

"Can you stay for a while and monitor the chats in case we get a hit?"

"Certainly."

"Good. I'll advise Jason of the plan so he can start trolling that board." Sloan left with Mitchell close behind.

Catherine regarded Rebecca with a soft smile. "You like Mitchell, don't you?"

"Why do you say that?" Rebecca arched an eyebrow in surprise.

"You're hard on people you like."

Rebecca winced. "On you, too?"

"No." Catherine moved closer and rested her hand on Rebecca's arm. God, it was good just to touch her. "I didn't mean it that way."

"I've missed you this week," Rebecca confessed, feeling her entire body sway toward Catherine as if she'd been offered water in the desert. "Can I take you home later?" At Catherine's look of hesitation, she added quickly, "I'll just drive you home. I won't stay or—"

"Oh, Rebecca," Catherine said quietly, a too familiar note of sadness in her voice. "Don't you know how much I've missed you, too? Do you think I don't *want* you?"

"I just didn't want you to think I meant...that all I wanted..." Rebecca swore sharply, then leaned the last few inches and kissed her gently. After a very long minute, she lifted her mouth away and murmured, "It's not just about sex. That's all I meant."

"Are you going out tonight?" Catherine asked, stepping back so she could think clearly. It *wasn't* all about sex, but the feel of her after days apart drove any semblance of reason from her mind.

"I'll be back in a few hours."

"I'll be here."

Chapter Sixteen

Rebecca waited across the street from the all-night Gateway Diner on the corner of 13th and Locust. The early September night was chilly, and she hunched her shoulders inside her worn leather jacket. Secluded in the shadows beneath the awning of a shoe repair store, she watched the parade going in and out through the revolving doors. Some were bar patrons who had left the neighborhood watering holes in search of something to eat before wending their way home; some were prostitutes of both genders taking a break from working the streets or just socializing with friends; and some were merely lonely people with nowhere else to be and no one waiting for them to be there. At 1:15, as Sandy's message had said, the young blond approached, walking north on 13th and, a moment later, she joined Rebecca in the shadows.

"Hey," Sandy said. Dressed in a short black leather skirt, open-toed high-heeled sandals, a pale scoop-neck top that outlined her high firm breasts, and a thin jacket that clearly wasn't providing any warmth, she shivered visibly and wrapped her arms around herself as if to ward off the night.

"You're gonna have to start covering up if you don't want to freeze your assets off," Rebecca remarked.

"If they can't see it, they don't buy it," Sandy rejoined.

Rebecca glanced out into the street, knowing that the occupants of the cars slowly crawling by were cruising the sidewalks for hookers or hustlers, searching for a few minutes of company. "Did you ever think of getting into another line of work?"

"Yeah. Except no one seems to be hiring nuclear physicists at the moment. You know, space travel ain't what it used to be."

"There are programs available," Rebecca said quietly. "Places you could get job training or—"

"Frye, if you keep on with this social-work talk you're really gonna scare me. Now, do you want the information I've got for you, or not?" Sandy had no intention of discussing her choices with the tall blond cop. For one thing, it was none of her business. For another, the quiet concern in Frye's voice bothered her, and she didn't want to think about exactly why. When people cared about you, they ended up owning a little piece of you. She didn't want anyone to have even the smallest hold on her. Because then she was vulnerable.

Rebecca blew out a breath and rolled her shoulders, wondering what the hell she was trying to do. Sandy had probably been a runaway, most likely running from abuse, like the majority of young kids on the streets. *Not all of them,* she reminded herself, thinking of Anthony DeCarlo's teenage daughter, who had left home to punish her parents— an act of adolescent rebellion that had almost cost her life. But most of them arrived on buses or thumbed their way into the city, only to end up sleeping ten to a room and selling themselves in one way or another for a meal, or drugs, or merely some human connection.

Sandy had made a choice for survival, and she had used her wits and whatever else she had to make that happen. As far as Rebecca knew, the young woman wasn't using drugs, and she wasn't selling herself at truck stops or under bridges in the underbelly of the city. She had a decent apartment, and it looked as if she was eating well and taking care of herself. If she was using her body to make a life for herself, there were worse things she could've done. And no matter what she was doing, Sandy was a source of information and that was all.

Rebecca finally replied, "Yeah, tell me what you've got."

"Let's go somewhere and get a drink. I'm freezing out here."

A few minutes later, they were seated at a back table in the Two Four Club, an after-hours place that catered to a mixed clientele whose only common bond was that they didn't want to go home until they had no other choice. Rebecca walked to the bar and asked for a cup of coffee for herself and a beer for Sandy. The bartender grimaced at her request but poured lethal-looking liquid into a Styrofoam cup and passed it to her across the bar. She carried the cup and Sandy's bottled beer back to the table, then fished four folded twenties out of her jeans and put them underneath the beer bottle.

"I know a girl who made some movies." Sandy deftly extracted the bills and slid them into a pocket under the waistband of her skirt.

"Name. When and where. Details this time."

Sandy shook her head. "First of all, who she is isn't going to help you, and I'm not telling you. *I* know what she knows. Take it or leave it."

"Give me what you got." Pressing wouldn't help. Sandy was unyielding about protecting her friends.

"She says she and two other girls had sex with three or four guys."

"And that's news?"

"Well, it is when somebody's filming it for some kind of live TV."

"What do you mean by 'live'?" Rebecca's pulse quickened.

"She says one guy told them that everything they said and did was going to be viewed just like prime-time television—right when it was happening—so to be careful not to use their own names." Sandy sipped her beer, then continued with an expression of loathing on her face. "And to make sure they, you know, spoke up."

"Why?" Rebecca asked.

"He gave them a…what do you call it…a script to look over before they started filming. But apparently it wasn't much, just a list of things to say, you know…the usual…"

"Give me a for-instance."

"Oh, you know. The things guys like to hear. *Oh baby, you're so big. It feels so good. Don't hurt me. Hurt me. Don't come in my mouth. Come all over me.*" Sandy looked past Rebecca at some vision only she could see. "That kind of thing."

"Did your friend say who they were, describe the men in any way to you?"

Sandy shook her head again. "No names. She went along as a substitute for some chick who usually did it but couldn't make it because her boyfriend'd put her in the hospital. Says she didn't even know the other girls she was with very well."

"These girls. How old were they?" Rebecca asked quietly. Under the table, her hands were balled into fists, and she ignored the desire to break something.

"Thirteen, fifteen, and sixteen. But they all look about twelve, especially if they dress for the part."

"Christ."

Sandy glimpsed something very close to fury flicker across the starkly handsome planes of Frye's face. There it was again, that undercurrent of concern that touched something in Sandy that she didn't want to be awakened. It happened when she was with Dell, too. Even just being around Dell made it happen. Made her feel connected.

"What?" She was startled, realizing that Frye was speaking.

"Did she tell you where this was?" Rebecca repeated.

"Two different places—and apparently the girls don't know where it's going to be until that night. Someone picks them up and takes them there, and it's all very, you know, 007. Darkened windows in the van, that kind of thing. A warehouse is all she told me." She finished her beer and pushed the bottle aside. "I'm pretty sure it's in the city, though, because she said it wasn't more than half an hour, and it seemed like they were driving in circles for quite a while."

Rebecca felt the familiar thrill of the hunt. This was a real lead. "She give you anything else?"

"Uh-uh. Just that she did two of these runs—one was about six months ago and the other three weeks ago."

"How often do these live films get made?"

"She's not sure." Sandy gathered her things. "Look, I can probably find out more. I just thought you'd want to know about this operation."

"You did plenty," Rebecca said seriously. "I'll take it from here." She'd have Watts get with someone from Juvie and pull the files on all the girls under seventeen known to be turning tricks and still on the streets. One of them would know someone who'd been in on one of these shoots. The community was too close for this to be a secret. Eventually a location or a name or a description would pop up.

"You know, I could pass, Frye," Sandy said quietly. "I do it all the time."

"What?" Rebecca asked sharply, her attention suddenly completely focused.

"For fourteen or fifteen. If I send out the word that I want in..."

She should do it. She should use her. It was probably a better route to whoever was behind the whole operation than waiting for Sloan and Jason to sift through hundreds of pedophiles in hopes of finding one who could open a door for them.

"No. You're done with this." Rebecca stood, shrugging into her jacket. "Thanks."

"Hey, Frye?" Sandy asked casually. "Who's Catherine anyway?"

Rebecca regarded her impassively for a long moment, then smiled. A brief, quicksilver smile. "Anybody ever tell you that you ask too many questions?"

Then she was gone, leaving Sandy grinning at her back.

❖

When Rebecca returned to Sloan Security, she found Jason, Sloan, and Catherine crowded around the large central work station while messages scrolled on three of the four computer monitors simultaneously. Glancing over Jason's shoulder, she asked, "Any progress?"

"Lots of action," Sloan responded as Jason continued to chat electronically with someone by the name of Everhard1040. "No sign of LongJohnXXX yet."

"Mitchell go home?"

"Under duress," Sloan said with a laugh. "She'd been here since 8:00 yesterday morning, so I told her to take off."

It was 2:30 in the morning, and Rebecca felt the dull edge of fatigue clouding her brain. She shook herself mentally, annoyed that she still didn't seem able to function at full speed. "How long are you going to keep at it?"

"A while longer," Jason muttered. "He might still show up."

"Catherine, I think you can probably call it a night," Sloan said with a sigh. "We'll keep an eye on things here for a bit."

"If you get anything that looks promising," Rebecca said, "call me. As soon as we have something solid, I want to take this to my captain and start discussing what we'll need for a warrant."

"You might as well start the wheels moving—you know how long the DA's office takes to make a decision. At the very least, we're going to need to confiscate any computer equipment we find so I can work on it back here," Sloan advised with an optimism Rebecca did not share. "Once I have just *one* CPU that's been receiving these live feeds, I can start tracing where the broadcasts are coming from."

"We'll probably need your crime scene techs on the scene to log everything we find and remove also," Jason remarked. His eyes were still fixed on the constantly changing messages, and he occasionally typed a message, too.

"Fine. I had planned on giving my captain an update tomorrow. I'll call you in the morning before I meet with him if I don't hear from you first."

"Good enough," Sloan agreed.

Bending down, Rebecca murmured to Catherine, "Are you ready to leave?"

"Yes." She was used to dealing with people—emotions—in the intimate confines of therapy, one-on-one, face-to-face. Watching the disembodied phrases stream across the screen, knowing that somewhere there was a person attached to them, but having no sense of who that person truly was, disturbed and disoriented her. It left her with a compelling need to feel connected, to see and be seen. "More than ready."

"Is your car here?" Rebecca asked as they stepped out onto the deserted street. Sloan's building on Front Street faced the river one block away and Delaware Avenue, the sometimes-busy thoroughfare that ran along the waterfront. But at this hour, no one was about.

"Yes, I'm parked just down the block," Catherine informed her, "but I'll probably come back to review more transcripts some time tomorrow, so I don't mind leaving it here overnight. Let's just take one car."

"Fine. I'll drop you off tonight and then swing by and pick you up at your place in the morning before I go in to see the boss." Rebecca unlocked the passenger door of the Corvette and held it open for Catherine. After walking around to the driver's side, she slid in behind the wheel and reached to put the keys in the ignition. Catherine's soft touch on her wrist stilled her motion. Turning to face her passenger, she said quietly, "What is it?"

"Let's go to your apartment."

"*My* apartment?" Rebecca said, startled.

"Yes. It occurred to me over the last few days that all of our time together has been spent at my place. I don't know where you go when you leave me."

"I don't go anywhere." Rebecca was still for a long moment, then she said in a low voice heavy with feeling, "When I'm not with you, Catherine, I'm either working or waiting to be with you again."

Catherine smiled fondly, struck by how much Rebecca's simple words stirred her, because she knew they didn't come easily. Insistently, she said, "I want to see where you sleep. I want to be able to imagine you there when I'm in bed alone." She didn't add out loud, *I want to be able to imagine you somewhere other than Sandy's apartment...or a hospital bed.*

"Okay. I have to warn you, though, it's the maid's week off."

Catherine laughed and settled back into the bucket seat. "I promise not to look under the bed."

From Sloan's, Rebecca drove south on 4th Street into Queen Village, a pocket of small row houses and restaurants sandwiched between the newly trendy South Street business district and South Philadelphia, the historically working-class Irish and Italian area. Ten minutes later, they were climbing the stairs to Rebecca's second-floor apartment above a mom-and-pop grocery store that had been owned by the same family for over fifty years. Rebecca tried frantically to remember exactly in what condition she had left her apartment, but she drew a blank. She so very rarely paid attention to her surroundings when she was there. It was a place to sleep, make coffee, and shower before going back to her real home, the city streets.

After unlocking the door, she pushed it open and said, "Come on in."

Catherine stepped through and waited for Rebecca, who pulled the door closed, bolted it, and flicked on a wall switch to her right. After her eyes adjusted to the light, Catherine looked around, smiling to herself when she found that the apartment was very close to the way she had envisioned it. One large living room with a door to the left that opened into a small kitchen and another on the right that most likely led to the bedroom and bath. A utilitarian sofa with the requisite coffee table in front of it, a very nice stereo set coated with a layer of dust that suggested it rarely saw any use, and a high-end television comprised the furnishings.

She strolled a few steps forward. An end table supported a haphazard stack of paperbacks, and a gym bag lay open on the floor to her left, apparently having been abandoned there after Rebecca removed her soiled workout clothes. It looked like a bachelor apartment, which, of course, was what it was.

"As I said," Rebecca began in an apologetic tone, "it's not much to look at—"

"On the contrary," Catherine said. "It seems very much like you. Utilitarian, and a little bit…" She quirked an eyebrow, grinning at Rebecca. "Spartan."

"Spartan, huh?" Rebecca laughed, too, and began to relax. "Can I get you something? I've got soda, I think, and…" Her voice trailed off as she followed Catherine's gaze.

"Is that yours?" Catherine asked quietly, her tone carefully neutral. Her heart was pounding furiously, but she knew that her voice sounded calm. That was the benefit of years of training.

Rebecca stared at the half-empty bottle of Johnnie Walker Black on her coffee table. "Yes."

"Are you drinking?" It terrified her more than she would have ever dreamed to think of Rebecca in any kind of trouble, physically or emotionally. If she was drinking again, then something was very wrong. To realize that something so serious could be happening to someone she loved and that she wouldn't even know, wouldn't even *suspect*, made her wonder what exactly had happened to the two of them. How could they have drifted so far part?

"Rebecca?" Catherine asked again into the silence.

Rebecca took a deep breath. "No, I'm not."

"But you bought it?"

"Yes. I did. Four nights ago." *The second night we were apart.* She shrugged out of her jacket and released the clasp on her shoulder holster, removing it and stowing it in its customary spot on top of the bookcase next to the door to her bedroom. Turning, she asked, "Can I take your jacket?"

Catherine simply nodded and slipped it from her shoulders. Approaching Rebecca, she held it out in one hand.

Rebecca took it and carefully placed it on a hanger in the small closet next to the front door. Then without hesitation, she walked to the table, lifted the bottle of scotch in one hand, and carried it into the kitchen. She returned empty-handed and sat on the sofa. Catherine sat down beside her.

"Why?" Catherine asked, leaning toward her but not yet touching her.

"I've asked myself that every day for the last four days," Rebecca said at length. "I can't tell you exactly why, but I was lonely, and I was angry, and I was tired. I can usually deal with one or two of those things at one time, but when they all come together, I mostly just want to forget."

Those words and her expression shredded Catherine's soul. "Is it me?"

"No," Rebecca said, her voice a whisper. "It's me."

❖

"Who is it?" Sandy called irritably.

"It's me."

She opened the door and regarded her unexpected visitor. "You okay?"

"Yeah."

Neither moved; each leaned against the doorjamb on opposite sides of the threshold, regarding one another as if uncertain what to say next. Finally, Sandy said, "It's three o'clock in the morning, Dell. What's going on?"

"Did you talk to Frye tonight?"

Sandy's eyes sparked with sudden anger. "We're not going there."

"Just tell me you're not doing something crazy for her."

"What I do for her or anyone else isn't any of your business," Sandy said, moving to close the door.

Mitchell straight-armed the door before it could close completely, but she made no move to enter the room. "You met her tonight, didn't you?"

"Are you *following* me?"

"No. I guessed."

"Leave it alone, rookie."

"I don't want you to tell me what you told her," Mitchell insisted. "Just tell me if you're doing anything except passing on information."

"Go home, Dell," Sandy said, but her voice was softer now.

"Please, Sandy," Mitchell said with a note of quiet desperation. "I can't sleep. I keep thinking…these guys…"

"There's a reason we can't be friends," Sandy said, her eyes impossible to read but her tone bitter. "And this is it. For a little while, you can forget what I do, what I am…but not all the time, right, Dell? And this is what happens."

"You're wrong," Mitchell whispered. "The only thing I can't forget is the way you looked lying in that alley with your face covered in blood. I don't want anyone else to hurt you."

Sandy blinked. The torment in Dell's deep blue eyes was impossible to ignore. She wasn't certain what brought the tears to her own eyes—the fact that Dell was hurting or the fact that the young cop could feel something like that for her. All she knew for certain was that no one had made her cry in a very long time, and she had sworn that no one ever would again. In a voice she didn't recognize, she asked, "Are you coming in?"

"No," Mitchell said hoarsely, her entire body trembling.

"Why not?"

Because I want to so bad.

❖

Breathless, Catherine rolled over and pushed Rebecca away. "I have yet to determine how it is that every time I intend to have a serious conversation with you, I end up in bed with you instead."

"Sorry," Rebecca gasped. "I think I started that."

"Well," Catherine murmured, linking her fingers with Rebecca's as she stared at the ceiling in the semi-darkness, "you definitely had help finishing it."

Rebecca waited for Catherine to continue, wondering what she was going to ask or what she hoped to hear. When the silence between them expanded to fill the room, Rebecca spoke out of a desperate need to break through the barriers between them. "Every night, I poured a glass of Scotch and sat staring at it...I don't know for how long. Then I'd get up and pour it down the sink."

Catherine turned on her side to study Rebecca's profile in the moonlight. "Does anyone know?"

Startled, Rebecca replied, "Who would know?"

I should know. But this wasn't the time for that. "Watts...or Whitaker?"

"No," Rebecca replied abruptly. Then, aware of her defensive tone, she added more softly, "I can't talk to Whitaker about this, Catherine. I'm still waiting for him to sign off on my incident evaluation. The last thing I can tell him is that I feel like getting drunk."

"I understand, believe me. I see people every week who don't want their employers to know they're in therapy. Still, it would probably help if you talked to...someone about this," Catherine said carefully. "A friend or...me." Gently, she stroked the length of Rebecca's arm. "But keeping it inside is going to make it harder not to drink."

"I know. I think I'm past it now. I emptied the bottle down the drain tonight."

Catherine felt a small swell of relief, but she knew it was never that easy. "And the next time?"

After a pause, Rebecca answered quietly, "Next time...I'll tell you."

"Thank you," Catherine whispered. "What you did, not drinking, was incredibly difficult, Rebecca. I'm proud of you."

Rebecca turned on her side to face Catherine, her palm resting on the crest of Catherine's hip, their bodies only inches apart. "I want to make things right between us. And I don't know how."

"What we're doing right now will make things right between us," Catherine said, her voice tight with emotion. "I need to know you, Rebecca. Not just all the strong, brave, wonderful parts of you, but the parts that are uncertain or lonely or...frightened."

"I need practice at this."

"So do I," Catherine admitted. "I haven't cared about anyone like this before. You bring up feelings in me I didn't even know I was capable of having. Before you, my life was ordered; everything made sense. I was settled...comfortable."

"Doesn't sound too bad," Rebecca said with a hint of laughter.

Catherine laughed, too. "No, it wasn't. It wasn't bad at all; it was just not *remarkable*. Being with you is quite remarkable."

"Captain Henry told me that I could be promoted to lieutenant if I wanted it," Rebecca said in a low voice. "I could tell him yes."

"Do you want that?"

"I wouldn't be on the street as much. I'd have more regular hours."

And you'd hate that. Catherine leaned closer and kissed the point of Rebecca's shoulder. "You'd do that for me?"

"No," Rebecca said, her eyes meeting Catherine's. "I'd do that for us."

"Maybe someday," Catherine said softly, stroking the edge of Rebecca's jaw with her fingertips, feeling the muscles bunched tightly beneath her fingers. "Right now, I'd rather you just share your life with me, not change it for me."

"I don't think I've ever done that with anyone, but I'll try. I swear to God, I'll try."

"Good. You can start in the morning." Catherine slipped her fingers into the hair at the base of Rebecca's neck and guided the other woman down on top of her. "But right now, I'd rather not talk."

Rebecca slid her thigh between Catherine's legs and leaned on her elbows, staring down into Catherine's face. "I feel like part of me is missing when I'm not with you."

Maybe it was her words, maybe it was the pressure of warm firm muscle against her nerve centers, but a surge of desire so powerful it caused every muscle in her body to tense wrenched a sharp cry from Catherine's throat. She wrapped her calves around Rebecca's leg and thrust hard into her, forcing the blood to pound faster through her already swollen flesh. Pressing her lips to Rebecca's ear she whispered raggedly, "I don't want to…think. Make it so I can't."

First, Rebecca kissed her until Catherine couldn't speak. Then she found her nipples, and teased them, tormented them, until Catherine couldn't breathe. Then, she touched her, stroked her, and finally filled her…until Catherine couldn't do anything except feel.

Chapter Seventeen

The phone rang at 6:40 a.m. Rebecca groped for the receiver and fumbled it to her ear. "Frye."

"You up yet?" Sloan's ever-present, clearly irrepressible energy crackled over the line.

"No. Damn...you been to bed yet?"

"Nope. But I've got something for you."

Rebecca sat up in bed, and Catherine rolled over to rest her head against Rebecca's stomach, wrapping one arm around her waist. Rebecca threaded the fingers of her free hand through the thick tresses at the base of Catherine's neck.

"Tell me."

"LongJohn finally showed up last night, and he's dangling bait in front of BigMac's...nose. You'll have to see the transcript, but basically, he's offered BigMac a show. A *live* show."

"Excellent," Rebecca rejoined, her mind already prioritizing her day's work. "I need as many details as you can give me. I'll be over in an hour."

"I'll put the coffee on."

Rebecca leaned toward the nightstand to hang up the phone.

"What is it?" Catherine asked sleepily.

"Sloan's got something for us."

"I take it that means we're getting up?"

Rebecca slid down into bed and settled Catherine into her arms. "We've got a few minutes. You can sleep a little longer."

Catherine ran her palm along Rebecca's ribs and down to the base of her abdomen, her fingers settling lightly in the cleft between Rebecca's thighs. "I wasn't thinking of sleeping. The last thing I remember from last night is feeling as if my entire body had disintegrated. It was wonderful, but at about the point where my arms and legs disassembled, I think I lost consciousness." She laughed softly, edging her fingers lower as she spoke.

Rebecca's body had come to attention, and she murmured huskily, "Like I said, we've got a few minutes."

Catherine pressed closer, her mouth against Rebecca's neck. Teasingly, she murmured, "I might need a little longer than that."

"Uhh," Rebecca gasped as fingers closed around her length, "take all the time you want."

❖

If Sloan was surprised to see Catherine arrive with Rebecca, she didn't show it. Hair wet from the shower, in a tight black T-shirt and black jeans, she met them at the elevator with a handful of printouts in her fist. Her eyes alight with excitement and the thrill of the hunt, she said, "Come on down to the conference room."

Jason was there waiting, looking immaculate in a crisp white shirt and blended silk trousers. Grinning at them, showing not the slightest hint of fatigue, he said, "Looks like I might have a date this weekend."

They all helped themselves to coffee and then sat down with copies of the most recent chat transcript.

Transcript Six - Excerpt
```
LongJohnXXX: Hey big man, wondered where
you were
BigMac10: Looked for you earlier, but you
were nowhere
LongJohnXXX: Busy arranging entertainment
for some friends
BigMac10: entertainment? Anything hot?
LongJohnXXX: sizzlin
BigMac10: live action?
LongJohnXXX: Next best thing — live on
screen
BigMac10: oh man, how sweet
LongJohnXXX: turn you on?
```

```
BigMac10: you know it. Room for one more?
LongJohnXXX: could be - not exactly an open
house, you know
BigMac10: I understand, but I've got the
green. No matter the price
LongJohnXXX: You know liberty place?
BigMac10: like my own backyard
LongJohnXXX: Cybercafe at 17th and market,
Log on Sunday 7 pm
BigMac10: and then?
LongJohnXXX: then we'll see-come prepared
to party
```

"What does this mean?" Catherine asked. "Why does he want you to go to this cybercafé?"

"It's a test," Jason explained. "One, to see if I'm serious, and two, to make sure I'm not trying to trace him from my computer. I suspect he's been logging on somewhere other than his house just to protect his equipment."

"He'll probably be there—in the café," Sloan added. "Trying to get a look at Jason and see if he looks legit or like a cop."

Jason smiled, spreading his arms wide. "What do you think?"

"You don't look like a cop—more like a choir boy," Rebecca said seriously. Only the slight quirk at the corner of her mouth suggested she was teasing. "This looks good," she added as she leaned back in her chair. "I'll take copies of these and the CI reports to my captain this morning. We'll have the necessary support and paperwork if we get to the point where we can move on this guy."

"It's far from a lock," Sloan warned in an unusual show of reservation. "This guy is very smart. We're not talking about amateur hacks making videos in their basement. The fact that he wants Jason to contact him from a commercial machine means that he's aware that he can be traced. That shows a fair amount of sophistication."

Jason nodded in agreement. "He's been very careful so far not to spell anything out. Not once has he mentioned kids or ages or any details of what he's offering."

"We'll have to talk about putting someone inside that café with you, Jason," Rebecca said thoughtfully. "At the very least, we'll need to be able to follow you so we can set up outside his house once you get there." Glancing at Sloan, she asked, "How do we play this once Jason's inside? Is there any chance we can put an undercover cop in his place? I can probably find someone who is computer literate enough."

"I wouldn't recommend it," Catherine interjected. "Not at this point. Jason and this man have a relationship. There's a certain style of speech, a certain way of responding to verbal cues, that Jason has established with him. No one else is going to have that flow."

"I agree," Jason said. "Besides, we have no reason to think this guy's dangerous."

Rebecca didn't necessarily agree. If this was an operation being run by the local organized crime syndicate, then anyone involved was capable of violence. The hierarchy within organized crime dictated that everyone, at every level, protect the integrity of the organization at all cost. "What about once he's inside this guy's place? How will we get the signal to go in?"

"Ideally, we'll want to wait until they're receiving the live feed," Sloan explained. "I want as much information downloaded into that CPU as possible before we confiscate. Plus, it will preserve Jason's cover if you bring him in along *with* this guy, just in case we need to use him again where he'll be visible. Remember, this perp is just a link to the big guys—not the payoff."

Rebecca regarded Sloan sharply. The cybersleuth had been a cop, all right, because she still thought like one.

Again, Jason nodded, the same predatory glint in his eyes as Sloan's. "You can bet this guy is going to be wired for everything. Count on it. Anyone receiving this kind of feed will be recording and probably uploading to their own server. He'll have a sophisticated wireless system that Sloan should be able to hack into from outside the building. She ought to be able to see what we're seeing."

"This is loose," Rebecca insisted steadily. She knew she didn't have to tell Sloan, or Jason for that matter, what she meant. There were a dozen ways something could go wrong.

"It won't be by the time we get ready to roll," Sloan said just as steadily.

"We'll need to inform Clark," Rebecca added with a sigh.

"Let's tighten it up first," Sloan suggested.

"Right," Rebecca said brusquely, slapping her hand on the tabletop. "Okay then. I'll take it to my boss."

Catherine rode down with Rebecca in the elevator and walked her to her car. "I'm going to stay here for a few minutes, then I have a few patients to see."

Rebecca nodded, tossing the file folder with the transcripts onto the front seat. "Okay." She started to turn away, then as an afterthought added, "Uh, I'll be at the station house most of the day doing this paperwork and making phone calls. See you tonight?"

"Yes," Catherine replied, smiling at Rebecca's effort to explain her day. The detective tried, even when it was foreign to her, and it made Catherine feel more cherished than any other gift possibly could. "That would be just perfect."

❖

When Rebecca walked into the squad room later that morning, Watts was seated at his desk, his chair turned toward the door as if waiting for someone. The minute he saw her, he got to his feet and walked quickly to her.

"Man, am I glad you finally called me. If I had to chase down one more flasher at the mall, I was going to have to start taking drugs. Have you got something? Because I've been working the computers every chance I get, and I still can't spring any names. It seems like every time I get close, I run into another dead end. It's uncanny. In fact, if I didn't know better, I'd say someone had been erasing files."

Rebecca regarded him closely, because she had learned that Watts rarely said anything that he didn't mean. Only people who didn't know him very well thought he was all empty talk. "There are still some things you and I need to look into along those lines, but not right now. I've got something to take to the captain, and I need you assigned officially from here on out."

Watts beamed and then, looking around the squad room as if to make sure that no one had seen him, added, "Anything I need to know before we go in there?"

"No surprises," she assured him. "Just try for once to follow my lead, and keep quiet...if you can."

He just grinned as she turned and walked away. Five minutes later, they sat facing Captain John Henry across the expanse of his desk, waiting for him to finish a phone call. When he put down the receiver, he immediately said, "It's Saturday morning. What have you got that can't wait?"

Rebecca began unhurriedly to explain. "The task force you assigned me to has turned up a lead here in the city on a kiddie porn ring. We need to stake out a suspect who we believe is receiving live child pornography over the Internet, marketing it to people he meets in chat rooms, and possibly broadcasting it as well. We think that he may have an indirect connection to the people making the videos, and they're the ones who are using kids for sex."

Henry regarded Rebecca quietly for a moment. "This task force, it's being run by Justice, right?"

"Officially, yes. Most of the work has actually been done, though, by the private computer consultants which Justice brought on board. The feds have pretty much taken a backseat up until now. I'd like to keep it that way. Any arrests should be ours, and if there's a connection to anything local, I want to know about it first. You know what Justice is like—they'll snatch up a couple of these guys and offer them immunity to turn state's evidence on somebody higher up the food chain, and we'll never bring anybody to trial."

"The civilians—who are they? You trust them?"

"I do," Rebecca informed him. "It's an outfit by the name of Sloan Security. They're experienced and highly skilled. In fact, Sloan could probably get this new electronic investigation division that the commissioner has been harping about off the ground. I don't think we've got anybody in-house who can actually do it."

Henry merely grunted, then glanced at Watts. "And Detective Watts figures in this, how?"

"We're going to need manpower for stakeouts, plus I have information from a confidential informant that some of the younger prostitutes may be involved in making these films. I don't have any names yet, and I'd like Watts to work with Harris in Juvie to track down some of the younger girls and question them."

Rebecca took a deep breath. She knew she was asking for a lot and needed to make the case firm. "We really need to work through the juvenile unit because they've got all the records and most likely can find these kids a lot faster than we can. Plus, Harris is a good detective. I'm willing to bet she has relationships with some of these kids and can help us get the information we need."

"So, what's the rush to go to the DA? You know they're going to be running with a skeleton staff, and finding a judge to sign off on a warrant is always tricky on a weekend. Plus, it usually pisses off the judge to get paged during a golf game, and that doesn't help matters."

"It's possible that we're going to have contact tonight or tomorrow night with one of these Internet guys dealing with the live video broadcasts. We're going to bring him in for questioning, go through his place looking for verification of child porn, and confiscate all of his electronic equipment. I'd like to have a warrant to cover that."

"Which means we're gonna need the crime scene techs, too," Watts added. "That's a lot of overtime, and it will help to have the DA on board to back us up with that."

"Thank you, Detective," Henry said dryly. "I'm well aware how the fiscal distribution of my division works."

Rebecca squelched a smile, but she knew that Watts had made a good point. Administrators like Henry, even the ones who had once been good cops as he had been, were highly motivated by the bottom line, which was usually financial. The more paperwork he had to back up his allocation of funds and manpower, the better the final accounting of expenditures would be.

He pushed back in his chair and sighed. "Okay, put the paperwork on my desk and I'll make some calls."

"Thank you, sir," Rebecca said, preparing to rise.

"You stay, Frye."

Watts hesitated for a second, glancing quickly from Frye to Captain Henry, and then left the room when it became apparent that no one was going to say anything until he did.

After Watts had closed the door behind him, Henry said, "How actively are you involved in this investigation?"

"Just gathering the information as it comes in."

"I still haven't seen anything on you from Whitaker."

"I'll see that he gets it to you."

"See that you do, Sergeant."

"Absolutely, Captain."

Once outside, Rebecca glanced at her watch and decided that

Whitaker probably wasn't available on a Saturday afternoon. Monday would be in plenty of time.

❖

"What are you thinking about?"

"Hmm? Oh," Rebecca exclaimed with a wry smile. "I was thinking how nice it was not to be thinking about anything."

They were walking hand in hand through the narrow streets of Old City on First Saturday, a monthly event when artisans of all persuasions displayed their wares on the sidewalks for passersby to peruse, musicians played in alcoves and on street corners, and the many bistros and cafés served drinks or cappuccino at tiny tables lining the walkways. It had a certain Mardi Gras flavor with the historical charm that made Philadelphia famous. They'd had dinner at a small, intimate restaurant and then had taken to the streets along with scores of others to luxuriate in the still-warm September evening.

"You might have been thinking that five minutes ago," Catherine said with a faint laugh, "but now you have that look of complete and utter detachment that spells cop mode."

Rebecca blushed, an occurrence so rare for her that it was nearly reportable. It was true, she *had* been thinking about the case, and she had no idea that it showed so plainly. All she'd wanted, when the evening had begun, was to somehow show Catherine how crazy in love with her she was, and now, not three hours later, here she was obsessing about the job again. *Jesus.*

"I'm sorry," she said quickly, "I was just—"

"Don't apologize. I have to admit that I've been wondering what was happening with Sloan and Jason, too. This waiting for something to break can get very wearing."

"You were?" Rebecca was pleasantly surprised. It hadn't occurred to her that Catherine could become as absorbed in a case as she, although she certainly *should* have realized that after their experience with Raymond Blake. Then, Catherine had been as persistent as any obsessive detective in bringing him to justice. "You know, we're just around the corner…"

"I was just thinking the same thing." Catherine stopped walking and regarded Rebecca with an eager glint in her eyes, then glanced at her watch. "It *is* after 9:00 on a Saturday night. Think anyone is still around?"

"Can't hurt to see."

Ten minutes later, Jason's now-familiar voice rumbled from the speaker above the door. "Come on up. Might as well have a party."

When they had ascended the elevator and disembarked on the third floor, they discovered Jason and Mitchell hunched over the monitors and murmuring conspiratorially. Rebecca regarded Mitchell impassively when the young officer turned at the sound of footsteps. Mitchell gazed back, a faint hint of challenge in her eyes. It was the first time Rebecca had ever seen her any way but appropriately respectful.

"Mitchell," she said with a perfunctory nod.

"Sergeant," Mitchell said stiffly.

Turning to Jason, Rebecca asked, "Anything?"

"The usual. Saturday night seems to bring out all the perverts. LongJohn hasn't shown up, though." Dividing his attention between the screen and the newest arrivals, he crossed one elegantly trousered leg over the other and asked, "How's the warrant situation?"

"Captain Henry's working on it. I should have something by show time."

"Good," he replied distractedly. "I'm not entirely certain that our guy will contact me tonight, since we already have a specified meeting for tomorrow. On the other hand, I want to be here if he does log on."

Catherine nodded in agreement. "He may very well want to be sure that you're still interested, and I wouldn't be surprised if he sends a few more verbal tests in your direction—to verify your authenticity. He's got to be suspicious that you—BigMac, I should say—might be law enforcement. I would suggest you appear enthusiastic but don't probe too overtly for more information at this point."

"Gotcha." Jason reached to his right and thumbed through an inch-high pile of computer printouts. "These are from the last couple of days, and there might be some other possibles in here. We might as well take down as many of them as we can when the time comes." Glancing then at Catherine, he asked apologetically, "Have you got a few minutes?"

Catherine hesitated, looking at Rebecca, who shrugged infinitesimally. By unspoken agreement, they had thus far kept their personal involvement private from the others in the group, for no other reason than that they both preferred to separate their professional and personal lives whenever possible.

"Sure," Catherine said. "I'll just take them back to the conference room and go through them."

As Catherine lifted the pile and turned to leave, Rebecca looked pointedly at Mitchell and said, "Officer, let's take a walk."

"Yes, ma'am," Mitchell said and rose instantly.

The two of them headed toward the far end of the vast loft space, in the opposite direction from the conference room, finally stopping beneath an expanse of windows that afforded a view all the way into southern New Jersey. Between them and the industrial center of Camden ran the Delaware River, illuminated by the lights of oil barges and other ships.

"Captain Rodriguez called me this afternoon," Rebecca began without preamble, referring to one of the uniform commanders and Mitchell's superior. "He told me that all they need is your paperwork cleared up and you'll be reassigned to street patrol."

"I don't want to be reassigned," Mitchell said immediately. She was in jeans and a work shirt, but despite the casual garb, she stood at parade rest, as if she still wore her Army lieutenant's bars.

"Is there some problem in-house?"

Mitchell glanced at her sideways, surprised by the question. It was rare for detectives to take any interest in uniformed officers, and rarer still for them to question the workings of other divisions. Frye was essentially asking her if she had a problem with her superiors or her fellow officers, which, to her knowledge, was unheard of.

"No, ma'am. No problems."

"Okay." Rebecca expected no other answer. Mitchell was clearly a by-the-book cop, and if she was having problems, she'd keep it to herself like any good cop and try to handle it on her own. Rebecca didn't intend to push her on it, not now. They had other issues to get clear. "Then why don't you want to go back to your regular duty?"

Mitchell squared her shoulders even further and said directly, "Because I want to stay on this assignment. I like working with Sloan and McBride...and I like working with you."

Rebecca turned her head and regarded Mitchell steadily. "Every uniform wants the gold shield, at least any uniform worth anything at all."

"Yes, ma'am."

"You've got a long ways to go before that, Mitchell."

"Yes, ma'am."

"But you've made a good start." Rebecca slid her hands into her pockets and rocked slightly on the balls of her feet as she watched the night slide by on the river below. "I'll see what I can do about keeping you around."

"Thank you very much," Mitchell said, trying not to sound as relieved as she felt. Frye was not the type you kissed up to.

"One more thing."

Mitchell looked at her questioningly. "Yes, ma'am?"

"You want to tell me about you and Sandy Sullivan?"

Mitchell's heart began to race. Suddenly, for the first time since the day she had stood on the parade ground at West Point as a new cadet, she felt her knees shaking. In a clear voice that she willed not to waver, she answered, "No, ma'am, I do not."

"If you get between me and this investigation, or any other investigation, I'll have your badge."

"Understood."

"Good," Rebecca said. "We'll meet here tomorrow afternoon at 4:00 p.m. to review the details of the operation."

"Yes, ma'am," Mitchell said, hoping that the shock didn't show in her voice. Frye had just invited her along on a high-level tactical maneuver. This was more than a dream come true; it was a career-making opportunity. And that was after her asking about Sandy. How in *hell* had she known?

"And Mitchell," Rebecca added as if in afterthought, "don't ever turn your back on the night. You never know who might be watching."

❖

For the next hour and a half, Jason and Mitchell occupied themselves inputting data into one of their seemingly endless analysis programs. Rebecca sat with her feet up on the counter, leaning back in a swivel chair, watching a computer monitor and thinking about Mitchell. After the third time she'd seen her in the Tenderloin late at night and out of uniform, she'd decided to find out what the rookie was up to. It hadn't taken long. She'd followed them from the diner to

Sandy's apartment earlier in the week, and now she had to ask herself why she was allowing another cop to have anything to do with one of her confidential informants. Maybe it was the way she'd heard Sandy laugh at something Mitchell had murmured to her as they'd walked close together, their arms brushing with each step.

"Hey there, Detective," Catherine said softly as her hand passed across the back of Rebecca's neck.

"Hey." Rebecca grinned, grateful for Catherine's reappearance so that she didn't have to analyze precisely *what* she'd felt when she'd seen the two young women together. "How's it going?"

"I've pulled three that I think have promise. Officer Mitchell," Catherine said, "I've circled the identifiers that I'd like you to cross-reference."

"I'll get on it right away."

"Tomorrow will surely be soon enough," Catherine said with a smile. Glancing at her watch, she added, "It's nearly 11:30. I don't know about the rest of you, but I need a break. Where's Sloan, by the way? She seems to be the only one of us with any common sense."

Jason laughed. "Don't you believe it. She went to the airport to pick up Michael. If it hadn't been for that, you can bet she'd be right here."

"Ah," Catherine said, still somewhat surprised. She would have thought Sloan was a lesbian, but perhaps that was just because she found her attractive. Smiling inwardly, she reminded herself that appearances were most often deceiving. "Well then, I'll say good night."

"I'll walk you out," Rebecca said, getting to her feet. "Jason—call me if anything comes up. Mitchell—go home."

Both of them nodded, but they were already engrossed in some bit of electronic information, their heads bent close together over a printout. Neither of them said good night.

Chapter Eighteen

Michael Lassiter glanced at her passenger. "I could have taken the train from the airport, you know."

Sloan reclined in the passenger seat, her left hand resting loosely in Michael's right, their fingers intertwined. Smiling, she replied without opening her eyes. "I know that. I just wanted to be there when you came home."

"I'm glad you were," Michael said softly, her voice thick with a panoply of emotions—wonder, gratitude, desire. In all the years of her marriage to Nicholas, she had never felt this kind of welcome or the peaceful sense of well-being that came from knowing precisely where she belonged in the universe. "I love you."

"Good thing," Sloan said drowsily. "Because I'm mad about you."

Michael had rarely seen Sloan exhausted, but she had known when she'd left for Boston that it was unlikely that her lover would sleep at all in her absence. From everything she had gathered, things were moving so quickly on the new investigation that even had she been in town, Sloan would probably have been working nearly twenty-four hours a day. It was only her quiet insistence that her lover get an occasional hour or two of sleep that ever brought Sloan upstairs during this kind of intensive assignment.

As Michael turned off the four-lane highway that ran along the river onto the maze of one-way streets in Old City, she stated emphatically, "When we get home, you're going straight to bed."

"Promise?" Sloan rejoined, turning her head on the headrest and finally opening her eyes. With a grin, life clearly returning to her features, she added, "I think you're exactly what I need to jump-start my engine."

"Well, you can just motor down, hotrod," Michael said with a laugh. "Maybe in the morning I'll take you for a ride."

"I'll be sure to pencil you in on my schedule, then."

Michael was about to launch a comeback as she turned onto their block. Slowing, peering at the unexpected obstacle in her path, she muttered in frustration, "For God's sake, who would leave that right in front of the driveway?"

Had Sloan been less tired, perhaps she would have been faster to make a connection. As Michael downshifted into park and opened the driver's door to get out, Sloan glanced idly out her window toward their building. A shopping cart, turned over on its side, lay on the sidewalk in front of the wide double doors leading into their garage. *Odd*, she thought, as she dimly registered the sound of an engine starting nearby. Suddenly, some long-ingrained distrust pulsed through her brain. She turned just as Michael stepped from the car.

"Michael, no—"

Her words were lost in the sound of squealing tires, a muffled scream, and the rending of metal as the driver's door of the Porsche was torn off and catapulted down the street. The Porsche then caromed sideways half onto the sidewalk from the force of the impact. By the time Sloan extricated herself from the car, which had been pushed into a parked minivan, the vehicle that had struck her lover was gone.

Ten feet away, Michael lay motionless in the road, a dark pool spreading on the pavement beneath her head.

❖

"My God, did you hear that?" Catherine exclaimed as she and Rebecca stepped from the elevator.

"Sounds like a hell of a fender bender," Rebecca muttered, instantly alert. "And it was awfully close."

Suddenly, the sounds of frantic shouting were audible from just outside, and Rebecca hurriedly pushed through the door to the street. Directly in front of her at the foot of the steps, Sloan's Porsche was canted onto the sidewalk with the engine still running. She glanced inside through a spiderweb of shattered safety glass. Empty. From the far side, she could hear strangled cries. "Catherine, stay here for a minute."

"Rebecca, someone's hurt. I'm a doctor," Catherine said urgently from just behind her. "I need to attend to the victims."

"I know that," Rebecca snapped, not used to having her authority questioned at a scene. "But you'll have to wait. I don't know what happened here. It might not have been an accident, and I don't want another victim." *Especially not you.*

There was no time for discussion, and the detective didn't wait for a reply. Instead, she climbed over the rear bumper of the parked minivan—which now housed a portion of the front of Sloan's abandoned vehicle—her cell phone in one hand and her weapon in the other. Even as she assessed the activity in the street, visually searching for possible assailants, she called for an ambulance and backup in clipped, commanding tones.

From the corner of her eye, she checked the figures in the street. Sloan, blood streaking her face and arms, was on her knees above the supine body of an unconscious blond woman Rebecca did not recognize. She couldn't tell how badly either was injured, and she couldn't allow her concern to divert her mind from more important tasks—ensuring that there were no further threats remaining in the immediate area and preserving any evidence of the crime.

Catherine clambered over the wreck after her, and Rebecca cursed. "Keep down at least," the detective barked, blocking the three women from the street as best she could with her body while she scoured the windows in the buildings on both sides of them, searching for any kind of movement behind the many darkened windows. She saw nothing suspicious, but it was impossible for her to tell if any of the people in the densely packed buildings might represent a danger. Curious onlookers were approaching from down the block, but fortunately there were no vehicles to be diverted yet. She glanced down once more and saw a widening pool of blood beneath the blond's head.

"Catherine, keep them right there until backup arrives."

"Don't worry," Catherine said grimly after one quick look. "No one is moving her without a backboard."

Mitchell and Jason burst from the building. "Oh God," Jason gasped, stopping in his tracks and staring in horror.

Rebecca, turning at the sound, ordered, "Mitchell, secure the scene.

Backup is on the way. I'll call for the crime scene unit and find out where the fuck the ambulances are. This was a hit-and-run at least."

"Right," Mitchell responded crisply, her face tight with shock but her voice strong as she clipped her badge to the waistband of her jeans. After glancing once at the badly smashed car, she asked in a quiet voice only Rebecca could hear, "Intentional?"

"We have to assume so, until proven otherwise," Rebecca affirmed, noting with approval Mitchell's quick, intelligent assessment. "Keep your eyes open. Just because this was a vehicle hit doesn't mean there won't be someone in the crowd or on a rooftop with a gun. I'll call Watts down to canvass with you."

"I'm on it." Mitchell headed off in the direction of a rapidly approaching group of civilians.

"Jason," Rebecca added brusquely, "you get back inside."

Unsurprisingly, he ignored her and made his way to Sloan.

"Fuck," Rebecca muttered in surrender and phoned Watts.

Sloan, still on her knees, was curled protectively over Michael's motionless form. She gripped her lover's limp hand, a world of anguish on her face. "Please, please...call an ambulance..." she implored to no one in particular, her eyes fixed on Michael's pale face. "Oh, Jesus, please...Michael, baby..."

"Sloan," Catherine said gently, carefully placing her hand on the dark-haired woman's shoulder. "I need to be where you are so I can evaluate her." The injured woman lay nearly under a parked car and Catherine couldn't get room to assess her status. *So this is Michael.*

"No." The sound was choked, agonized. Sloan looked up into Catherine's face, eyes unfocused, and insisted desperately, "No. I'm not leaving her."

"No, of course you're not," Catherine assured quietly. "Just let me close enough to help her."

Sloan seemed not to have heard, but leaned closer to the unconscious woman, whispering in a choked voice, "Baby, it's me. It's okay. It's going to be okay. Please, baby...ohgodgod..."

Jason knelt next to his friend. "Sloan—let Catherine help Michael. Just move back a little bit. You don't have to leave her."

Sloan looked at him as if she didn't recognize him; then she blinked, and her eyes seemed to clear for an instant. "It was supposed to have been me, Jason. It's my car. She was driving..."

"It's okay. We'll worry about it later." His voice trembled on the words.

Mutely, Sloan shifted a fraction, tenaciously gripping Michael's right hand. Catherine gently displaced her further until she could lean down and place her fingers on the injured woman's neck, searching for a pulse.

Automatically, as often happened when examining a patient no matter whether physically or psychologically, Catherine observed many things at once, assimilating impressions almost unconsciously. While her fingers registered the faint, thready beat of blood through the artery she probed, her mind noted how achingly beautiful the injured woman was. The perfect unmarred features, fit for an artist's canvas and incongruously free of any sign of pain, as if she were only peacefully slumbering. The left hand lying gently between her breasts, a heavy platinum band glinting in the halo of light from the streetlights overhead. The lover bending to her, devotion etched in every line of her hauntingly handsome face. Only the maroon circle of blood, rapidly darkening to black, cast a nightmare pall over the ethereal tableau.

Catherine wrenched her gaze from Michael's face. Quietly, she murmured to Sloan, whose shallow, tortured breathing spoke of unbearable grief. "Listen to me. She's alive. That's all that matters. We'll have her in the hospital in a few minutes where she can be taken care of. Do you hear me? Sloan?"

Sloan coughed and tried to catch her breath. She couldn't think; she couldn't feel. She wasn't even certain her heart was beating. All she could sense was terror. "Please…please don't let her die." She looked at Catherine, her eyes fathomless pools of anguish. In a voice beyond torment, she repeated, "Please…I can't…without her…I can't…"

Catherine couldn't offer the one promise Sloan begged for, so she said nothing. She placed the fingers of one hand beneath Michael's chin, lifted enough to keep her airway open, and carefully slipped a folded handkerchief, which Jason had supplied, behind her head to staunch the flow of blood from a large open wound. Rebecca paced back and forth in front of them, one eye on the street, the other on them, snapping orders into her cell phone. Mitchell, amazingly, had found crime scene tape somewhere and was cordoning off the street while instructing gawkers to stay back.

In the distance, sirens approached.

❖

An hour later, Rebecca walked into the brightly lit trauma unit waiting room where an anxious group had gathered. Catherine rose to meet her, her green eyes dark with concern.

"Any word?" Rebecca asked in a low voice, running one hand down Catherine's arm in lieu of a kiss.

Catherine shook her head slightly, but some of the tension left her chest at the sight of her lover. The waiting room, the waiting, Sloan's torment—all of it brought back too many images still too fresh. Not long ago, it had been Rebecca. Rebecca lying so still, so pale, bleeding…so much bloo—

"Hey," Rebecca said softly, alarmed by the faint trembling she felt beneath her fingertips. "You okay?"

"Yes," Catherine said hoarsely, forcing the memories back behind barriers still too fragile to contain them. "No word yet. I've been doing what I can to get updates, but because it's Saturday night, it's a madhouse in there. All I know is that she's still being evaluated."

Rebecca nodded, looking past Catherine to the other occupants of the cramped windowless space that might have been any of a dozen such hospital rooms she'd waited in during the course of her career. She concentrated on deflecting the pain that filled the air, needing to keep her distance so she could work. "Who's the redhead?" she asked, remarking on the woman in the blue print shirt and chinos sitting with one arm wrapped protectively around Sloan's waist.

"Sarah Martin," Catherine replied, following her gaze. "Jason's partner…and Sloan's best friend, apparently."

"Huh," Rebecca remarked with interest. *Now I'll bet that's a story.*

"What's happening back at Sloan's?" Catherine asked, needing to think about something, anything, other than this nightmare.

"I finally got Watts out of bed, and he and Mitchell are running the scene. They're canvassing the neighborhood, interviewing anyone who was around. Or anyone who will *admit* to being around. There's a tavern on the corner, and they'll need to talk to everyone they can chase down who was there. That'll most likely take all night and a good part of tomorrow. Flanagan's team showed up; they're getting the crime scene photos, analyzing the impact patterns, looking for identifying tire treads. The usual. Flanagan's fast, but it will still be at least a day or so before she has anything concrete. This kind of crime leaves a ton of physical evidence to sort through."

Neither of them laughed at the irony of that statement.

"Was it intentional?" Catherine asked quietly, because she had to know. She had to know how close death had come this time.

Rebecca hesitated, then exhaled raggedly. "Looks like it, yeah. Someone was expecting Sloan to come back and had set it up so she'd have to get out of the car. Obviously, it didn't go down the way they planned, because Michael was driving."

"Why Sloan?" Catherine asked carefully, fighting to ignore the churning in her stomach. "Why not...you?"

"What?" Rebecca's eyes shot to Catherine's, instantly concerned. "It wasn't me. It's not *going* to be me."

They both knew there was no way to guarantee that, but it wasn't the time to discuss something they couldn't change.

"Still, why Sloan?"

"More importantly," Rebecca said darkly, "why *now*?" Although she hated to do it, she needed to find out. "I have to interview her."

"Oh, Rebecca," Catherine murmured. "She's so vulnerable right now. Can't it wait?"

"This was attempted murder." Rebecca heard the censure in her lover's tone, and it hurt, but nothing showed in her face. "No, it can't wait."

Catherine watched her walk away, wishing she could take back the words. She of all people should know what it cost Rebecca to do the job she did. If the image of Sloan's agony hadn't been so fresh in her memory, she would have remembered that.

❖

Rebecca set a cup of weak vending-room coffee in front of Sloan, then walked around the small table and sat down across from her. They were alone in an unadorned, harshly lit consulting room down the hall from the trauma waiting area. "How you doing?"

The other woman shuddered as if with a sudden chill, then met Rebecca's gaze with eyes that were slightly dazed. "If I could just see her..."

"Catherine's working on that right now. She'll come and get us if there's any word."

"I can't believe this is happening." Sloan passed a hand over her face. "One minute we were just talking, laughing about making lo—" Her voice caught. "Oh, Christ…I don't know what I'm going to do."

"Sloan," Rebecca said gently, "I need your help."

Violet eyes gone nearly black with pain flicked to hers, caught, then held on. "I'm so fucking…scared, you know?"

"Yeah…I know." She wanted to touch her, because she could feel the agony radiate from her skin, but sympathy wasn't going to help find who had done this. "Michael needs your help, too."

"No one knew I was going to the airport," Sloan said lifelessly, as if anticipating Rebecca's questions. "Well, Jason knew, of course. But he was the only one."

Rebecca said nothing, preferring to let Sloan tell it in her own way. The security consultant wasn't a suspect to be interrogated, but a witness, and a traumatized one at that. Her recollection of the event would be distorted by grief and fear and the mind's natural desire to block out the things too terrible to contemplate, but fortunately, she was also a trained investigator. Instinctively, she would know what they needed to do and the things that Rebecca needed to know.

"Obviously," Sloan continued in a weary voice, "someone set it up so I'd have to get out of the car to move the cart, and they were waiting for me. I can't tell you exactly what happened next, because I didn't *see* anything. It was over in a few seconds, and for most of that time, the Porsche was moving from the impact. I'd already unbelted, and I was getting tossed around pretty good." As she spoke, she unconsciously twisted the band on her ring finger, something Rebecca had never seen her do before. Rivulets of sweat ran down her face, despite the fact that the room was cool.

"What about after you got out of the car?" Rebecca asked quietly. "Did you see anything then?"

Again, Sloan shivered. "All I was thinking about was Michael. By the time I got out of the car and into the street, all I could *see* was Michael…she was lying on the pavement, and she wasn't moving…" Her voice trailed off, and she closed her eyes. "Sorry," she whispered.

Rebecca waited. She knew very well that Sloan was reliving those few terrifying seconds, seeing and feeling it all over again. After a minute, as kindly as she could, the detective probed, "Did you see the taillights of the vehicle? The license plate?"

"No."

"Anyone on the street—someone who might have been watching the building?"

"No," Sloan repeated hoarsely, opening her eyes and bracing her forearms on the table, staring at the speckled gray surface, trying not to see the spreading pool of Michael's blood. "Nothing. No one."

"Okay." Rebecca curled her fingers around the rigid arm and squeezed firmly. "Thanks."

For now, that would have to be enough. Tomorrow, she would ask Sloan again. Right now, the woman was clearly numb with shock and fear. When the horror had receded just a bit, she might remember more.

"It was supposed to have been me," Sloan said dully. *It should have been me. I wish to God it had been. Oh, baby, I'm so sorry...*

"That's my read on it, too," Rebecca said, knowing that only the truth would help ease Sloan's guilt. "The timing is too damned coincidental for this to be anything else. Who knows about the operation tomorrow night besides you and Jason?"

"No one." Sloan's face hardened, and anger began to dispel the mind-numbing dread. "Michael...Michael left town before the whole thing came down, and I didn't tell her when I spoke to her on the phone." *I didn't want her to come home early. Didn't want her to worry.*

"What about Jason?"

Sloan shook her head. "Jason may have told Sarah; you can ask him. But Sarah's ex–State Department. She'd never say anything to anyone."

"I'll double-check with him just to be sure," Rebecca commented, but she was inclined to agree that the leak hadn't come from the three of them.

Suddenly, Sloan stiffened. "Clark. Clark called this morning...uh, Saturday—yesterday morning—and I told him we had something. That we expected an operation to go off before the end of the weekend."

Rebecca was silent, considering Sloan's information. Clearly, their plans had been revealed to someone who felt that Sloan, as the person most likely to uncover someone via the computer traces, was the biggest threat. The choices for the source of the leak were limited.

Besides Sloan and Jason, Mitchell and Catherine knew of the upcoming meet. Neither of them had the right kind of contacts, even if they *had* slipped and mentioned the plans, which she doubted.

She herself had told Captain Henry when she'd briefed him about the warrant. Recalling Trish Mark's observation that after Captain Henry and the chief of detectives had met with her boss, the investigation into Jeff Cruz's and Jimmy Hogan's murders had been dropped, Rebecca considered that it might have been him. It was hard for her to believe that John Henry was on the payroll of the organized crime syndicate— or dirty in any way, for that matter, but it wasn't beyond the realm of possibility.

Then there was Avery Clark, who had come out of nowhere and put together an elite but highly unusual team. Their small group resembled the black-ops units that worked undercover, often employing less than sanctioned avenues of investigation—just like Sloan had been doing, and as Clark must have known she would. And just as with those covert units, if something went wrong, the government would be largely unaccountable. Clark remained a cipher, as did his true motives, and that made him a very good suspect.

"I'll get to the bottom of this, Sloan. You have my word," Rebecca said stonily. "For now, we have to assume that no one is above suspicion."

CHAPTER NINETEEN

A li Torveau slid the CAT scan onto the view box and pointed. "Linear nondisplaced skull fracture, right here in the occipital area. Big scalp laceration over it—lot of blood loss from that. Brain looks okay, although I'm sure there's a significant contusion."

Catherine studied the scan, nodding. "What about systemic injuries?"

"In addition to the head injury? Bilateral pulmonary effusions, fractured left renal pelvis, and a hemarthrosis of the left knee. Basically, she got bounced around big time, but most of the major organ systems were spared long-term damage."

"What about the kidney injury? Is it going to require surgery?"

"Probably not," the trauma surgeon said. "We'll repeat the CAT scan in six hours and follow her hemoglobins, but the perirenal space is so tight, hemorrhage usually stops on its own. Fortunately, her pulmonary status is stable right now, too, and I just took out the endotracheal tube. There's always a possibility that she could develop acute respiratory distress syndrome, but we'll cross that road when we come to it."

"What about the intracranial injury?" Catherine inquired. "Any idea what to expect in terms of her regaining consciousness?"

"She's likely to have increased brain edema over the next few hours—maybe days." Again, Torveau shrugged. "She'll wake up when her neurons recover from being shaken all to hell. I can ask neurology to come and see her, but you know damn well they're going to say they can't tell us anything."

Catherine smiled. She was well aware that surgeons had little regard for medical specialists who generally were unable to give a hard and fast prognosis. "If you're confident that there's no surgical problem, I'm sure her family will be, too. Can I see her for a minute before I talk to her partner? I just want to be able to prepare her before she sees Michael."

"Sure," Torveau said. "She's in trauma bay one. Bring her partner in whenever you want. I've got to go; there's a spleen that wants to be liberated waiting for me upstairs in the OR. The family can catch me later if they have questions."

"Go ahead, and thanks for letting me take up your time."

"No problem." And then she pushed through the double doors and was gone.

Catherine walked through the treatment area to one of the cubicles where stabilized patients awaited transfer to regular hospital rooms. Nodding to a nurse who was busy charting the events of the resuscitation, Catherine approached the bed where Michael lay. On the far side of the small room, a rack of monitors gave continuous readouts of her status while IV poles hung with resuscitation fluids stood silent sentinel.

"Michael," Catherine said softly, bending down close to her. It was impossible to tell what an unconscious person heard or stored in their memory to be recalled weeks, months, or even years later. She always assumed they were listening, and she always spoke to them as if they would remember. "My name is Catherine Rawlings. I'm a friend of Sloan's."

To her surprise, Michael's eyelids fluttered and her left hand twitched. Reaching for her hand, Catherine cradled the slender fingers in hers. "Michael?"

Michael opened her eyes, her pupils wide and unfocused. "Slo… an?"

"She's outside. She's just fine."

Catherine thought she saw a flicker of a smile before the other woman drifted away again. "And she'll be much, much better now," she whispered, gently releasing Michael's hand.

❖

Rebecca and Sloan walked out of the consultation room, and the first person they saw was Avery Clark. Rebecca wasn't even aware of Sloan moving, but in the next instant, the security expert had the federal agent up against the wall with her hands fisted in the folds of his jacket.

"It's about time you told us what the fuck is going on," Sloan snarled, inches from his face. "Justice is famous for keeping secrets, and one of your secrets almost got my lover killed." She punctuated each word with a shove that bounced him against the wall.

For an instant, Clark looked stunned, and then Rebecca saw his hand move under his jacket in the direction of his weapon. In all likelihood, it was an automatic response to Sloan's unexpected attack, but Rebecca wasn't about to let weapons come out.

"Sloan," she barked, "let him go."

Sloan appeared not to hear as she pushed Clark's body hard against the wall again. Rebecca moved to separate them, grasping Sloan's left shoulder with her right hand and wedging herself between them.

"Back off, Sloan."

This time, Sloan might have heard, because she appeared to loosen her grip on Clark's jacket. Apparently, that had been the opening Clark was waiting for, because he brought both arms forcefully up between Sloan's, breaking her grip and shoving her back at the same time. The force of his blow deflected off Sloan's arms as she let go, and his swinging fists caught Rebecca in the chest with the force of a sledgehammer. Rebecca rocked back on her heels, pain exploding in her chest.

By that time, they had drawn a crowd. Jason jumped between Clark and Sloan, and the two men began shouting. Sarah grasped Sloan's side, gently but firmly pulling her away. Rebecca sagged against the wall, one hand pressed to her chest, struggling to get her breath and trying to see through a red-hot wave of pain.

"For God's sake!" Catherine exclaimed, having seen the last of the altercation as she hurried down the hall toward them. "Have you *all* lost your minds? Sarah, take Sloan back to the waiting room. I'll be there in a minute."

She was nearly running by the time she reached Rebecca, her heart in her throat. Agony was carved into every line of the detective's body, and for one terrifying second, Catherine flashed back to Rebecca as she had seen her the night in Sandy's apartment—gasping for breath, one lung down, on the brink of full arrest. *Oh no, not again.*

"Rebecca!"

Rebecca forced herself to focus and took a slow, shallow breath. "I'm okay," she managed, reading the panic in Catherine's face. After taking another shaky breath, she repeated, "I'm okay. He just... surprised...me, that's all."

"You need to sit down," Catherine said in a voice that she hoped sounded calmer than she felt.

"Okay, right. Just...give me a minute," Rebecca said, uncertain that she could actually make it across the room. Still sagged against the wall, she looked around, putting together the events of the last few furious minutes. "Where's Sloan?"

"Sarah has her. Rebecca, please," Catherine said, slipping her arm around Rebecca's waist. "Come on, darling."

"What about Clark?" Rebecca said through gritted teeth. *Christ, my chest hurts.*

"With Jason, I think." Catherine gave up trying to keep her lover quiet and simply guided her slowly across the room to the row of orange plastic molded seats. "Sit. I mean it."

Rebecca sank down willingly and leaned her head back against the institutional tan wall. "What a fuck-up."

"I'll be right back," Catherine murmured. Returning a second later with a stethoscope borrowed from one of the trauma nurses, she leaned down, unbuttoned Rebecca's shirt, and slipped the bell under the material. "Breathe."

Rebecca took a breath, and then another. It hurt, but she was getting air. "I'm...okay."

"Shh," Catherine admonished, moving the stethoscope over both sides of Rebecca's chest. Finally satisfied, she sat beside her and slipped the instrument from around her neck. "You sound okay. We should probably get a chest x-ray just to be sure."

For a moment, Rebecca looked as if she might protest, then she nodded. "Can it wait until I get everybody settled down here?"

Catherine didn't want to negotiate where Rebecca's well-being was concerned, but she recognized the attempt at compromise. Inwardly, she was still trembling, but Rebecca was trying to meet her halfway, and she needed to try, also. "All right, that's a deal. But not more than an hour."

"Good enough," Rebecca said, bracing one hand on the back of the plastic seat and getting just a bit shakily to her feet. "I'll find you before then, and we can get the x-ray."

"Promise?"

Gently, Rebecca brushed the wisps of hair back from Catherine's temple. There had been too much fear for one evening. For one lifetime. And she couldn't swear it wouldn't happen again. But this she could do.

"Yes. I promise."

❖

Down the hall, Sloan approached the narrow steel stretcher with her stomach roiling. Michael looked so frail attached by a myriad of lines and wires and tubes to machines that metered out her life in an impersonal series of beeps and flashing readouts. Swallowing hard against the rise of acid in her throat, Sloan took the slender hand that rested motionless on the white sheets between both of hers.

Leaning down, she whispered, "Hey, baby…it's me." She kissed the unconscious woman's forehead. "Catherine says you'll be okay."

Michael's chest rose and fell steadily, but she gave no sign of recognition. Sloan's head grew light, and for an instant, panic surged through her. *Oh God, Michael, you have to be okay. I'm not gonna make it if you aren't. I need you, baby. Please…*

In the midst of her terror, Catherine's words came back to her.

She's seriously injured, but nothing that won't heal. She's young and strong, and she has everything to live for. She has you, Sloan. Just be there for her. That's all she needs.

Sloan took a long slow breath. "I love you. Everything is gong to be okay. You're going to be just fine."

As she lifted Michael's hand to her lips, she closed her eyes and prayed.

❖

An hour later, Sloan, Rebecca, and Avery Clark gathered in yet another unmemorable conference room at University Hospital. They had to meet there, because Sloan wouldn't leave the building until Michael's repeat CAT scans were done and Torveau decided if surgery was needed on her damaged kidney. Rebecca watched warily as Clark and Sloan eyed each other across the ten-foot space, ready to dive between them yet again if the tension in the air became physical.

"If I've got some reason to apologize," Sloan said flatly, watching Clark's face, "I will. But I'm not convinced that I do. You find out in the morning that I'm close to nailing someone and that evening a car tries to run me down. That seems just a little too coincidental."

Clark looked from Sloan to Rebecca, judging the battle lines and allegiances. Shrugging as if to acknowledge that he was outnumbered, he then sat down and gestured with a hand for them to do the same. "Look," he began resignedly, "I can tell you what I know, but I don't have the answers you're looking for."

"*Any* answers would be a start," Rebecca interjected sharply. "There are holes in this investigation big enough to drive a truck through. What's the real purpose behind what you've got us doing?"

"This *is* a legitimate attempt to expose the child pornography ring that we believe is operating in this area," he insisted. "We don't know yet how deep or how far this kind of Internet crime extends, but it's much broader and already more technologically sophisticated than we ever dreamed. And the dispersion of the actual pornography is just one small piece of it. It ties closely to child prostitution, and *that* ties strongly to organized crime. Because of that, it's a priority with any number of federal agencies as well as your own department. We're the advance team, in a sense."

The two women waited in silence. There was more; there was always more.

"The situation in this city is slightly more complicated." He hesitated, glanced at Rebecca, then shrugged. "We've suspected for a long time that organized crime had compromised local law enforcement at the highest levels. It's a legacy that goes back forty years or more. It's less overt now, but it's still there."

"Every city has that kind of corruption to some extent," Rebecca remarked impatiently. "It's a fact of life. What's that got to do with us?"

Clark shook his head angrily. "Every time we get close to the syndicate in this region, our eyewitnesses disappear, our evidence gets lost, or some jurisdictional *oversight* results in the case being thrown out before we ever get to court."

"So you've got a leak," Sloan said through gritted teeth, frustrated with the typical circumspect vagaries she thought had been left behind when she'd left Justice. "Or else *you're* the problem."

"It's not our leak." Clark sagged slightly, looking suddenly drained. "We were close to getting names a few months ago. We had a good pipeline to inside information—an undercover agent who was putting together the links we needed to go right to the top." His expression darkened. "And then someone took him out."

"Someone was cleaning house," Rebecca said grimly. "We lost cops then, too. My partner was one of them."

"That's something we have in common, Detective," Clark said with a frustrated sigh. "Jimmy Hogan was one of mine."

"What?" Rebecca exclaimed sharply, body tensing. "Hogan was an undercover narcotics agent for the Philadelphia PD."

"He was also a United States Justice Department investigator."

For a moment, the room was silent, and then Rebecca said quietly, "So Hogan was doing double duty, and he was going to help you make a federal case against the Zamora crime family. That was his ultimate agenda, and the narcotics angle was just a cover—right?"

"I'm not at liberty to say."

"Screw that! Did you know he was going to give us the intel on the kiddie prostitution ring?"

"It was important for his cover that he function as a cop as well, and it seemed fair to feed you some information on that. We were only interested in the guys at the top."

"But someone found out about it," Rebecca said. "And took him down. My partner just happened to be with him."

"That's how we read it," Clark acknowledged unhappily. "When we set up this task force, I wanted to keep it small so that something like what happened to Jimmy wouldn't happen again. The fewer people who know what we're doing, the safer I figured we'd be."

"Any ideas about the identity of the leak?" Sloan asked grimly, her attention on Rebecca now. Apparently Clark had convinced her of his veracity.

"Theories, nothing more at this point," the detective replied with a shrug. First and foremost, she was a cop. She didn't indict other cops without evidence, and she had none. Avery Clark might be telling the truth; in fact, she thought that he probably was. But that didn't mean he was telling *all* of the truth, and it didn't mean he could be trusted. Until she had something concrete, and maybe not even then, she didn't intend to share what she knew. Or even what she suspected.

"It looks like we'll need to shelve tonight's operation," Clark said.

Sloan's head snapped around to him. "Why?"

"We're compromised," he pointed out. "Someone clearly felt threatened—and they know your name."

"I don't think that means the operation is blown," Rebecca disagreed. "If the leak is inside the department somewhere, they don't know the details of the meet or who it's with, just the general plan. They only know we're getting close to *someone*—a connection which might eventually lead right up the ladder to the child procurers and video distributors…and finally to the money men. It makes sense that they'd go after the individual who was the greatest threat to exposing that connection, and right now that person is Sloan."

"I say we keep going," Sloan said, a cold hard rage filling her chest. "It's my lover they put in the hospital. I want them."

"I agree," Rebecca added. "If we don't move now, eventually they'll get word to all their people to lay low, including these Internet entry men. We'll never have a better shot at it than tonight."

"They may be waiting for you," Clark pointed out. "They missed Sloan. They might try again at the meet. With McBride inside, you'll have a potential hostage situation."

Rebecca's face was unreadable. "That was always a possibility. We'll be prepared for that."

"You're running the ground show, Frye. It's your call."

"Then I say we go."

"I want my people on board for the arrest," Clark stated.

"They can ride backup," Rebecca countered flatly. "We have to go in fast to protect Jason and secure the computers before this guy has a chance to destroy the evidence. That means a small strike force. I'll run it with my people." *People I can trust at my back.*

"You should bring in the TAC squad and a hostage negotiator. Just in case it goes bad."

"No," Rebecca objected. "You know those guys would bring in two dozen men and a half dozen armored vans, and we'd lose the element of surprise. We go small and quiet."

He looked for a moment like he would argue; then, seeming to relent, he replied, "At least bring your team shrink. You'll have a negotiator present."

Rebecca's jaw clenched. "No way."

Sloan regarded her steadily, suspecting that she knew the reason for Frye's resistance. When Catherine Rawlings was in the room, something softened in the detective's hard eyes. She said quietly, "Jason could be at risk."

Rebecca hesitated a heartbeat, then blew out a breath. "Okay. But she rides backup with you, Clark. And she stays *in* the vehicle."

"Fine," he said, rising. "I'll see you tonight then."

"We'll brief at 4:30 at Sloan's," Rebecca said tightly as he made for the door. When he'd closed it behind him, she turned to Sloan. "How's Michael?"

"In and out. She..." Sloan faltered, her voice breaking. "Ah, fuck..." After a minute, she continued, "She opens her eyes for a second every now and then, but she doesn't seem to recognize me."

"That's to be expected at this point, I guess." She couldn't think of a single thing to say that would help. Had it been Catherine...even contemplating that made her stomach roll with dread. "Jesus, I'm sorry, Sloan."

Sloan looked away, swallowed once, then found her voice. "Thanks."

"Is there anyone you can call in to help Jason tonight? I'll need Mitchell for the strike force, and I don't know if she's computer savvy enough to handle your job anyhow."

"I'll be there," Sloan said sharply.

"Look, Sloan," Rebecca said evenly. "Things have changed. This operation is hot now, and we don't know what we're walking into tonight. You're in no shape—"

"I'm okay."

"Like hell you are. You haven't even been to bed for almost two days."

"They tried to kill me. They nearly killed Michael instead," Sloan seethed. "I'm *owed,* Frye."

"I need to be able to count on you. You've got..." She glanced at her watch. It was 3:50 a.m. Sunday morning. "You've got fifteen hours until this goes down. If you don't sleep most of it, you'll be a danger to all of us."

Sloan rubbed her face with both hands and sighed. "I'll sleep here. You have my word."

"I need you sharp tonight, Sloan."

"I know what I need to do. I'll do it."

Rebecca took a chance and took her at her word.

"I just reviewed your chest x-ray with the radiology resident. It's normal." Relief clearly evident in her voice, Catherine informed Rebecca of the good news as she emerged from the conference room.

"Good," Rebecca replied. "How do *you* feel? You look beat."

"I feel about how I look," Catherine said with a wry smile. "How's Sloan?"

"Ragged, but calmed down a bit."

Catherine sensed an uneasiness in Rebecca's voice. "What is it?"

"Clark thinks it would be a good idea if you came along on the operation tonight. A precautionary thing." Just saying the words made her chest tighten with anxiety.

"What do you think?" Catherine asked carefully.

"I think he's right, and it's exactly what I did *not* want to have happen," Rebecca said sharply. A glimpse of Blake, his gun to Catherine's head, flashed through her mind. "God *damn* it."

"It will be fine, Rebecca. It's nothing like the last time." When her lover merely nodded curtly, she commented gently, "We're both tired. Let's talk about it later." Again Rebecca nodded silently, and Catherine asked, "What are you going to do now?"

"Drive back to Old City and check in with Watts and Mitchell." As if anticipating Catherine's next words, Rebecca added quietly, "Just for a few minutes. Then I'm sending Mitchell home and leaving the follow-up to Watts for the time being. I'll meet you at your place in less than an hour."

"All right." Catherine understood that Rebecca couldn't rest until she had taken care of these last details. She understood it, and she tried hard to accept it. It wasn't easy, seeing the deep shadows under her lover's eyes and remembering the pain on her face just hours before. Then again, she doubted that any of them looked fit for public presentation at the moment. "I'm going to leave in just a few minutes, too. I just want to check on Michael one more time."

Rebecca grasped her hand and drew her around the corner into the deserted alcove in front the elevators. Then she pulled her into her arms and kissed her, hard. Finally releasing her, she said fervently, "You were incredible tonight. None of us would've gotten through this without you."

"If things keep up this way," Catherine said with a shaky laugh, "I'm going to have to take an emergency room medicine residency."

"It's not always like this," Rebecca assured her swiftly.

"So you've said," Catherine murmured softly, laying her head against Rebecca's chest, just enjoying the solid comfort of her. "Come home soon. I want to hold you."

Rebecca kissed her forehead, then held her tightly, refusing to think about anything beyond the moment when they could be together. "Sounds like just what I need."

She wondered if Catherine had any idea how very true those words were.

CHAPTER TWENTY

S arah Martin quietly pushed open the door to room 614 and stepped inside. The vertical blinds over the one window had been closed and the room was suffused in the pale yellow light of late afternoon. A steady beep from the monitor above the bed and the faint rasp of breathing were the only sounds. She walked to the figure slumped in a chair by the bedside and whispered softly, "Sloan." When she got no response, she leaned down and gently shook the other woman's shoulder.

Sloan's eyes flew open, and she straightened with a start. Immediately, she looked toward the bed and then sagged slightly in disappointment. Michael had not regained consciousness since the one brief moment with Catherine nearly twelve hours before. Turning to her companion, she rubbed her face with both hands and asked, "What time is it?"

"It's 3:30. Jason is on his way to the office for the briefing."

"Right," Sloan rejoined wearily, rising slowly. "Show time."

Sarah stilled her friend's motion with a hand on her arm. Quietly, she whispered, "Maybe you should call it off."

"No. We might not get another chance." Sloan moved to the bedside and ran her fingers lightly over Michael's cheek. After leaning down, she threaded the fingers of her left hand through her lover's and murmured close to her ear, "I won't be long. I love you." She kissed her fingers, then, gently, her lips.

With a determined gait, she walked out of the room and didn't look back. Outside in the hall, she turned to Sarah, who had followed. "If Jason doesn't make contact with this guy tonight, he'll get spooked and suspect we're on to him. We don't know how closely he's in contact with other members of this organization. He might not know anything; he might be a central player. We can't afford to tip them off at this point."

"Jason said the same thing," Sarah said with a sigh, remembering their strained conversation only an hour before. She hadn't wanted him to be the one to make contact, and he'd insisted it would be fine. "Look, go home and take a shower. If Jason's going through with it, I'll feel better if you're there with him. The three of you mean more to me than anyone in the world. Having Michael hurt is all I can take."

Sloan glanced at the closed hospital door, knowing that everything that mattered in her life was on the other side. "I don't want her to be alone."

"I'll stay with Michael, and you'll be back soon—right?"

"If she wakes up…" Sloan swallowed hard and continued, "*When* she wakes up, if I'm not here, tell her I'll be right back. Tell her I lo—"

Smiling faintly, Sarah took Sloan's hand. "Sloan, believe me, Michael knows that. Go get this thing done."

Sloan nodded, a hard glint in her eyes. "Jason and I will see you in a few hours."

❖

Catherine and Rebecca dressed silently on opposite sides of Catherine's bedroom. Catherine pulled on navy cotton chinos and a short-sleeved polo shirt, topping it off with a blue blazer. Rebecca slipped into jeans and a button-down-collar shirt, strapped on her shoulder harness, and covered it with a dark blazer of her own. They had slept most of the day and had said very little after rising and showering together.

"Be sure you stay with Clark," Rebecca said quietly, her back to Catherine. From her gym bag on the floor, she pulled two extra magazines for her automatic and slipped one into each of the front pockets of her jacket. "We'll all be miked, and you should be able to hear everything that's going on. Even if things get…chaotic…stay in the car. Don't come forward until I personally call for you."

"How likely is this to turn into some kind of standoff?" Catherine registered Rebecca's anxiety for her safety, but considered it unfounded. Of much greater concern to her was the possibility that *Rebecca* would be in the middle of a firefight. "I know you don't want to hear this, but you're in no condition—"

"We have no reason to believe that this guy will resort to violence," Rebecca said immediately, facing her lover now. "I just want to be prepared for any contingency. On the off chance the situation does heat up, I don't want you at risk."

"If someone has to go through a door," Catherine said persistently, "let it be Watts. Not you. Not this time."

Rebecca looked past Catherine out the bedroom window, struggling to find some balance between who she knew herself to be and who she needed to be if she was to keep Catherine in her life. "If we have to go through the door, I'll let Watts go through first today—but I can't promise you that I won't be right behind him." She met Catherine's eyes. "That's the best I can do."

"All right."

Rebecca's piercing gaze intensified. "And what about you? Will I have to worry about you while I'm trying to control the scene?"

"I'll stay with Clark until I'm summoned. I promise."

They both moved at once and met each other in the middle of the room. Simultaneously, each slipped her arms around the other's waist as they pressed together for a fierce kiss. A minute became two until finally each drew back a fraction with a regretful smile.

"Time to roll," Rebecca said softly, gently releasing her.

❖

Mitchell ran through her mental checklist. Automatic loaded. Backup .32 in her right ankle holster. Extra ammo in the right front pocket of her jeans. Badge in the opposite front pocket. Cuffs in her left rear pocket where she could reach them while holding her gun on a suspect with her dominant right hand.

She stopped by the front door of her apartment and snagged her black leather jacket off the clothes tree. She was in jeans, sneakers, and a short-sleeved football jersey. She couldn't think of anything else she needed—or needed to do. Fleetingly, she thought about making a phone call, but then thought better of it. It seemed as if there should be someone, but there never really had been.

Her family had never understood her reasons for wanting to go to West Point and had understood even less her reasons for leaving the Army. Of course, it hadn't helped that she couldn't tell them why she had resigned, because she would have been betraying secrets that were not hers to reveal. Now she was a cop, something else that no one in her family of business executives and investment brokers could fathom. The only person she could think of, in fact, the only person she really *wanted* to call, was someone who considered the police her enemy. In the end, as it had always been, she was alone.

She stepped through her door and went down the two flights of stairs out onto the sidewalk. A car was idling at the curb, and she slid into the front seat.

"You all set, kid?" Watts asked.

"Yeah, I'm ready."

❖

When Rebecca and Catherine arrived at Sloan's shortly after 4:00 p.m., they found Sloan, Jason, and Mitchell waiting for them in the conference room. Avery Clark, along with two men who were apparently DOJ agents, joined them soon thereafter. Once they had all gathered around the table, Sloan and Jason flanking Rebecca at one end and Clark at the opposite end, the detective and the federal agent regarded each other expressionlessly, as if a silent debate was taking place as to who would speak first.

Finally, Clark said, "Why don't you go ahead and lay it out for us, Detective Sergeant."

"Okay. Mr. McBride is to make contact with the subject at the Upstairs Connection, a cybercafé at 17th and Market at 7:00 p.m. tonight." As Rebecca spoke, none of her surprise at the fact that Clark had allowed her to take control of the operation so easily showed in her face. It wasn't her experience that federal agents ever relinquished the lead to local law enforcement. It might simply indicate that Clark was the straightforward agent he represented himself to be, one whose only interest was in breaking the case. Only time would tell.

She continued speaking, letting every thought except those of the upcoming engagement fade from her mind. "As instructed, he will log on as BigMac10, his Internet persona, in the usual chat room and wait for contact. Presumably, he will be given further instructions at that point. Sloan will be monitoring from a wireless unit in the lead trace car, both there and at the final destination. At this point, we have no reason to assume that the subject, LongJohnXXX, suspects Mr. McBride to be anything other than someone interested in viewing live sex with minors and a potential customer for future live broadcasts."

She threw Jason a quick glance and received a slight nod. "Therefore, we don't expect resistance. Nevertheless, the exact location on this subject within the hierarchy of the organization is unknown, and he's considered a potential threat risk."

"Are you going to wire him?" one of Clark's agents interrupted, indicating Jason dismissively. This drew a quick flicker of disapproval from Clark.

"No," Rebecca answered calmly. "We considered it, but that's the one thing we think that the subject might check for, given even a normal level of suspicion. We don't want to blow McBride's cover before he gets inside the subject's house and we have access to the most recent downloads."

As Rebecca continued to outline the upcoming maneuver, Catherine watched her and the others at the table. She loved to watch Rebecca work. When Rebecca was in charge of an operation, every ounce of her considerable personal presence emerged—her strength and confidence and skill were undeniable. There was something both comforting and exciting in the unshakable certainty she exuded as she enumerated each detail—the order and positioning of the stakeout vehicles, each team's role in the apprehension of the subject, and the contingency plans if the subject deviated from the scenario they predicted him to follow.

It was fascinating and terrifying to listen to the individuals, seated around the table, discuss the upcoming maneuver, which could potentially result in injury or death to any one of them. All in a day's work, it seemed. To be able to confront that reality and ignore it required tremendous powers of both denial and self-assuredness. It also required a tremendous amount of trust. She began to understand the bond between police officers in a completely different way. It was more than just the connection that grew between two people who worked together. When you relied on someone for your very life day in and day out, the allegiance and commitment formed a bond that very little could break.

She wondered what it would be like to have to work within that tight community and *not* have the support of one's fellows. For an instant, she thought of Mitchell and her experience that night in a dark alley when she had called for backup and no one had come. She glanced at the young officer and saw dedication and determination etched in each intense line of her face. Then her lover's voice penetrated her consciousness again, and she saw only her.

"So," Rebecca said, her tone shifting as she wrapped things up. "Once we have the subject in custody, the crime scene team will be standing by to oversee evidence documentation."

She looked around the room, assessing each individual. Clark seemed calm; his two agents fidgeted slightly as if impatient to get on with things. Jason had listened intently, but she had a feeling that he and Sloan had already had their own briefing. They appeared far less interested in the tactical maneuverings of the police than they probably were in their own plans for information assessment and transmission during the operation. Watts slouched next to Jason, looking bored as usual. Mitchell, next to him, had never moved her eyes from Rebecca's face during the entire briefing, as if she were memorizing each word. To her left, Sloan had not moved during the entire time either, and Rebecca detected a faint tremor in her hand where it rested on the table. On the far side of the security consultant, Catherine sat composed as always, quietly watching, absorbing, and evaluating.

"Sloan?" Rebecca wanted to be sure she had her attention. "Anything to add?"

Sloan cleared her throat and straightened slightly in her seat. "The success of the operation depends upon us hitting fast with absolutely no warning. Anyone with something to hide who knows anything about computers might program a destruct sequence, which can be initiated with a keystroke or two. Depending upon this guy's level of knowledge and his degree of suspicion, he may very well have something like that in his system. We'll have almost no time between entry and immobilization if we're going to preserve the critical evidence on his hard drive."

She glanced to Jason once, an unreadable flicker of understanding passing between the two of them. "The most important thing is that LongJohn have absolutely no reason to believe this is anything other than a meeting with a prospective client and fellow connoisseur."

"What about arming McBride?" Clark suggested. "He would be the logical one to subdue the subject if it seems as if he's about to destroy critical evidence."

Rebecca shook her head. "Not advisable. The subject is very likely to search him for evidence of weapons or a wire. We'll have front- and rear-entry teams, assuming there are two entrances, or a tandem front strike force. We'll be moving very quickly. Hopefully, the element of surprise will be all that's necessary. In addition, I don't want McBride exposed as one of us. I intend to arrest him along with LongJohn and take him in to preserve his cover. Tonight is just the beginning of this sweep."

Clark nodded. He and every law-enforcement officer at the table knew that the individual at most risk in the entire operation was Jason, who would be unprotected and unarmed in the middle of a potentially violent situation.

For his part, Jason looked relaxed and calm, perfectly at ease. "Once we start receiving the live download, Sloan will be able to pick it up. I'll be expecting you, and he won't." He shrugged as if that settled things.

"All right," Rebecca said, standing. "We need the surveillance teams to move into position at 6:00. Assume that LongJohn is smart enough to check the area before he enters the café, so keep an eye out for anyone looking into parked vehicles."

Everyone rose, then moved into separate groups. Rebecca motioned to Catherine with a faint tip of her chin, and the two of them stepped out into the corridor.

"If we're lucky, we won't need you," the detective said quietly.

"I think that I should ride with you and Sloan," Catherine said just as quietly. "Sloan's going to be monitoring the actual conversations that Jason and LongJohn are having, isn't she?"

"That's the plan." Rebecca could see where Catherine was going with this tack and searched furiously for an argument to counter it.

"In that case, I need to know what is being said between them as well. That's the only way I can judge the tenor of the situation, and it will give me a much better idea of LongJohn's state of mind. If I can be of any help at all, it's going to be in evaluating the threat risk. And to do that, I need to know what's being said."

"She's right," Sloan said from a foot away, having approached without their notice. "I was about to suggest the same thing, but I didn't want to do it in there."

Her blue eyes sharp as lasers, an acid retort on her lips, Rebecca whirled to face Sloan. With effort, she managed to contain her temper, because the professional part of her knew that what Sloan and Catherine said made sense. And had she been thinking more like a cop and less like a lover, she would have suggested the same thing herself. "You're right," she admitted with a sigh.

Sloan, in black jeans and T-shirt, looked worn beyond exhaustion. Her normally vibrant eyes were dull with pain. Directing her next words to Catherine with just a hint of her old charm, she asked, "I assume that you can be trusted to stay in the vehicle if things get crazy?"

"Word of honor," Catherine agreed, her eyes on Rebecca.

Rebecca rubbed the bridge of her nose with one hand, rapidly making mental readjustments. "Okay, Catherine, you'll ride with us. I'll advise Clark and meet you two downstairs." She turned and walked away, leaving Catherine and Sloan alone.

"How are you doing?" Catherine asked gently.

"Okay," Sloan lied.

"Michael?"

Sloan shook her head. "She hasn't regained consciousness yet." Her eyes searched Catherine's face. "Are you *sure* she woke up earlier when…"

Catherine placed her hand on Sloan's arm and squeezed gently. "I'm absolutely positive. She's just healing, and when her body has restored itself enough, she'll wake up. It's going to be all right."

"Thanks." Sloan sighed, accepting Catherine's comfort gratefully.

"You don't need to thank me. Just take care of yourself. Michael will need you strong when she wakes up."

Sloan nodded again, then squared her shoulders, her eyes clearing and determination hardening in her face. "We have a long way to go before we get to the people behind this. Tonight's just the opening move."

"Well, then," Catherine replied as they moved down the hall toward the elevators, "let's be sure to win this round."

❖

Rebecca, Sloan, and Catherine sat in a nondescript beige Ford sedan half a block down and diagonal to the Upstairs Connection. Rebecca continuously scanned the street, watching for anyone who appeared to be watching for *them*. They had arrived an hour before Jason's appointed rendezvous time. At 6:45, they had seen him come down the street from the direction of the 15th and Market Street subway-surface car stop, which he had taken to get there. At 6:50, he had passed through the street-level door that led to the second-floor cybercafé and disappeared from their view.

Sloan worked silently, monitoring the connection she had established to the Internet using a sniffer software program that allowed her to hack into a local wireless network. She was completely unaware of anyone else's presence in the vehicle. Right now, keeping Jason safe and apprehending the suspect were her primary objectives. As long as she focused on the screen and the multiple programs she had running, she didn't think about Michael for at least a few minutes at a time. While she worked, she could almost ignore the constant ache in her chest.

In the backseat, Catherine waited patiently, having learned how to separate herself from the anxiety and distractions of others during her hours of therapy sessions. She had also learned to dissociate herself from her own internal issues and concerns. Doing that in the presence of her lover, whose health and well-being were of paramount concern to her, was more difficult than she had anticipated, however. She found that if she concentrated on trying to understand just what Sloan was doing, it helped. Thus far, from what she could glean from the occasional update provided to Rebecca, she knew that Sloan was now monitoring the chat room where Jason was to meet LongJohn.

"Anything?" Rebecca asked calmly. She sat behind the wheel of the sedan, as relaxed as she usually got during a stakeout.

The long hours of waiting could lull an unsuspecting, inexperienced officer into a state of lassitude, which could result in dulled reflexes and impaired powers of perception. That meant you could be taken by surprise, and *that* could get you killed. She had learned long ago to maintain her level of alertness despite the boredom of inactivity. She constantly surveyed her surroundings, looking for anything out of the ordinary. It wasn't beyond the realm of possibility that LongJohn might have brought along an accomplice who was watching for them just as they were watching for LongJohn and Jason. She needed to be certain that they were not followed when *they* followed their quarry.

Sloan shrugged and muttered, "I'm in the chat room. Jason just logged on. No contact yet from LongJohn."

"Is it possible that he won't actually come to this location?" Catherine asked. "Physically, I mean?"

"Possible," Rebecca answered. "He may just have wanted Jason on an unfamiliar machine where he couldn't use exactly the kind of programs that Sloan's using now to trace him. I'm still betting that he'll show here though. He'll want to get a look at Jason."

"I agree," Sloan offered. "Otherwise, I think he would have simply given Jason instructions for the meeting privately, in any of a million rooms they could have gone to. If he's gotten this far, he trusts that Jason is who he says he is."

"Either way, if we follow Jason when he leaves here," Rebecca added, "we'll get to LongJo—"

"LongJohnXXX just logged on," Sloan advised, her voice sharp and her attention riveted to her laptop.

"Read out the conversation," Rebecca ordered.

```
LongJohnXXX: You there, Big Ten?
BigMac10: You know it. Primed and ready.
LongJohnXXX: What are you wearing?
BigMac10: LOL. Changing horses on me now?
LongJohnXXX: No way, buddy. You know what
makes me stiff -- young and pretty and
female. But hey, to each his own.
BigMac10: Olive green Dockers and a tan
shirt. Pass inspection?
LongJohnXXX: Can't be too careful
BigMac10: No kidding. What next?
LongJohnXXX: You about ready to take care
of business?
```

```
BigMac10: Can't be too soon. I'm hurtin for
something to ease my strain
LongJohnXXX: Give me 15, then wait outside.
Your chariot's on the move.
BigMac10: The service is appreciated. I'll
be there.
```

Rebecca keyed her mike to the frequency Clark and his people were using as well as the radio in Watts and Mitchell's unmarked car. "Anticipated contact, fifteen minutes. No make or model on subject vehicle."

A chorus of *Roger*s floated through the air, and then silence.

"Everything seems aboveboard," Sloan said. Glancing over her shoulder, she looked to Catherine. "What do you think?"

"It seems that the whole purpose of this meeting was for LongJohn to inspect Jason. If he's not actually inside with Jason right now, he's somewhere he can watch him come out. I don't see anything amiss at this point."

Rebecca set her watch to fourteen minutes and continued her silent vigil.

Jason logged off and checked his watch. He and Sloan had previously discussed communicating via aliases on-line after LongJohn had contacted him but had decided against it. There was no telling if LongJohn had associates who might be monitoring the chat room after his log-off. And it was possible that LongJohn himself was still on-line under yet a different alias, checking to see if there was any unusual activity after his and Jason's conversation. It seemed safer at this point to follow instructions until they were closer to LongJohn in the flesh.

He looked around the room, which was one large space with a dozen small tables equipped with Internet terminals. At the far end of the room was a small bar that served coffee and a limited selection of junk food. Almost every table was occupied, and no one looked particularly suspicious. Of course, what did the typical pedophile look like? Anyhow, no one seemed to be paying special attention to him.

And at this point, he wasn't particularly nervous. Playing roles was something that came naturally for him. The threat of physical danger didn't particularly worry him either. He wasn't a kickboxer like Sloan or a Kung Fu master like his lover, but he could handle himself in an altercation, if need be. However, if things played out the way he and Sloan had theorized, when the time for the bust came, he doubted that LongJohn was going to pose much of a threat.

He glanced at his watch and smiled to himself. Five minutes till show time.

❖

"Smoke?" Watts asked.

"No thanks," Mitchell replied.

"You mind?"

Mitchell stared in surprise. "It's your car, Detective."

"Yeah, but the sarge always busts my balls about it."

"Well, I guess she can."

"Yeah." Watts fumbled through the pocket of his jacket until he found the crumpled pack of Camels and fingered one free. After cracking the window a couple of inches, he made an attempt to direct the smoke in that direction. "You ever been on a No Knock bust before?"

"No, sir."

"I'll go through the door first, and I want to feel your balls...uh, your...whatever, right up against my backside the whole way. You stick to me like we're two dogs screwing."

"I can handle that," Mitchell said expressionlessly. She wondered if Watts had any idea what cadet training was like at West Point. She could crawl through ditches under live fire without flinching. Had done it, leading a platoon of cadets.

"Good. I don't want you getting separated and end up shooting me."

"You don't have to worry about that, Detective."

He glanced at her, assessing her tone and expression. She looked perfectly steady and certain. "You scared, kid?"

"No, sir."

"Good." He settled his butt a little more comfortably on the seat and continued to smoke in silence. Until he had gotten hooked up with Rebecca Frye, he'd never worked with a woman before. Not one-on-one. Now he couldn't get away from them. It sure was a different world.

❖

Precisely fourteen minutes after his log-off, Jason McBride exited through the doors of the Upstairs Connection and walked to the intersection of 17th and Market. A blue Mercedes SUV, driving south on 17th, pulled up next to him, and the driver's window descended smoothly.

Rebecca saw Jason lean down, nod once, and walk around the front of the vehicle to slide into the front passenger seat. She keyed her mike and started her engine. "We have contact." She gave a verbal description of the vehicle, knowing that Mitchell and Watts would run it through VI, Vehicle Identification, as they drove.

She pulled into traffic allowing several cars and a minivan to move between her and the SUV. They drove just below the speed limit through the city to the on-ramp to Interstate 95. A minute or two later, Mitchell's voice came over the radio.

"No identification on the vehicle," Mitchell reported. "The plates are not registered."

"Forged, probably," Rebecca muttered. "Roger that."

After another minute, she dropped back, and the black Buick driven by Watts pulled out from several cars behind her and passed to take over the lead position. They would alternate like this as long as needed until Jason's vehicle stopped. Somewhere behind them, Clark followed as well. If the SUV began to take evasive maneuvers, suggesting that the tail had been spotted, the third car would split off to triangulate an interception point. For now, whoever was driving the Mercedes ahead of them did not appear to be aware of their presence.

"Do you think that's LongJohn driving?" Sloan asked at one point.

"Most likely," Rebecca said, eyes fixed on the traffic ahead of her. "I can't see him inviting someone else to the party at this point. Any potential customer might get spooked meeting someone they hadn't anticipated. These guys are pretty suspicious as a group."

"I wonder what the hell they're talking about?" Sloan mused.

Rebecca shook her head. "I've got a feeling it's not the weather or sports."

"Well, whatever it is," Catherine interjected, "Jason is fast on his feet, and he and LongJohn have a relationship. That's why no one other than Jason could have done this at this point. He'll be okay."

He better be, Sloan thought. *Because I can't take one more person I care about getting hurt.*

Twenty minutes later, they had circled nearly the entire city on expressways and arterials. They were approaching an area less than a mile north of Sloan's loft that still retained the flavor of a working-class neighborhood. Called Fishtown, the neighborhood consisted of row houses and singles interspersed along narrow streets where a few trees still managed to grow.

"Here we go," Rebecca said as the Mercedes signaled and pulled right toward an exit ramp. After following a few blocks, she once again opened the frequencies to the other members of the team. "Subject vehicle has turned right into a driveway on the corner of Girard and 4th. Single, two-story, white frame house—no number visible. Detached garage, front and rear entries likely. I am proceeding around the block and will approach from the north."

Giving instructions as she drove, Rebecca deployed the other two vehicles where the police officers and federal agents could easily approach the house from opposite directions. She and Sloan needed to be as close as possible so that Sloan could hack in and monitor the live download. Two minutes later, they were parked between several vehicles on the adjacent cross street in a spot from which they had a clear sightline to the house. Lights were visible in a room on the first floor.

"We might be lucky," Rebecca said. "The doors should be fairly easy to breach, and if they're in that room with the lights, we should be inside and have containment in less than ten seconds."

Sloan didn't reply. Head lowered over her screen, she was feverishly running through programs, attempting to establish a strong enough signal to trace the activity from LongJohn's computer. Finally, after what seemed like an interminable wait, an image flickered and then stabilized on her monitor.

Three pairs of eyes focused on the fifteen-inch color screen. For a moment, the images were indistinct, and then the focus cleared and they were able to see two young girls as they walked naked into a room furnished with a large bed and not much else.

"Got you, you son of a bitch," Sloan whispered.

Chapter Twenty-one

"Should we go in?" Rebecca asked Sloan, an edge in her voice as she thought about Jason. She hated having a man out of sight and hearing, particularly inside a building with a perp of unknown violence potential. Especially while she sat in a car watching the radio.

From the backseat, Catherine placed a hand lightly on Rebecca's shoulder and urged, "Wait a few minutes if you can." She had been sitting quietly, watching the figures on Sloan's screen. A man had entered the room, joining the two young girls. He wore a nondescript uniform, apparently supposed to represent a delivery person of some kind. The two naked girls feigned surprise and awkward shyness, all of it clearly staged but not nearly as artificial as she might have expected. There was a sense of cinema verité that was all too professional and deeply disturbing given the subject matter. "I'd give…this…a while to run, because I think LongJohn is more likely to be preoccupied the longer this goes on."

Rebecca glanced back sharply, aware of the hollow note in her lover's voice. Stakeout operations like these were never easy, not when pent-up, adrenalized excitement and the fear of something going wrong invariably combined to make you crazy. This time it was even harder, because she was certain that Catherine must be feeling tremendous compassion for the young girls being degraded and victimized while they all sat watching.

"No matter what we do here," Rebecca reminded her gently, "it won't make any difference to them. Not tonight, at least."

"I know," Catherine replied tonelessly, not looking directly at Rebecca. "Ten minutes. That should be about right."

Rebecca keyed her mike and instructed the other teams, "We'll go in ten. Team one, you have the front; team two, the rear. Move into position and wait for my signal." After terminating the transmission, Rebecca glanced at Sloan. "Are you getting what you need?"

"Looks like it," Sloan said without glancing up. Intensely concentrating, she was still rapidly sequencing through programs and downloading as much information as she could.

"Okay, good." Rebecca itched for action. "You two stay here until the all-clear." She handed Sloan a handy talkie. "I'll contact you on this as soon as we've secured the location. Then you can get a look at his system."

"Good enough." For the first time in the last hour, Sloan lifted her gaze from the computer monitor. "Look out for Jason, will you?"

"Absolutely." As Rebecca lifted the handle, swung open the door, and put one leg out, she glanced briefly again into the rear seat. Catherine was watching her. "I'll see you in a few minutes."

"Yes," Catherine responded softly, her eyes on Rebecca's face. Memorizing it, as if it hadn't already been indelibly carved on her heart.

Rebecca slipped away into the darkness, and Catherine wondered once again what it was that made someone do that. What was it that allowed an individual to place herself in imminent peril to right some wrong or correct some injustice? She continued to stare at the house, barely able to make out a flicker in the surrounding shadows, which she imagined would be Watts and Mitchell and perhaps the Justice agents.

She tried to imagine what they were thinking and finally decided that there was no way she could, not without having experienced it. Suddenly, she understood some of why it was that police officers rarely had friendships outside the force. She also understood why they had such a high rate of divorce. How could anyone who did not do this on a daily basis possibly understand what it was to go out day after day and face the unknown? An unknown that could very well kill you.

"She'll be fine," Sloan said as if reading her mind.

Without taking her eyes off the front of the building, where she could just see the door but could not see the figures, who she knew must be crouching in the shadows, Catherine said once more, softly, "Yes."

❖

"Did I tell you or did I tell you?" LongJohn said with a note of both excitement and pride in his voice. "This is the real thing. Primo, man."

The two men were seated in front of a twenty-one-inch flat-screen computer monitor in small comfortable easy chairs with a TV tray-table between them. Two open bottles of beer sat on the table flanking a bowl of peanuts. On the screen, the now naked thirty-year-old man, a big beefy guy who looked like a college football player gone to fat, stood by the side of the bed while one of the preteen girls performed fellatio on him. Kneeling on the floor next to them, the other girl fondled him. His large hand roamed over her barely perceptible breasts.

"Oh, yeah, it's everything you said," Jason said, facing the screen and fixing his gaze on a point two inches above it. He had watched enough to know that this was what they had been waiting for. He didn't want to see the details. "Worth every penny, guy. And more so. I wouldn't mind getting this on a regular basis."

"Like I said, that can be arranged," LongJohn said, his eyes riveted to the screen. "All you need is a little green and the right connections. We'll pipe this straight to your bedroom."

"Just tell me where to sign," Jason replied. The live download had been running for almost ten minutes, and he wasn't certain how long it would last. More importantly, he estimated that the strike force would make their move soon. Now was the time for a little diversion.

"You know, I've been waiting all weekend for this," Jason said, purposefully lowering his voice and hesitating as if he were having trouble catching his breath. "I'm afraid I might pop in my pants if I don't do something about it pretty soon."

"Go ahead, man. Feel free. I'm in need of a little relief myself," his companion answered.

Out of the corner of his eye, Jason could see LongJohn rhythmically squeezing the crotch of his jeans as he stared fixedly at the monitor. Jason made a show of unbuttoning his chinos and lowering his fly. He wasn't worried that LongJohn would watch him, because LongJohn wasn't interested in what Jason had between his legs. He was interested in watching the children performing sex acts on the man on the screen.

Jason slipped his hand inside his trousers and faked a moan. He wasn't hard, but LongJohn would never know that. He spread his legs wider and murmured, "Oh yeah, that's better."

Next to him, he heard the sound of a zipper sliding down followed by a grunt as LongJohn reached inside his jeans. The sounds from the speakers were mostly moans and strangled grunts and fragmented bits of dialogue that combined with Jason's intentionally audible breathing and LongJohn's escalating groans.

Jason hoped the noise would help mask the sounds of the police entry and add to the general confusion when the strike force descended upon them. His only concern now was that LongJohn would be quicker to the finish line than he had anticipated. The guy had freed himself from the confines of his pants, and from the sound of his breathing and the rapid creaking of the chair as the other man rocked his hips in an ever increasing crescendo, Jason feared that his diversion would be shot before Frye and friends arrived.

And he hadn't planned a second act.

❖

"On three," Rebecca whispered into her mike. "One, two, three... GO."

Watts hit the door with his considerable bulk, and it broke loose from the frame, crashing inward with a splinter of wood and popping screws. Rebecca was surprised at the speed with which the big man moved. In an instant, he had disappeared into the darkened room, Mitchell close behind. Distantly, she heard an echoing crash from somewhere in the depths of the house. *Clark's team.*

Rebecca moved low through the doorway, stepping up quickly next to Mitchell. They turned their backs to one another, guns extended in two-handed grips, each of them scanning opposite sides of the room. Watts was out in front, beside the door on the wall opposite the entry, peering around the corner into the next room.

"Clear!" Mitchell shouted.

"Go," Rebecca ordered, and they all surged forward. Within a matter of seconds, they were in a large recreation room filled with computers, video machines, and graphics equipment. A large monitor sat on an elevated shelf displaying the sexual scene they had observed from the car. Moans and cries and hoarse *oh yeahs* provided a backdrop to the surprised exclamations of the two men in the easy chairs.

Watts yanked the suspect, a youngish white male in a T-shirt and jeans, from the chair and pushed him spread-eagled onto the floor. Kneeling with one meaty leg in the center of the stunned man's back, Watts glanced up at Rebecca with a satisfied smile. "What do you think, huh, Sarge? Caught the scumbags with their dicks in their hands."

"Well, just get him zipped up and read him the card," Rebecca said, referring to the Miranda warning.

Mitchell had Jason, who was loudly protesting for all to hear that he'd had no idea LongJohn planned to show a sex video, in the same position on the floor as the perp. She secured cuffs onto him as she recited his rights in a flat monotone.

Rebecca lifted her radio and said, "Sloan, come on ahead." Then, switching frequencies, "Dispatch, this is Detective Sergeant Frye. I need the crime scene team at—"

"That won't be necessary, Detective," Avery Clark said as he and his two agents converged on the scene from the rear of the house. "We'll be taking the equipment into custody."

"The hell you will," Rebecca snapped, ignoring the faint sound of the dispatcher calling her name over her radio. "This is *my* crime scene, and I'll log the evidence."

Clark shook his head. "Sorry, Frye. We have jurisdictional priority here." He turned to one of the two federal agents with him. "Go ahead, Reynolds. Start packing this stuff up. Call and get the rest of the team down here to give you a hand."

Sloan caught his last statements as she entered the room. "You lying son of a bitch," she seethed, stalking toward Clark from across the room. "Is this what you call a joint investigation? We lead you to the suspect and then you take all the evidence?"

Rebecca edged forward as she noted all three of the Justice agents stiffen, ready to intervene if Sloan put hands on him. She had no doubt that this time Clark or one of his men would get physical.

"Well, now. If we find any little thing we can pass along to you in the way of other guys like this," Clark said, nodding toward LongJohn, "we will. We're after the big fish here, not the pervs sitting around getting off on this garbage."

"What about what happened to Michael?" Sloan demanded

angrily, raising her voice above the cacophony and attracting further attention from Clark's two underlings, both of whom edged closer. "We need to follow the trail from *here* to find out who targeted me."

Clark met her hot gaze impassively. "You'll get info on a need-to-know basis."

"I'll get the fucking info *right fucking now*," she grated, heading toward the CPU that was guarded by the bigger of the Justice agents. Clark stepped to intercept her, but before he could, Rebecca grasped Sloan's arm and stopped her in mid-stride.

"Hold up, Sloan," Rebecca cautioned. Leaning close, she whispered harshly, "You touch one of them, and you'll end up spending the night in a cell down at the Federal Building. And I can't help you there."

For a fraction of a second, something dark passed through Sloan's eyes. It was a mixture of fury and pain. "Son of a bitch," she whispered hoarsely.

"Yeah," Rebecca muttered through clenched jaws, echoing Sloan's frustration and rage. But it hadn't been the first time, and it most likely wouldn't be the last, that when it came time to reap the benefits of a joint operation, the local authorities were left with nothing. A hand still on Sloan's arm, she ordered, "Watts, get those two down to headquarters."

"You can have *him*," Clark said amiably, nodding toward Jason. "I want first crack at this guy." He indicated LongJohn with a sweep of his hand.

Rebecca stepped very close to Clark, her chest nearly touching his. She was an inch taller, and for an instant his smile faltered. "To do what? Offer him a deal?"

"We just want to talk to him. Then you can have him."

"You're all heart, Clark," Rebecca snarled, walking to where Watts and Mitchell waited.

Sloan followed reluctantly in her wake, as Rebecca growled, "Come on, let's get out of here."

❖

"What's happening?" Catherine asked as Sloan and Rebecca flung themselves into the sedan and slammed the doors. "Is Jason all right?"

"He's fine," Sloan replied, suddenly weary beyond belief. The only thing she wanted was to get back to Michael.

"Did you get LongJohn?"

"Yeah, and we've been screwed," Rebecca seethed as she cranked the ignition and pulled away from the curb in one rapid motion. "Clark's taking first crack at the suspect *and* the evidence."

"Which means," Sloan added darkly, "we'll never get anything out of any of it."

Catherine stared from one to the other of the women in the front seat of the careening vehicle. The level of fury and frustration was incendiary. "What about the task force—the investigation?"

Rebecca laughed bitterly. "My guess is it will be tabled while the feds play games trying to get this guy—LongJohn—whoever he turns out to be, to name names or lead them to the next guy who will." She took a calming breath; she didn't want to bark at Catherine. "With a real live perp, and one who is connected enough to be brokering sales of these sex videos, Clark probably figures he's got a hotter lead than anything we can turn up from the Internet." Another deep breath. "At least for now."

She needed to keep her anger at bay while she considered her options. Clark might have stonewalled her for the time being, but the investigation wasn't dead. There was still a porn ring to break and a leak somewhere to plug. And Jeff's killer to find.

"And the children?" Catherine asked quietly. "Where do they fit into this plan?"

There was an uncomfortable silence, then Rebecca answered, "Eventually, the pornography ring will be exposed—either during the feds' sweep, if they ever make a case, or by one of us at the local level. Someone will get them."

"That could take months, couldn't it?" Catherine struggled to understand how the politics of this jurisdictional battle could be allowed to affect the welfare of these innocent victims, but she knew in her heart that there would never be any sense to it.

"Clark's agenda is to bring down the organized crime syndicate that controls drugs, racketeering, prostitution, protection—you name it," Sloan said resignedly. "In one way or another, it affects thousands, and the federal government isn't particularly interested in saving the few. They want the big payoff."

"But then, what about the pornographers?" Catherine insisted. "Are they going to get away with this?"

"No," Rebecca responded firmly. "Special Crimes has always been after the guys who were marketing kids. This Internet search was one way to get to them, but it's not the only way. We know more about how the ring works now—we'll just have to go back to the streets and do it the way we always have."

She was thinking of what Sandy had told her about the young prostitutes who had been involved in making sex films. She and Watts needed to track them down. She remembered, too, Sandy's offer to sign on for one of the films. *"I can pass, Frye. I've done it before."*

Rebecca blew out a frustrated breath. "I've still got some leads."

"You've got more than that," Sloan responded with a hint of her usual fire.

Rebecca glanced at her sharply. "What do you mean?"

"I've got the download of tonight's video." Sloan lifted her laptop. "All of it. There's information I can get from that. I might not be able to tell you a street address, but given enough time, I can probably give you a sector location. It'll be a place to start."

"You're likely to be unemployed by tomorrow, Sloan," Rebecca reminded her. "If Clark gets anything out of this guy, he'll probably work that angle in preference to anything else we might get from the Internet."

"I told you before," Sloan replied evenly, "I don't work for Clark. Someone behind this pornography operation, or someone working *with* whoever's running it, tried to have me killed. Instead, they put my lover in the hospital. I'm not done with this yet."

"No," Rebecca agreed, thinking that this *someone* was probably the same person who had her previous partner killed, "neither am I."

❖

"What a fuckarow," Watts grumbled. "Although we should have seen it coming. You can never trust the feds."

Jason rubbed his wrists, trying to erase the slight indentations the cuffs had made. He was also trying to erase the mental images he still held of the scene on the monitor.

"You okay?" Mitchell asked with concern, looking over the back of the front seat at him. "I didn't mean to ratchet them so tight. Habit."

"I'm fine," he said quickly. "Just pissed off. I *know* that guy knows how this whole part of the operation works. Did you see the setup he had in that room? He's a *relay* station. I'll bet he remasters those feeds and makes high-quality wholesale products. He's probably got customer lists, for Christ's sake."

"Well, if he does," Watts grunted, "the feds will find them in about a year. You know damn well if they had anyone who could actually do the kind of voodoo you and Sloan have been doing, they'd have used them to begin with instead of coming to you."

"Maybe." Jason smiled wryly at Watts's veiled compliment. "Then why cut us out now, when we've finally got something to work with?"

"Because they don't want to spend time and resources on the street side of the operation," Mitchell said cynically. "All they wanted was a key—someone they could twist who would lead them inside the organization. They'll probably turn this guy and send him right back out to work. He could be back in the kiddie smut business in a day or two. Except this time he'll be feeding the feds information while he peddles skin to other guys like BigMac10. That's how federal cases get made. Inside informants. Rats in the garbage dump."

Watts looked at the young woman beside him intently. *Smart kid and good in the crunch, too.*

Jason sighed. "I know, believe me. I've seen the wheels of Justice turn, and most of the time, they're moving in reverse. What a colossal waste."

"Yeah, maybe," Watts muttered almost to himself. "Maybe not. We know some things we didn't know before."

And knowing Frye, we're not about to let this go.

❖

"Has she said anything?" Sloan asked quietly, moving carefully through the dimly lit room to the bedside where Sarah sat waiting.

"No," Sarah replied gently, rising. "She's just been sleeping."

Sloan brushed her fingers lightly over Michael's hand where it lay motionless on the sheets, lingering for a moment on the wedding band she had placed there. "Jason's fine," she added, her eyes moving to her lover's still face.

"I know," Sarah answered. "He called me from the office. Said you were probably on your way here. I'm going to go pick him up now and take him home."

"Good," Sloan said wearily, settling into the chair by the bed. "He's okay, Sarah, but the whole thing was ugly. To say nothing of pointless."

"He sounded drained," Sarah agreed. "And *you* look it. I don't suppose you'd consider going home for a few hours?"

Sloan shook her head, a faint smile on her face as she continued to stroke Michael's arm. "No. There's no reason to go anywhere—not while Michael is here."

"Okay, then." Sarah brushed her hand through her friend's dark hair, letting her fingers rest on her cheek. "Try not to worry."

"Sure."

When the door had closed, Sloan leaned forward and took Michael's hand. "Hey, baby," she murmured softly. "I love you. I'll be right here."

❖

Rebecca leaned against the shower wall and let the steaming water pound her, hoping it would drive some of the tension from her body and the disillusionment from her consciousness. The door slid open and Catherine stepped inside.

"Mind company?"

"Nothing I'd like better," Rebecca answered, reaching for the shampoo. "Turn around. I'll wash your hair."

Catherine turned her back, resting her hips against Rebecca's thighs, and tilted her head so that her lover could work the lather through her hair. As strong fingers massaged her scalp, she groaned, "God, that feels criminally good."

"You *look* criminally good," Rebecca murmured, leaning forward until her breasts pressed into Catherine's back and her pelvis moved against Catherine's rear. For the first time in hours, she realized that she wasn't thinking about anything at all—anything beyond how the faint brush of her nipples over Catherine's skin started a pulse thudding between her legs. She moved her soapy hands from her lover's hair and slid her palms over the tops of Catherine's shoulders, then down her arms. "I love you."

Catherine closed her eyes, aware of the tingling wherever Rebecca touched. Reaching for those clever hands, she drew them to her breasts, gasping as willing fingers closed over her nipples. "Oh, God."

Rebecca braced her back against the wall, cradling Catherine in her arms, still back to front, working her nipples, massaging her breasts, brushing fingers lightly down her belly and then back up again. "You make me so hot," she whispered, her lips close to Catherine's ear. "You make me wet just thinking about touching you."

"Then...don't just...think," Catherine replied, her legs shaking. "Touch." Reaching behind herself with one hand, she insinuated it between their bodies, working her palm down Rebecca's abdomen, feeling muscles tighten under her caress. When she reached the space between her lover's thighs, she slid a finger on either side of her clitoris, squeezing steadily until Rebecca groaned against her neck. "'Cause I'm way past hot already."

"Careful...you'll make me come," Rebecca warned, her voice low and tight. Catherine seemed not to hear and continued to milk her length until she jerked against Catherine's hand, a fist of pleasure threatening to burst inside. "Oh fuck..."

"Uh-huh," Catherine gasped, her free hand on Rebecca's wrist, guiding her hand. Moaning at the first press of Rebecca's fingers, she turned her head, her teeth catching skin at the base of Rebecca's throat.

As Catherine worked her relentlessly toward orgasm, Rebecca pushed deeper between Catherine's thighs until she was inside her, enclosed by the smooth grip of firm muscles. Then she took her with quick, hard, driving strokes that echoed the blood pounding fiercely through her depths—the fury of her thrusts propelled by Catherine's sharp cries of encouragement. Shuddering, barely breathing, she locked her knees to keep from falling as she came, supporting her lover's body as Catherine stiffened, then convulsed in her arms.

Eventually, they managed to finish the shower, both of them quiet. When they stood together naked, toweling off, Catherine said, "What the hell was *that*?" At Rebecca's quizzical glance, she added, "The last thing I was thinking about when I joined you in there was sex. I wasn't certain, after watching that awful video, when I *would* think about it again. Then, I'm practically ready to come the second you touch me."

"Adrenaline," Rebecca replied matter-of-factly, reaching for an old pair of gym shorts. Pulling them on, she continued, "It happens after that kind of operation—the fear and the stress come out like that sometimes. The sex helps to burn the edge off."

"What did you do when you were unattached?"

"When I was still drinking, I drank. After I quit, I went to the gym. Once in while," she shrugged, grinning sheepishly, "I'd find company."

"Hmm," Catherine mused, slipping into her robe. "See that you come directly here should the occasion arise in the future."

"That was my plan," Rebecca responded, pulling her close.

"What else are you planning...about...all of this?" Catherine asked, threading her arms around Rebecca's waist.

"I'll be back on regular duty in a day or so, and I'll have new cases to worry about." Rebecca rested her cheek against Catherine's hair and closed her eyes. "It happens like this in police work. You work your ass off and then you can't make the case because of a technicality, or you *do* make the case, but the perp plea bargains it down to nothing."

"So you're letting this go?" Catherine asked, surprised.

Faintly, Rebecca shook her head. "Clark will pull the plug on this task force—he's probably already made the call. But I'll keep doing what I'm trained to do until we make this right—for Jeff, for Michael, for those young kids."

"Yes," Catherine murmured, "until justice is done—for all of them."

About the Author

Radclyffe is a retired surgeon and full-time award-winning author-publisher with over thirty novels and anthologies in print. Seven of her works have been Lambda Literary finalists including the Lambda Literary winners *Erotic Interludes 2: Stolen Moments* edited with Stacia Seaman; *In Deep Waters 2*; and *Distant Shores, Silent Thunder*. She is the editor of *Best Lesbian Romance* 2009 and 2010 (Cleis Press), *Erotic Interludes* 2 through 5 and *Romantic Interludes* 1 and 2 with Stacia Seaman (BSB), and has selections in multiple anthologies including *Best Lesbian Erotica* 2006–10; *After Midnight*; *Caught Looking: Erotic Tales of Voyeurs and Exhibitionists*; *First-Timers*; *Ultimate Undies: Erotic Stories About Lingerie and Underwear*; *Hide and Seek*; *A is for Amour*; *H is for Hardcore*; *L is for Leather*; *Rubber Sex, Tasting Him,* and *Cowboy Erotica*. She is the recipient of the 2003 and 2004 Alice B. Readers' award for her body of work and is also the president of Bold Strokes Books, one of the world's largest independent LGBTQ publishing companies.

Her latest releases are an all-Radclyffe erotica anthology, *Radical Encounters* (Feb. 2009) the romantic intrigue novel *Justice for All* (April 2009), and the romance *Secrets in the Stone* (July 2009). Her forthcoming works include *The Midnight Hunt* (writing as L.L. Raand, March 2010) and the first in the First Responder Series, *Trauma Alert* (July 2010).

Books Available From Bold Strokes Books

The Pleasure Set by Lisa Girolami. Laney DeGraff, a successful president of a family-owned bank on Rodeo Drive, finds her comfortable life taking a turn toward danger when Theresa Aguilar, a sleek, sexy lawyer, invites her to join an exclusive, secret group of powerful, alluring women. (978-1-60282-144-6)

A Perfect Match by Erin Dutton. The exciting world of pro golf forms the backdrop for a fast-paced, sexy romance. (978-1-60282-145-3)

Truths by Rebecca S. Buck. Two women separated by two hundred years are connected by fate and love. (978-1-60282-146-0)

Father Knows Best by Lynda Sandoval. High school juniors and best friends Lila Moreno, Meryl Morganstern, and Caressa Thibodoux plan to make the most of the summer before senior year. What they discover that amazing summer about girl power, growing up, and trusting friends and family more than prepares them to tackle that all-important senior year! (978-1-60282-147-7)

In Pursuit of Justice by Radclyffe. In the dynamic double sequel to Shield of Justice and A Matter of Trust, Det. Sgt. Rebecca Frye joins forces with enigmatic computer consultant J.T. Sloan to crack an Internet child pornography ring. (978-1-60282-147-4)

The Midnight Hunt by L.L. Raand. Medic Drake McKennan takes a chance and loses, and her life will never be the same—because when she wakes up after surviving a life-threatening illness, she is no longer human. (978-1-60282-140-8)

Long Shot by D. Jackson Leigh. Love isn't safe, which is exactly why equine veterinarian Tory Greyson wants no part of it—until Leah Montgomery and a horse that won't give up convince her otherwise. (978-1-60282-141-5)

In Medias Res by Yolanda Wallace. Sydney has forgotten her entire life, and the one woman who holds the key to her memory, and her heart, doesn't want to be found. (978-1-60282-142-2)

Awakening to Sunlight by Lindsey Stone. Neither Judith or Lizzy is looking for companionship, and certainly not love—but when their lives become entangled, they discover both. (978-1-60282-143-9)

Fever by VK Powell. Hired gun Zakaria Chambers is hired to provide a simple escort service to philanthropist Sara Ambrosini, but nothing is as simple as it seems, especially love. (978-1-60282-135-4)

High Risk by JLee Meyer. Can actress Kate Hoffman really risk all she's worked for to take a chance on love? Or is it already too late? (978-1-60282-136-1)

Missing Lynx by Kim Baldwin and Xenia Alexiou. On the trail of a notorious serial killer, Elite Operative Lynx's growing attraction to a mysterious mercenary could be her path to love—or to death. (978-1-60282-137-8)

Spanking New by Clifford Henderson. A poignant, hilarious, unforgettable look at life, love, gender, and the essence of what makes us who we are. (978-1-60282-138-5)

Magic of the Heart by C.J. Harte. CEO Susan Hettinger and wild, impulsive rock star M.J. Carson couldn't be more different if they tried—but opposites attract in ways neither woman can resist. (978-1-60282-131-6)

Ambereye by Gill McKnight. Jolie Garoul is falling in love with her assistant. The big problem is, Jolie is a werewolf. (978-1-60282-132-3)

Collision Course by C.P. Rowlands. Tragedy leaves Brie O'Malley and Jordan Carter fearful and alone. Can they find the courage to take a second chance on love? (978-1-60282-133-0)

Mephisto Aria by Justine Saracen. Opera singer Katherina Marov's destiny may be to repeat the mistakes of her father when she becomes involved in a dangerous love affair. (978-1-60282-134-7)

Battle Scars by Meghan O'Brien. Returning Iraq war veteran Ray McKenna struggles with the battle scars that can only be healed by love. (978-1-60282-129-3)

Chaps by Jove Belle. Eden Metcalf wants nothing more than to flee from her troubled past and travel the open road—until she runs into rancher Brandi Cornwell. (978-1-60282-127-9)

Lightbearer by John Caruso. Lucifer dares to question the premise of creation itself and reveals that sin may be all that stands between us and living hell. (978-1-60282-130-9)

The Seeker by Ronica Black. FBI profiler Kennedy Scott battles ghosts from her past, deadly obsession, and the evil that haunts her. (978-1-60282-128-6)

Power Play by Julie Cannon. Businesswomen Tate Monroe and Victoria Sosa are at odds in the boardroom, but not in the bedroom. (978-1-60282-125-5)

The Remarkable Journey of Miss Tranby Quirke by Elizabeth Ridley. When love enters Tranby's life in the form of a beautiful nineteen-year-old student, Lysette McDonald, she embarks on the most remarkable journey of all. (978-1-60282-126-2)

Returning Tides by Radclyffe. Insurance investigator Ashley Walker faces more than a dangerous opponent when she returns to the town, and the woman, she left behind. (978-1-60282-123-1)

Veritas by Anne Laughlin. When the hallowed halls of academia become the stage for murder, newly appointed Dean Beth Ellis's search for the truth leads her to unexpected discoveries about her own heart. (978-1-60282-124-8)

The Pleasure Planner by Larkin Rose. Pleasure purveyor Bree Hendricks treats love like a commodity until Logan Delaney makes Bree the client in her own game. (978-1-60282-121-7)

everafter by Nell Stark and Trinity Tam. Valentine Darrow is bitten by a vampire on her way to propose to her lover Alexa Newland, and their lives and love are placed in mortal jeopardy. (978-1-60282-119-4)

Summer Winds by Andrews & Austin. When Maggie Turner hires a ranch hand to help work her thousand acres, she never expects to be attracted to the very young, very female Cash Tate. (978-1-60282-120-0)